ABOUT *HEY SUNSHINE,*
BOOK ONE OF THE *HEY SUNSHINE* TRILOGY

Avery Kent knows that life can change in an instant:
One second you're on your way out of small-town life, the next you're left heartbroken and stunned when your thrill-seeking high school boyfriend runs off in pursuit of a potentially dangerous dream.

Four years later, everything is different. When Chase returns, admitting he made a mistake and asking for a second chance, Avery wants to think she can trust him again.

But when the arrival of a handsome, quiet stranger named Fox shifts Avery's focus, she realizes that things are about to get a lot more complicated.

When is a lot of history enough reason for a future? And how do you ignore the way someone makes you feel, especially when they were **the last thing you ever expected?**

"Romance is ON POINT."
— Brianna's Bookish Confessions

"Not only is this book one of my favorites of 2015, it's one of my new all time favorites."
— Taylor Knight at Bibliophile Gathering

"Hooked from the very first page."
— Monica @NightReads

"Incredible romance and the perfect amount of drama to keep you turning every page until the end."
— Allissa Lemaire @ABookishLoveAffair

Also by Tia Giacalone

HEY SUNSHINE
NIGHT FOX

FORTUNE

ISBN-13: 978-1-950449-02-6
ISBN-10: 1-950449-02-5

Tia Giacalone
Visit my website at www.tiawritesbooks.com

BRIGHTER DAY

Tia Giacalone

To Rove
♡ Yia xxoo

To Lou

Emma xxoo

This book is dedicated to true love — in all of its forms.

PROLOGUE

FOX

I knew I would always dream of fire. It was in my bones, in my blood—the smoke, the ash, the creaking sounds wood made when it was charred completely through and about to crash down around you. In the heart of a fire, in full gear, with the heat pressing from all sides and the roar of oxygen in your mask—there was a sort of quiet. It was just you and the flames until someone won.

I preferred to be the winner, of course, but I didn't always get what I wanted. And when that happened, I played the game again and again in my dreams.

"I need to get in there." I grabbed a jacket off the rig and shrugged it on.

"Sir, you really can't—"

"He can go with me." The assistant chief glanced my way. *"You need a helmet."*

The fire was low and sparse, mostly just embers skittering across the scorched floor looking for more fuel but finding only clumps of wet ash. An old building burned fast and bright—and didn't leave much behind. The blackened hulls of the stove and ovens stood stark and alone in the mess. Most of me hoped I'd find nothing, but a deep, dark corner of my chest knew otherwise.

Was this it? Would it all end here?

I swept one side of the devastated diner, ducking under charred beams and listening for the telltale signs of collapse. Then I searched the other side, all the way through.

Nothing. No one.

The wind picked up, howling, encouraging any flame left to find a dry place to spread. I shouldn't be here. Something wasn't right.

"I warned you."

I whirled around as I heard his voice behind me.

"You did me wrong, Fox. This is payback."

Still no one.

"I tried to help you," I told the wisps of smoke.

The embers sputtered, dancing through the haze.

"It wasn't enough."

You couldn't save someone from themselves. I knew that.

And yet.

"What do you want?"

Completely alone now, with no lights from the fire rig, no shouts of the firefighters as they worked. It was me, this husk of a building, and that voice.

"Everything."

The words faint now, the embers starting to die.

"I'll find you," I said to no one.

I could see the stars overhead through the charred roof. The only light to guide my way back. Back to reality? Back to Avery? I didn't know.

"I'll find you," I said again.

The stars winked out.

I wasn't afraid. Darkness meant no fire.

I'd won—and still lost.

CHAPTER ONE

AVERY

Every day for the past four years—save the weeks I'd spent in Seattle while Fox recuperated—I'd done some version of the exact same thing.

Up every morning before eight, that was never-changing. I'd fed Annabelle her breakfast, which had gotten way easier over the years. I don't know who set the low bar of sliced bread as the pinnacle for great things, but cereal definitely beat it—especially for a bone-tired mama trying not to show her weariness to her toddler. I'd dressed myself and my baby—she usually looked better than I did, but we were both covered in all the right places so I counted it as a win.

Stacking blocks on the living room rug gave way to playdates with her little friends, which morphed into a whole new world when she started preschool. I cooked dinner, I did laundry, I cleaned my tiny house. In between everything, I found time for classes, to study, to work, to volunteer at her school, to write papers, to read both to myself and to her. Those little variances made the years fly by—it wasn't monotonous, it was my life and I loved it. I worked hard for it to mean something and propel me forward. I raised my baby, I fell in love, I graduated from college and dreamed of the future.

Everything was connected by one constant—Kent's Kitchen. No matter how my life had grown over the years, the Kitchen was always there. I put on my apron five days a week and brought good food to good people.

Kent's Kitchen wasn't just a building. Everyone in Brancher knew it. The diner stood for something in our town—the American dream and the idea that there could be a spot of kindness, a place of welcoming and generosity, in a world that sometimes seemed like a hopeless place.

To watch it burn right in front of our eyes felt like the death of a family member.

The fire could've taken so much more—could've taken Fox—but we got lucky. He'd already left by the time my parents' diner burst into flames. I was grateful for that every day. I was still mad, still so very, very angry, but I was also grateful.

Because I'd gotten a taste of life without Fox, and it didn't suit me. He was supposed to be here, with me and Annabelle, forever. I'd made my peace with my ex's actions before the fire, but I'd never forgive J.D. Warren for trying to take Fox away. He'd gone too far, he'd threatened not just my husband but our friends who worked at the diner, my parents, and their livelihood. And for what? Money that he hadn't earned but still felt entitled to.

Would I think of things in two eras now—before and after the fire?

If I were being truly honest, life hadn't been the same since that morning all those months ago when Fox woke up from his coma and couldn't remember that he loved me. Going back even further, maybe it had changed irrevocably when I got the phone call that he'd wrecked the bike to save a highway full of people and his future was uncertain.

Or maybe it was the day he got off the bus in our tiny town, hurt more deeply than his limp belied, so very lost in every sense of the word, even with a transit schedule in his hand. In that moment we'd first glimpsed each other, even with the entire history of my life and the weight of his past all around us—our futures shifted.

I'd changed the entire structure of my world once before, when I found out I was pregnant with Annabelle. Nothing was more important to me than being her mother. And that path I'd chosen, the one for me and her, had led to everything we had now, including Fox. I would've been long gone from Brancher otherwise, ostensibly never knowing what I was missing. Except... would I? Would some part of me have known that Fox was out there somewhere, waiting for us?

I believed in fate. I believed in chain reactions, in cause and effect, in signs and wishes and things that seemed too good to be true. Hell, I'd believe just about anything these days, because the world had dealt me the unimaginable over and over again. Some of it wondrous, and some of it devastating.

But there was always new life after that, fresh starts and second chances after devastation. Fox had taught me to look for it, to own my strength and trust my resilience. So now—it was up to me.

⁓◟⁓

I'd been dreading the insurance meeting out at the ranch, and it turns out my feelings were warranted. It only took ten minutes for our worst fears to be confirmed. The diner was underinsured, which we'd already known. The policy was old, the building's appraisal outdated. It was a loss we could've weathered, given enough time and fundraising.

But then came the loophole. To get even the paltry payout, the investigation needed to be closed—and that could take months. With no income from the diner, and no budget for a rebuild, we could lose the ranch. My father had already put his breeding venture on hold until the spring in order to adjust the schedules after Fox and I moved to Seattle.

"Mr. Kent, we hate to be the bearers of bad news, but there's nothing else we can do."

My dad's face was impassive as he surveyed them. My mother sat next to him, the shock written all over her face. "I understand."

What would happen to us now? How would my parents make a living? The ranch was all they had left. When my grandfather died, it had passed on to my father—and it would continue to pass down until someday it would be Annabelle's. The realization sunk my stomach to the floor. How had I never considered this before? I couldn't lose this place for her, not when it held so much of our family history—my very favorite memories of growing up, learning to ride and to love the land. But I was leaving, wasn't I? Was I coming back? Suddenly everything seemed so up in the air.

Getting to my feet, I took a deep breath, trying to calm my racing heart. "Thanks for your time," I said, but it came out too thin. Too scared.

Fox wasn't finished. "There has to be a way."

The agent shrugged and averted his eyes. "If the police find a suspect and prosecute for arson, everything will move more quickly. But until the investigation comes to a conclusion, my hands are tied."

"That's ridiculous," Fox bit out. "We're already taking a loss here, not to mention any delays. Has your company ever been sued for impediment and loss of revenue?" The agent looked at Fox blankly. "Fantastic. Looking forward to it."

I loved my husband when he was like this, all smart and sarcastic and sexy. It was almost enough to distract me from what was actually happening. But not quite.

The man shuffled his papers again as he collected himself. "I'm assuming that the change in ownership you contacted us about a few months ago will not proceed at this time?"

What? "Change in ownership?" I knew my voice sounded as stunned as I felt. "What are you talking about?"

He raised an eyebrow at me, and I saw Fox shift in his chair. "Your family considered putting the restaurant on the market last year, did you not?"

The silence in the room sent a cold shiver down my back. For a moment, no one took a breath, including my husband, who was doing his super-still-and-ready thing. My heart sank and broke at the same time. I knew this was a complicated situation, but I wasn't expecting that.

"Daddy?" I looked back and forth between the two men. "You wanted to sell? Why?" *Why was everything changing?*

"We thought about it, ultimately decided no." My dad's voice was rough. "Don't see why that matters now." His chair scraped the kitchen floor as he rose to his full height. "I think this meeting is over."

And not a moment too soon, because what I heard in my father's voice was enough to break my heart all over again.

Once the agent left, I brewed another pot of coffee for everyone as we sat in the kitchen. My mom looked drained, devastated, and my dad's stoic face showed his years. It was something I'd never seen before. Nothing ruffled him, nothing broke him, not even close. Except maybe this.

There was so much to unpack here, so much I hadn't realized. Knowing the ins and outs of a business I didn't plan to run wasn't on the top of my priority list, and now that felt like a betrayal. I took a seat next to my mother at the table. *Where did I start, when there was so much to say?*

"I'm sorry, Mama," I whispered, my voice breaking slightly. "Were you going to sell the Kitchen because we were moving? I—"

My mother's head jerked up and she looked at me sternly. I'd seen that face before, many times. "This is not your fault, Avery. Or yours," she said, her eyes finding Fox. "Not one bit of it."

I couldn't accept that, not when it was my former bad decisions coming back to haunt us. I didn't mean Annabelle—she was perfect. The man who'd helped me conceive her was another story. "But I—"

"No." She put her arms around me, and it took everything I had not to burst into tears. "We wanted to start up the breeding ranch again as you know, and we weren't sure if we could do both. But we love that old diner, and we needed the income—it just didn't seem right to sell. So I'll say it again—none of this is any of y'all's fault. We'll get through it. The important thing is that no one was hurt."

I nodded, pulling away to wipe my eyes, and in that instant, I made a decision. "Well, don't worry," I said, clearing my throat, "because we'll be here to help. We're not going anywhere."

My father flicked a concerned glance over to Fox, a crease in his brow. "What are you saying?"

I looked at my dad because I couldn't look at my husband. Not when he was being blindsided by this too. This was the only decision I could possibly make right now. I'd just have to pray that Fox understood. "I'm saying that I'm not moving to Seattle, not until this is all settled, and maybe not ever. I can't leave like this. I haven't gotten my letter yet, but I can defer again. It doesn't matter."

He shook his head. "No. Avery, you don't—"

"Daddy," I interrupted. "I can't even think about it. Please."

My mom pressed a kiss to my forehead like she used to do when I was little. "It'll keep for now. We'll find a way to make things right and move on. We always do."

When Fox and I got into the truck to head home, I knew I owed him an explanation. He hadn't batted an eye when I said we were staying in Brancher, but it wasn't just my life to direct at whim. We were partners. His anger over the insurance settlement was no surprise to me—he was invested in our lives here, especially as his memory precluded him from remembering much from before he'd worked his last fire season. He was in this with me, I had no doubt about that. But that didn't mean I could make huge decisions without even considering him.

"Fox?" I asked softly. He hadn't said a word since we'd walked out of the house. I watched his hands flex on the steering wheel as he turned the truck onto the main highway.

"Yeah?"

"I'm sorry I didn't talk to you about staying in Brancher. I just — I just can't leave now. But you have plans for grad school too… I'm sorry. I should've asked you first."

I knew Fox wouldn't blame me for wanting to stay and see everything through. I also knew that neither he nor my parents wanted me to once again reconfigure my life. But what they didn't understand is I would do that and a million other things, as many times as I had to, for everyone I loved to be safe and happy.

That was it. That was all I wanted.

"Avery, I would never leave your parents in the lurch like that. We don't even know our admission status yet since we applied to UW. Like your mom said, we'll find a way to make it right, and then we'll reevaluate, okay? It's still nearly a year away."

He turned for just a split second to look at me, and even though I knew I was probably a huge mess of tangled hair and red-rimmed eyes, the way Fox looked at me gave me hope. We could rewind all of this—his accident, the J.D. mess, the fire, and most of all the feeling of loss and subsequent uncertainty. We could make it whole again.

"Okay," I said, and his dimple popped. "But Fox, about J.D.— there's no reason to go looking for trouble."

His hands clenched the wheel again. "Avery—"

"Please, Fox. Don't do anything reckless, okay?" I pried one of his hands from the steering wheel and brought it into my lap. "I wouldn't ask, but I— please." I'd been thinking a lot about this. I had my theories and ideas, but deep down I knew it was better to leave it to the police.

"I promise. But we need to find him, Avery. It's the fastest way to put this behind us, and get the diner rebuilt. I…"

I know you're afraid, is what he wanted to say. And I was, still.

I wanted to help find J.D.—but not because I didn't think Fox could find him on his own. It was because I worried about what would happen if he *did*.

CHAPTER TWO

FOX

"**F**ox?"

I was sweating. It was hot in here and my limbs felt heavy, my breath harder to draw. After my shower, I'd gone to my usual spot on the couch to watch reruns, but now... where was I? Dreaming again?

"Hello?" The weight on my chest shifted. "Fox? Can you hear me?"

I pried one eye open to find my face millimeters from Annabelle's big blue eyes. I must've dozed off, and the afghan I'd pulled over myself was all tangled up around my legs. Combined with her position perched directly on my ribs—well, that explained the breathing issue.

"Hey, Bells," I said, lifting her slightly to try and free myself from the blanket. "What are you doing out of bed? What time is it?"

She shrugged. "I don't know time yet." My breathing regulated as she slid off the couch to her feet. "Can we have breakfast now?"

Seeing the world through Annabelle's eyes was refreshing. I hadn't had a lot of experience with children before this—I wasn't sure I'd be comfortable with them until I'd met her. In a lot of ways, she was like a tiny adult but with emotions heightened to the max. When she was happy, she laughed a lot and had a hard time sitting still. When she was sad, she cried, often uncontrollably. And when she was tired, she fell asleep nearly anywhere.

She had the best imagination of anyone I knew. For example, she insisted on sleeping with a nightlight in her room. I assumed it was because she was afraid of the dark.

"No, silly," she told me in her matter-of-fact tone, switching on the light before climbing into her bed. "How else will the bedtime fairies find me if they can't see? Then I'll have bad dreams!"

Admittedly, I'd never considered that scenario. But from Annabelle, it made perfect sense. Her childish wonder was infectious—and it was just what we needed right now.

I glanced at my watch—it was later than I'd thought. I hadn't been sleeping well, so maybe an extra hour was a good thing. "Sure. Where's Mama?"

Annabelle skipped ahead of me to the kitchen. "In the shower."

I figured as much, but I didn't say so to Annabelle. Avery thought I couldn't hear her crying if she was in the shower, but I knew what to listen for. There was no one in the world I was more attuned to than that girl. I knew every time she took a breath, every laugh, every tear that ran down her pretty face. It was my privilege to know everything about her, and I took it seriously.

"Annabelle, can you clear your books off the table and I'll be right back? I'm going to ask your mama how she wants her eggs."

She nodded, boosting herself up into her chair and reaching for the storybooks we'd left there last night. "Okay."

I had at least five minutes because that little girl was just like her mama—guaranteed to get distracted by a book. I turned and headed down the hall to the bathroom. Avery hadn't started taking long showers until recently. I'd let it ride for a couple days, but I couldn't stand to see her hurting—especially when she was trying to hide it from me.

"Avery?" I knocked on the door, and almost immediately her quiet sobs ceased. Another couple of seconds and the water shut off.

"Just a minute."

I waited patiently outside the door until she cracked it open and a waft of steam floated out. Avery was wrapped in a towel, the redness of her eyes easily explainable by a shampoo mishap, but I knew better.

"Is everything okay?" Her voice trembled just a bit. A less perceptive man might not have noticed—but again, studying this girl was my favorite subject.

She moved aside as I stepped in and shut the door gently at my back. "You tell me."

"I'm fine. Sorry I took so long. Did you need to get in here?" Her movements were efficient, almost businesslike as she sprayed something into her hair and began to brush.

As though we hadn't had another shower moment in our more recent history, as if I didn't know her nearly better than I knew myself. "Avery."

She put down the brush and turned to me. "I— I'm fine, Fox." The look in her eyes was almost pleading. "I have to be."

"You can talk to me about anything. You know that." I couldn't let it go. It wasn't in my nature to just accept Avery's sadness without trying to fix it.

Her hand brushed my cheek, and I turned my face into her warm palm. "I love you," she said softly. Tears threatened to spill over again, but she took a deep breath. "I just feel— I don't even know what I feel."

"We'll get through this. We are stronger than him, stronger than anything, Avery. One day at a time." It was an old adage for a reason.

"I know." She sighed again and picked the brush. "I just wish I knew what was going to happen."

No one wishes it more than me. I was not a fan of the unknown. I liked to be prepared, to have plan A and B and even Z. Avery and I were alike that way. It made me twitchy when things were out of my control, and sometimes that twitchiness manifested itself in strange distractions.

There was a time when I'd use the extra energy to work on my bike, to run, to hike, or to rock climb—those were the usual ways. But sometimes I tried other stuff too, like once I'd gone out on a crab boat for a few weeks in the middle of winter, just to get out of my own head. I liked the physicality of these things, the demand they put on my body to the point where my mind couldn't focus on anything else but moving my limbs. But now I needed to stay close to home for my girls, and running wasn't going to be enough. And if I was going to be home, I should make home the best place it could be.

"I was thinking about fixing up the backyard a little, maybe planting a garden and getting a spot fixed up for a swing set for Annabelle. What do you say?"

"Okay." I watched her in the mirror as she carefully attempted to paste a smile on her face.

"It'll be fun." *It'll be something, anyway.*

She nodded. "Sure. Sounds great."

If only I could believe that she meant it.

⁓﹏⁓

It wasn't often I wished I was unconscious. My dreams were largely kind of fucked up, and I didn't have control over them. I liked to be caffeinated, to be active, to be doing something with my body or at least my brain. That was probably why I didn't really enjoy my coma—if it was possible to enjoy comas. Awake and alert was my preferred state. But hour three in the detectives' office had me reconsidering.

"What time did you lock up the establishment, Mr. Fox? Earlier than

usual? Can we confirm that with the alarm company? What's that? No security system in place? Isn't that interesting, considering the elaborate setup at your home? Your waitress Claire said you let her leave early as well—any reason for that? Mr. Kent, where were you that evening? Can you confirm that? Any particular reason Mr. Fox took over your closing shift?"

I knew it was standard questioning, but it got under my skin. And when Avery's parents were dismissed, and the line of inquiry turned to J.D., my blood was set to nearly boil.

"Who? Annabelle's father? We have no record of his involvement with the child. What motivation would he have to destroy this business? An agreement? What sort? I see... More like an incentive, wouldn't you say? A bribe, even?"

The detectives were thorough, and ordinarily, I would've appreciated that if they hadn't made me start to doubt my own intentions. O'Connor and London knew what to do, I didn't doubt that. I just felt like they were heading in the wrong direction.

"You asked for my opinion, and I gave it to you. I'm sure J.D. set that fire. In his mind, he has every reason to want me dead."

"Because you lied to him?"

I fixed London with a pointed stare, but she didn't back down. "I didn't lie. I gave him a thousand chances. But after he broke into our house, I wasn't as polite, and he got mad."

"Broke into the house?" O'Connor flipped through a file. "I don't see a record of that anywhere."

"Right. In hindsight, that was a mistake," I said dryly.

Avery half-laughed, half-coughed. "Excuse me."

We were both punchy. I was operating on about three hours of sleep, and Avery—my wife had a spine of steel and the resolve to match. I knew that from Seattle. But when she was tired and world-weary—she looked for the humor.

"So he wasn't cooperating, he broke into your house, he threatened your family, and yet you were still going to give him money and send him on his way. And that doesn't seem strange to you?"

We'd circled back here yet again.

I fixed a steely gaze on O'Connor. "He's Annabelle's father. I tried to help him."

"And in return, he burned down your family business?"

"Not my ideal outcome." *Say it one more time for the people in the back.*

"I'm just attempting to understand the situation, Mr. Fox."

"It's really messed up," Avery told him honestly. "But we were trying to do the right thing."

"Look, I'm sure y'all are good people," London said. "But this is complicated and it doesn't play out well on paper."

"You have a witness account saying J.D. thought I was at the diner. You think I paid him to try and burn me alive?"

"I think you offered an unstable man a large sum of money. It's why you did it—and what he did afterward—that's in question." O'Connor and I stared at each other for several tense seconds before he spoke again. "You're not on trial here, Mr. Fox. I want to make that clear."

"J.D. does not know our daughter. He has no desire to remedy that. I wanted to make her adoption easy and official. He was in a bad spot, and I had the means to help him, which I hoped would, in turn, help my daughter's experience if she ever cared to meet him. We had no way of anticipating it would lead to this."

The conviction in my voice was genuine, and O'Connor heard it. Whether he believed it was up to him.

After a long moment, he nodded. "That's all for today."

My bones felt heavy as Avery linked her arm through mine and we headed down the hallway. I made it to the lobby before I couldn't take it anymore.

"Did I bribe J.D.?" I had to get it out, to set it free.

Avery gaped up at me. "What are you talking about?"

I kept my face calm, but it felt like fire burned under my skin as I spoke softly. "They think it looked like a bribe. Is that what I did? Did I bribe him to give me Annabelle?"

Avery's words sputtered out as she shook her head furiously. "No. Of course not. Don't let them put that on you."

"Throughout this entire fucking debacle I thought I was helping J.D.—but shit, Avery… maybe the reality is I simply enabled him."

─⊱⊰─

"This whole thing is bullshit," Lucas said heatedly, his loud voice crackling through my cordless earbuds. "The police know it was arson. What they don't know *for certain* is who did it. Ten people at Lucky's confirmed that they saw you leave the diner an hour before the fire started, not to mention the time-stamped security footage of you coming home. There are phone records proving the Kents' whereabouts. What did the detectives say? What's the problem?"

"The problem is, until the police can prosecute someone, there's no official conclusion. That leaves a loophole for delays, accusations, and general time wasting."

I heaved another bag of planting soil onto my flat cart, the midday Texas sun beating down on me as I stood in the outdoor section of the home improvement store in Midland. I could only run so many hours a week, and I was still bound and determined to do something productive. This was my third trip to the nursery section this week alone, which probably meant I'd already surpassed the hobby phase of this endeavor. Gardening was supposed to be soothing, but I wasn't feeling very Zen yet.

"Who burns down their fucking diner with inadequate coverage? This is beyond ridiculous, B. The Kents will take a loss no matter what. What motivation would they have?"

"Take your irritation level, magnify it by ten thousand, and you'll be somewhere in my vicinity," I muttered.

"So we just wait until J.D. turns up?" Lucas' voice dropped an octave, and I heard the unmistakable wail of a cruiser siren in the background.

"Are you getting pulled over?" I asked.

"What?" He sounded distracted now. "No, sorry. We have a police escort to the venue tonight. Crowds have been huge, and we want to make sure everyone stays safe."

Lucas was traveling on and off with one of his main clients, the insanely fucking famous band High Road Divide, as they embarked on a worldwide tour. I knew he had a lot on his plate already, but he'd made it clear he wanted to stay informed when it came to J.D., the diner, and life in Texas in general.

"You can call me later, Luke. It's okay." I pushed my loaded flat cart down the aisles, stopping to check prices in the garden fencing section before I headed to the checkout counter.

"No, B., wait a second. We can't sleep on this. If you want to mobilize something and really get out there to find him, I'm behind you. We can call Rambo Garrett—I'll put it together, and I'll be there. You know that."

Everything inside me was screaming that I couldn't just let this go, that we all needed the closure that would come with bringing J.D. in. We'd had a fairly pointless meeting with the investigators and their far-fetched ideas—and after the insurance meeting, I knew the case couldn't drag on forever if we wanted to see the policy settled. How long could my family hang in limbo? How long could the Kents hold on to their ranch with no income from the diner?

But going on a manhunt with Lucas would mean leaving Avery behind and breaking a promise to her—and that was something I swore I'd never do again.

"*Promise me.*"

The words triggered something, just another vague memory in the often dark void of my brain, images of shiny linoleum floors and long hallways, the smell of antiseptic and muted voices over an intercom.

"*Promise me you won't go outlaw, okay? We need you here with us.*" I *watched her lips move as she pleaded with me, under the flickering lights of the hospital elevator. Dempsey was out there somewhere, that asshole, drunk and completely oblivious to what he'd put my girls through tonight. My jaw clenched, but I cupped her face with steady hands. "Okay. I promise. For now.*"

The fragments of Annabelle's hospital stay after the Ferris wheel accident flashed in front of my eyes even as I trained them on the aisle in front of me. I wasn't sure any of this was a good idea but I had to do something—I'd taken up *gardening*, for fuck's sake, to keep myself busy and channel my excess energy. What good would I be to my wife, to her feeling of security, if I took off on the hunt for J.D.?

"I don't know," I admitted to Lucas, coming back to Earth. "I'm just trying to keep the status quo for now."

"What are the options, B.? Rebuilding the diner yourself? C'mon, you know just as well as I do that the best way to solve this problem is to come up with the cash to help the Kents save the ranch. Then we pool our resources, get J.D. convicted and put away, and life goes back to normal."

"I know, I know," I said distractedly. Without realizing it, I'd steered my cart over to the lumber section, right in front of a huge stack of two-by-fours. "I'll call you later, Luke. And thanks."

∼⁄∼

When Savannah Miller wants to have a video chat with you, the only answer is yes. I sat at the kitchen table with a cup of coffee and my iPad propped up on a few books, trying to conjure up an easy smile for my mom. She wasn't buying it.

"Tell me what I can do to help."

"I don't know, Mom. Honestly," I said when she tried to protest. "There's not much anyone can do." *Except maybe me. And Lucas. And his security spy shit.* But that was a no-go for now.

"I feel terrible for the Kents. What a loss." She folded her long artist's fingers in front of her chin as she studied me through the screen. "You look like you haven't been sleeping again."

"I'm—" For a nanosecond, I debated about how much I wanted to tell her. "I've been dreaming a lot lately." She'd sniff it out eventually regardless. "And thinking too much."

"I suspected that." Her smile was like Lucas's. "How's Avery?

And Annabelle?"

"Annabelle is great. Avery is… coping in her own way," I said slowly. "She feels guilty."

"Nonsense." Savannah's eyes flashed.

I laughed, a real laugh in spite of my somewhat disingenuous smile from before. "You sound like her mother."

"She's my daughter now, too. And we're both right." She leaned forward. "Listen to me, Beckett. I know you want to fix this. It's who you are. But there are some things that cannot be solved. They have to be healed."

"I'm not sure I know how to do that," I admitted.

"You'll figure it out. You always do."

We disconnected, and even though I'd been up since five that morning, I still had enough jittery energy left in my veins to consider prepping the side yard for sod. "There is something seriously wrong with you, man," I muttered to myself as I walked outside. "No one cares this much about grass."

But that was just it—I was terrible at sitting still. I had to come up with something else, and soon.

Something Lucas said had stuck in the back of my brain where I was still thinking of my mom's advice, and it all churned through my head as I stared at the lawn. I had a few rough sketches of improvements and additions I wanted to implement at home, and I'd always been interested in construction and architecture. Adding a bedroom was a far cry from a commercial build, but all any project really required was money and time.

I was lucky enough to have a bit of the former, and suddenly found myself with too much of the latter, hence my heaping pile of garden supplies and energy to burn. If I could accumulate the funds and find the manpower to facilitate it… would it be possible to rebuild the diner on my own dime?

Jim Kent wouldn't take a handout to save his spread, no matter how I sugarcoated it. Rebuilding was the only option. I couldn't sit around idly. With the Kitchen gone, we were all just drifting, waiting around for some sort of resolution, and like Lucas said—

that was bullshit. But could I pull it off?

Forget the sod for today. Phone in hand, I scrolled through my contacts until I found the name I was looking for. It would be only one of many calls today while I tried to see if my idea was even feasible, but it was a start. Maybe, just maybe, this could be the first step on the road to recovery for my wife, my in-laws, and the town I'd come to think of as my own.

CHAPTER THREE

AVERY

When someone tells you the truth only out of obligation, there is still a little bit of lie in it. Fox had told me what I wanted to hear when he first said that he wouldn't look for trouble, and he repeated the same thing when I pressed him for a promise after the insurance meeting.

"We'll see what they come up with, Avery." He'd taken his eyes off the road for a moment to glance in my direction. "I'm fine with it," he assured me.

There was the little bit of lie. We both knew it. It would keep for now, but not forever. Fox was right—J.D. was the key to just about everything amiss in our lives at the moment, but I hated to give him that kind of power. He'd had it once over me, when I was pregnant and alone, hoping he'd return my calls—I'd be damned if I let him have it again.

I never thought of Fox helping J.D. as a bribe. No one would if they knew our situation fully. The only thing Fox was guilty of was trying to make the best of a bad situation. But this time... I wasn't sure if there was anything even he could do.

We had to make this right, that much I knew. There was no other option than to finally put J.D. and his wake of havoc behind us. But I had to put my faith in the detectives assigned to the case —because my only other option was letting my husband loose to find J.D. through any means necessary. And after everything that had happened, and everything we still didn't know… I wanted Fox nowhere near him. We would find some other way.

My father had lived here in this town all his life, put his heart into running Kent's Kitchen, and kept up my grandfather's small ranch to boot. Just as it seemed like things were looking up and we could expand our livestock venture, everything went up in literal flames. It was devastating, heartbreaking, and I still couldn't wrap my mind around it. There were so many unknowns in our future as a family. Would there be enough money to ever rebuild? Would we lose everything my father and grandfather had worked for?

Almost absentmindedly I began cleaning, ruminating on the situation while aggressively dusting our built-in bookshelves, when I felt my phone vibrate in my pocket.

"Hello?" I stretched over and opened one of the living room windows, allowing some fresh air into a room that suddenly felt stagnant with what-ifs and furniture polish.

"Hey, girl!" Heather's voice came through the phone sounding much more chipper than I felt. "What are y'all up to today?"

"I'm just…" What was I doing, exactly? Distracting myself from reality? Or inventing new things to worry about? "…cleaning."

"Where's Fox?"

"Not here. He went to go get potting soil or something."

As a whole, the Fox family wasn't very good at distracting themselves with other things when they had a crisis on their hands. But if dirt made him happy, I wasn't going to complain.

"Well, I'll admit it," Heather began. "I already knew that since I'm parked in your driveway and his truck is nowhere to be seen. C'mon out here and go for a ride with me! I'm doing deliveries out and about around Odessa today."

I peeked out the front window and saw Heather waving frantically from behind the wheel of her little SUV. Without hesitation, I dropped my rag, hung up the phone, and grabbed my purse. I'd hoped for a distraction, and it showed up basically at my doorstep—and this one came with cookies. I closed the front door firmly behind me and ran down the porch steps to Heather's car.

"I have to be back by two to pick up Annabelle," I told her, sliding into the passenger seat.

"No problem," Heather replied as she backed down my driveway and pulled onto the street. "Thanks for keeping me company today. I drive more than ever now since the Kitchen…" she trailed off, flexing her hands uncomfortably on the steering wheel as we both tried to decide whether to pursue the subject of the diner. The Kitchen had been her very first account, the one that started her career—I knew she felt the loss on way more than just a financial level. "Anyway. You saved me from an afternoon of talking to myself."

"Same here. With Annabelle in school, I have a lot of free time."

I couldn't remember the last time I'd had nearly nothing to do. I'd worked in the diner since freshman year of high school, and I'd always had my studies to keep me busy. Then Annabelle came along, and college, and everything that went with being a single parent and head of your own household.

But now? There were still months before I started my grad program—if I ever made it there. I knew I was doing the right thing by wanting to stay, even if everyone disagreed with me. I couldn't feel good about Seattle until we'd come to some sort of resolution and I could be reassured that my parents would be okay.

Aside from that, Annabelle was occupied five days a week, and there were only so many hours I could spend cleaning. What were Fox and I supposed to do with all of our time? Spend the whole day in bed? I grinned for a moment in spite of myself, feeling a little shiver at the thought of Fox's strong naked body above me, holding himself up on tanned, muscled arms. Maybe we'd try that one tomorrow.

"Remember when Annabelle was a baby and y'all would come out on deliveries with me?" Heather's voice broke through my thoughts.

"Of course," I said. How could I forget when I was desperate for a way to make extra money that didn't take me away from my newborn, and determined not to ask my parents for a dime? "You were so nice to let me help you, Heather, but we both know you didn't really need me."

Heather shook her head as she turned onto the highway. "I sure did!" she exclaimed. "I wouldn't have half the accounts I have in Odessa and Midland if it wasn't for you. It was your marketing plan and pitch that got us into those restaurants and cafes, Avery. They never would've looked twice at some teenager with a home bakery otherwise."

"No way," I protested. "I just got you a foot in the door. After that, your baking did the work."

"And then Annabelle sealed the deal," she said, laughing.

At first, we'd tried to plan our new client meetings during Annabelle's nap time, where she would usually sleep like a cherubic angel in her car seat carrier. But after one disastrous timing mishap involving a diaper blowout (hers), a screaming fit (hers), and lots of tears (mine)—we learned that a happily awake baby was the key to making the sale. Heather had baked special teething biscuits that looked like some of her most popular cookie varieties, and the business owners loved to see my smiling baby chowing down on her treat while we talked about the products.

"She certainly did," I agreed. "Things seemed so complicated then, remember? At least they did for me. How to make ends meet, how to get out from under the shadow of who I was in high school and move forward? Now I have Fox, but I feel like in other areas things are even more of a mess than they were before."

"You're still essentially 'Most Organized'," Heather teased. "And everything else will work itself out, I know it will. But you're right about one part of it—some of us still haven't gotten that whole 'moving forward' thing down yet."

I shifted my eyes from the rural landscape to where Heather sat stiffly in the driver's seat. "What do you mean?"

"Lucas," she admitted.

"What? I thought things were going well!" I made a mental note to press Fox for information when I got home. If there was a problem in Lucas-and-Heather land, I didn't want to be the last to know about it.

"They are." She glanced at me with a slightly guilty look. "So well, in fact, that… I think I'm moving to Los Angeles."

My stomach flipped even as I smiled at her. "That's amazing, Heather! What do you mean you don't know how to move forward? This is going to be so good—no more long distance."

It'll be so good for you and Lucas, but terrible for me. I tried to shake the selfish, disloyal thought out of my head. *You were the first one who planned to move, Avery*, I admonished myself. *This was always going to happen.*

It was just… the way everything was going, I was deeply afraid that I would never see that dream of Seattle and grad school to fruition. I couldn't leave my parents and Brancher now. But how could I survive in this town without my best friend?

"Earth to Avery! Are you okay?"

I gave myself another mental head shake. "I'm really happy for you, Heather. I think this is exactly what you and Lucas need."

Heather opened her mouth to speak, then shut it again, looking at me carefully. "Avery," she began. "You know that Lucas tells me lots of things, right?"

I nodded. "You're pretty easy to talk to."

"Thank you, but that's not what I meant." She was still watching me closely. "You know he's said a few things about him and Fox going off and bringing J.D. in… but he tells me you're against it. At first, I understood why, what with Fox's accident and all I don't blame you for wanting to keep that man close."

"And now?" I knew what Heather wasn't saying, but her opinion mattered to me, and I needed to hear it straight from her.

"J.D. lit a fire in a small town, torched an empty building over what looks like a petty dispute with his baby mama. I'm not saying these detectives won't do their best for you, but I figure they probably have bigger fish to fry, you know?"

"I know," I admitted.

Fox had basically said the same. We believed in the system, and as a first-responder, Fox lived by it. But that didn't mean our situation would go as expediently as we hoped, no matter the good intentions behind everyone involved. Not to mention, I was fairly sure the detectives didn't have a clue where to start looking.

"I understand you don't want to let him go, Avery. Believe me, I do. But to make this right, eventually you might not have a choice." She pulled the car into a parking spot in front of her first restaurant delivery and turned to give me a long look. "I'm not leaving yet. First I'm going to help you however I can to get this mess straightened out, and then we'll both be on planes to the West Coast. Okay?"

"You don't have to—" I started.

"I'm perfectly aware of what I have and don't have to do." The no-nonsense tone was back in Heather's voice. "And I'm telling you, we always planned on leaving Brancher at the same time. None of that has changed—we just delayed it a few years, you know, extraneous circumstances and all that. And whether my destination is my own bakery in Los Angeles or to be the queen of wedding cakes in Dallas, I'm not leaving until you do." She winked at me.

I knew better than to argue with Heather when she sounded like that, wink or no wink. "All right. You win. Let's get these pastries inside."

CHAPTER FOUR

FOX

I got home from yet another trip to the home improvement store —not sure if landscaping was stress relief at this point or merely just a habit now—to find Avery and Annabelle sitting at the kitchen table, a plate of cut-up cheese and apples between them.

"How was school?" I asked Annabelle, kissing the top of her head before walking around the table to sit next to Avery.

"Good," Annabelle said, munching an apple. "Today we went to France."

I looked over at Avery in confusion. "What?"

"They're learning about cultures in other countries this week," Avery explained. "Tomorrow is Italy."

"So what you're saying is tomorrow we should have homemade pizza for dinner?" I asked. "Wanna help, Annabelle?"

"Yes!" Annabelle cried. "Yay, pizza!"

When Avery didn't comment, I turned to see a quiet smile on her face, but it didn't quite reach her eyes. "What's up?" I asked her softly.

She shook her head slightly. "Later."

I listened to Annabelle chatter about school for a few minutes, but my attention was on Avery. Something was bothering her lately, more than just the insurance thing or the detectives' progress. I knew our difference of opinion over how to find J.D. on top of everything didn't help, but there was something deeper here.

"Mama, I'm all done," Annabelle said, sliding out of her chair. She wiped her little hands on her pants. "Can I go play?"

"Sure, baby," Avery said, and Annabelle ran out of the kitchen toward her room.

I waited five seconds, listening to Annabelle's footsteps go down the hall, before I turned to Avery. "Want to tell me what happened?"

Her eyes widened for a second, and then she laughed once. "How do you always know?"

I pulled her from her seat into my lap. "I like to consider myself an expert on your face."

She draped her arms around my neck, and I pressed my lips to hers once, then twice. The feel of her body against mine made it very difficult to keep my hands at her waist, but I willed myself to keep it PG because Annabelle was roaming around and could pop back into the kitchen at any moment.

"You're pretty well-versed in the rest of me, too," Avery said, her voice low at my ear. She kissed the side of my jaw, her hands sliding over my shoulders and around to my back, but she stopped there—because she had willpower.

I wasn't as virtuous as my wife, but I was working on it, especially when little eyes and ears were around. *Me and my resolve could use a cold shower right about now.*

My hands tightened around her waist and I moved her back a bit so I could see her eyes. "Tell me, Avery."

"Lucas wants Heather to move to L.A."

Holy shit. *Good for Lucas.* "Wow. When?"

"She says she's not leaving until we do." Avery allowed herself a small smile. "I'm happy for her—I wish you had more brothers to go around."

I'd leave that idea alone for now. "Okay, so that's actually good news. What else?"

She sighed. "We already talked about it the other day."

I slid a finger over her lips. "Tell me again."

Her mouth twisted into another tiny grin which quickly disappeared. "I just—I can't stand the idea of my parents losing everything. Not *everything*, but you know what I mean. One second life is good, and the next the Kitchen is gone and maybe now the ranch too. How do I just move away and leave them with nothing? I want to do something, Fox, but what can I do?"

This was part of everything I'd been thinking about the past few days. "Avery, you're the best daughter anyone could ask for. You have to know that."

"I just feel kind of hopeless." She dropped her eyes down to her hands as she twisted them together, one of her other telltale signs of distress.

I didn't have things settled in my head yet, no solid plan. I wished I had more to offer her than just my words. But this conversation had strengthened my resolve to make everything happen. "You aren't *leaving* them, Avery. You know that, right? It's not selfish, what you've been working for. It's just incredibly fucking shitty timing and circumstances."

"It's not fair, Fox. It's not fair that after everything, he can still make me feel like this. Like I don't know what to do next. Who knows what this town thinks of me now? Do they blame me? I can't even imagine the gossip."

The sadness in her eyes just about did me in. There was only one other thing I could say to her, and I hadn't even realized I was going to say it until the words started coming out of my mouth. "Did I ever tell you what happened after Landry died? About the investigation?"

Her eyes snapped back to me like I knew they would. "No."

"I don't remember a lot of it, but I read the report when Woods gave me my file in Seattle."

"Why an investigation?" she asked. "It was a rescue."

"It's procedure, mostly," I said. "We lost a firefighter and a civilian, and people wanted to know what happened. I would feel the same way if I were fire chief or the family."

"Was it like a trial?"

I took a deep breath. "No, not exactly. We had to recount the events of the day, each of us separately, in a debriefing. Then they put it all together as a complete scene and assessed the actions of our crew."

It was easy, too easy, for me to go back there. To the smoke-filled skies, the broken ropes, the weight of Landry's death on my chest. To that desperate, almost maniacal hope that a little girl's heart would beat again.

No matter how I felt about it, even if part of me still thought I hadn't done enough, the powers that be decided that I had. For a long time—both before and after my motorcycle accident—I chose to dismiss the report, too angry and guilt-ridden to even consider that I hadn't been at least partially at fault. But the investigators knew every fact, searched intently for a flaw in our actions, and found none.

Now when I doubted myself, which was still more often than I cared to admit, I tried to remember that.

"That must've been hard. To have them rehash and dissect it I mean." Avery slipped her fingers through mine, and I brought her knuckles to my lips.

"It was." And it was still difficult for me to read about it, many months later. "But necessary. For the official record, for the families, and for us. The investigation was expository and uncomfortable, but it laid any speculation to rest and helped us all try to move on."

"What if we never get our resolution?"

"We will. I promise you that. But in the meantime—my point is, Avery, *you* know the truth in this situation. We all do. And we'll hold onto that until it comes to light."

She nodded slowly. "We'll find a way."

"Exactly." I kissed her hand again. "Let's get out of the house," I said suddenly. "Go somewhere. Anywhere." I wanted to tell her about my epiphany in the home improvement store, but it could wait.

Avery smiled, a real one this time. "Like where? Annabelle has school tomorrow," she reminded me.

"Isn't the drive-in movie tonight?"

Every few weeks, Brancher got together to show a family-friendly movie on the side of an old whitewashed barn just outside of town. Everyone came, tucked into blankets in the back of trucks, reclining in old sedans, or sometimes even set up with lawn chairs and coolers. The local market set up a little stall for concessions, and Brancher's only local radio station broadcasted the audio so you could tune in from your car stereo. I'd seen a flyer yesterday at the espresso hut—the movie wasn't from this decade, but I was still pretty sure that Annabelle would like it.

"I don't know..." she said hesitantly.

"C'mon, sunshine. Let me prove to you that this town is behind Kent's Kitchen, one hundred percent." Avery never gave herself enough credit. I had no doubt Brancher was with us.

Her eyes turned soft and bright, and I knew I had her. "Okay."

"That's my girl." I kissed her quickly before I jumped to my feet and yelled down the hall. "Annabelle! Get your sweatshirt! We're going to the movies!"

⚬⚬⚬

"Fox! Over here!"

When I pulled the truck through the gates and onto the field that served as a makeshift parking lot for the drive-in movie, we saw Joy standing up in the bed of her own truck, waving her arms to get our attention.

I was acutely aware of the apprehension on Avery's face as I maneuvered the truck around the other vehicles, and I hoped that this evening wouldn't turn out to be a stab in the back rather than a hand up after the Kents had been knocked down. Intuitively I felt like it would be the latter, and I had to go with that.

"Hi, Avery! Hey there, Annabelle!"

When people called out from nearly every car we passed, I had a feeling things would go the way I'd planned. We pulled up next to Joy and Henry and I jumped out of the cab, opening the back door to free Annabelle from her car seat.

"So glad y'all came tonight," Joy said. "I miss seeing your faces every day. Especially you!" She scooped up Annabelle in a hug. "Want to camp out over here in the truck with me and Henry? I brought ice cream," she added in a stage whisper, and Avery laughed.

"Go on ahead," she told Annabelle. "We'll be right here."

I grabbed the blankets and cooler I'd stashed in the back while Avery let the tailgate down. People were still walking around and chatting while we waited for the sun to drop low enough in the sky to start the film, and I watched with satisfaction as Avery talked and laughed with a few of her friends. Everyone said how sorry they were about the diner and that they missed seeing her there, and by the time the opening credits started, I felt pretty confident that this night was exactly what she needed.

Of course, all it would take was someone like Elise Dempsey to pop up and rain on the entire parade, but so far she was nowhere to be found—somehow an outdoor movie in the middle of a pasture didn't exactly strike me as being on a Dempsey-level of acceptable entertainment.

"Is that my parents?" Avery said goodbye to her friends and jumped up into the truck's bed, pointing out across the fields.

Sure enough, I saw Jim and Rebecca riding double on Jim's big gelding, cantering across the grass toward us. "I didn't know they were coming." That was only half true—I'd sent Rebecca a text when Avery agreed to go. But now that they were here too, it made me doubly glad that we'd come.

Jim pulled the gelding to a stop just before the far gate, dismounting and offering Rebecca a hand to help her down. The gelding wore only a halter, and after unclipping the lead he followed them like an obedient puppy on the opposite side of the fence line, safe from any late arrivers in their cars.

Like they'd greeted Avery, the residents of Brancher called their hellos, a bucket of water for the gelding was procured, and Jim had shaken about thirty hands before he reached our truck. Kent's Kitchen was a united front, and the town of Brancher was showing its solidarity. I didn't give a shit about being right, but this was one instance where I was definitely glad.

"Where's Annabelle?" Rebecca asked as she stepped up into the bed of my truck.

"Over with Joy," Avery replied. She looked over at her father. "I didn't know you were coming."

"Not many movie nights left before you go," Jim said gruffly. "Didn't want to miss it."

"Daddy, I told you—"

"Quiet now, chickie. It's starting."

There was a marked difference in the way my wife relaxed against me, her head on my shoulder, while we sat with her parents and the rest of our town and enjoyed the night air and a movie that had been made long before life had gotten so intensely complicated.

I knew that this evening wouldn't fix or erase anything, but I'd meant what I said when I told Avery about the Landry investigation—everyone who mattered would be on her side, and anyone with doubts would eventually come around. Until then, we'd keep doing what we always had, and keep being exactly who we were—like Jim Kent, who rode up to an entire town who welcomed him like a best friend.

After the movie, I collected a sleepy Annabelle from Joy and Henry's truck while Avery's parents helped pack everything else up. When we got home after a quiet drive, I sent Avery off to shower and relax while I put Annabelle to bed.

"Fox?" Annabelle said drowsily.

Someday she would call me Daddy. I felt like she'd come close a couple times, a hesitation before she said my name, but not yet. I wasn't sure how I'd feel when it actually happened, but "proud" came to mind.

"Yes, sweetheart?"

"Why can't we go to the Kitchen anymore?" She blinked her mama's blue eyes at me as she scooted down onto her pillow with her baby doll.

What was up with these girls throwing me for a loop today? Annabelle was half asleep in the truck the night of the fire, but she'd seen enough. For the second time in a matter of hours, I wasn't sure what to say.

"Well, it's closed right now, Bells. It needs to be fixed up before we can go back."

Annabelle nodded, seeming satisfied with my answer. "Okay. So when you fix it, then we'll go have a milkshake."

If she only knew what she'd just said. My resolve to make this project happen increased tenfold. I kissed the top of her head and switched on her nightlight. "Sounds good to me. Sweet dreams, Annabelle. See you in the morning."

When I made my way back into the living room, I found Avery curled up on the couch, writing in her journal. She didn't pull out the old notebook very often, but it made an appearance now and again. I never said as much to her, but I always assumed she wrote in it when she needed to hash something out with herself on paper.

I snagged a book off the shelves and sat down on the rug at her feet, one shoulder against her knees. After my conversation with Annabelle, I knew I had to tell Avery about my idea to rebuild the diner. The plans weren't fully formed in my head yet, but I couldn't go any further without her approval.

The click of her pen cap and the dull thud of the journal being set aside precluded Avery's warmth as she slid down off the couch to sit next to me, resting her head on my shoulder.

"Thanks for taking us to the movies," she said, her voice slightly muffled against my shirt. "It was a good idea. It was nice to spend that time with my parents, and Annabelle loved it."

"And you?"

She looked up at me, her eyes peaceful now. "I love *you*."

I tossed my book aside and slipped my arm around her shoulders. "I love you too, Mrs. Fox." I wanted to kiss her then, but more than that, I wanted to tell her what I'd begun to piece together about a rebuild. "I've been thinking," I began.

"Oh?" she said, her fingers running lightly up my bicep and disappearing under my shirt sleeve. "About what?"

My brain hovered right on the edge of clarity. How could I want her so badly when all she did was touch my fucking *arm*? "About—"

"I'm listening," she said, just the beginning of a sly smile appearing on her lips as her hand went to the hem of my shirt.

When her palm slid over my abdomen I almost gave in. *Gave in to what? Who was I kidding?* As if I ever needed any convincing to get naked with my wife.

"It's cool, I'm done talking."

In one swift movement, I pulled her over my lap, one hand at the nape of her neck and the other reaching up the back of her shirt, my fingers sliding over the indent of her spine.

I captured her lips with mine, feeling the catch in her breath as I stole it, loving the way she wrapped herself completely around me. It was easy to lose myself with Avery in my arms, our hearts pounding as we pulled each other closer. There was no room for anything between us, not her bra that I opened with a quick flick of my thumb, not her shirt that she raised her arms for me to remove. It was easy, so easy to get caught up in the moment with the girl who monopolized my every coherent thought.

But I couldn't love her here the way I wanted to, and we both knew it. My motorcycle injury was a distant memory, not anything that would prevent me from tossing her over my good shoulder and carrying her directly to our bedroom.

"Fox!" she squealed. "Put me down!"

"Can't yet," I said, gripping her butt and legs tightly as I strode down the hall. "Sorry."

Her laughter hushed as we passed Annabelle's door, and then we were in our room. I kicked the door shut and turned, sliding my wife's body down my own until we were standing chest to chest. Avery's eyes were heavy and lidded as she looked up at me, all traces of humor gone. Her lips parted, but before she could say anything my mouth was on hers again. It was just a taste of her— not nearly enough.

Avery tugged on my shirt, lifting it up over my torso until I broke away to shrug it off. "Better," she said, running her hands over me, her fingers hot and searching. She pulled me backward and we stumbled into each other before falling back onto the bed.

The air was cool in here, and I traced the goosebumps that appeared on Avery's skin as my hands skimmed down her sides, shifting her closer. Closer, always closer. We could never be too close, not even when I was inside her.

With that in mind, I shed the rest of my clothes quickly, and then my hands were touching her again. Skin against skin, kisses that went on and on, no breath except the ones we shared.

Avery came up for air, her fingers tracing my collarbone as she gasped against my neck. "I love you like this," she said softly. "Mine."

"Told you," I mumbled, my focus solely on getting rid of her jeans. "Done talking."

She nodded, lifting her hips for access. "Me too."

She overwhelmed me, this girl, my wife who knew me so well, who knew when I needed her skin and her body to center me, who knew when I needed her intelligence and compassion to guide me. Avery was everything I'd ever need, and I was greedy with her.

I wanted it all, all of her sighs and sharp intakes of breath, every way she moaned my name and all of the ways she touched me. I wanted her all over me, forever, just her and I until the end of our days or the end of the world or whatever came first.

When we were finally naked, I couldn't stop touching her. My fingers skimmed over her breasts, down the soft skin of her thighs, into her hair and down the line of her throat. And when she opened for me, I lost myself.

I pushed deeper, until her breath caught when I hit that secret spot, the one she saved just for me. Her eyes were locked onto my face, tracing every strained muscle, every drop of sweat that beaded on my skin. When she pulled her soft bottom lip between her teeth, I felt her body clench, her hands tighten.

But it wasn't over, not when I knew she wanted more. I was drunk on her, obsessed, willing to go to the ends of the earth and back again if that's what she asked. We'd stay wrapped up together until it was impossible to tell when she ended and I began. It was all I'd ever need.

CHAPTER FIVE

AVERY

I woke up the next morning more settled than I'd felt in the past month. Fox was sleeping soundly next to me, and for once he didn't awaken when I crept out of bed and dressed silently in the dim light of early dawn. After leaving him a note explaining my absence, I climbed into my old sedan and set out for my parents' ranch.

When I turned up the drive toward the house, I saw both of my parents out on the porch with the dogs, cups of coffee with rising steam spirals carefully cradled in their hands.

"Avery?" my mother called as I got out of the car. "What are you doing here? Is everything all right?"

"Fine, Mom," I said. "I just—I was up early and I thought I'd go for a ride."

I hadn't ridden much in the past few years, not since before Annabelle. There was a time it was vitally important to me, the hours I spent on horseback. I would take a book and a lunch and go out for the whole day, just roaming the pastures and fields behind the ranch. It helped clear my mind, helped me to feel free. There was nothing like the exhilaration of riding through a field with the wind in your hair—maybe that was how Fox felt when he rode his motorcycle. As much as I disliked the bike and nearly wanted to pass out at the thought of him ever climbing onto another Harley… when I related it to horses, I could understand.

Her worried expression cleared, and if I wasn't mistaken, she looked a little pleased. "All right, then."

My father took a sip from his cup. "Have fun, chickie."

There was so much we weren't saying. Always so much. Words were my passion and my vice, but lately, I was at a loss. But riding, this was something I could get back.

The usual morning barn sounds greeted me as I passed the ponies, Lobo and Tootsie, on my way to tack up one of our horses. My dad's big bay gelding stuck his head over his stall door to greet me, and I scratched his neck for a minute before moving down to the last stall in the barn where my favorite chestnut mare waited. She whinnied excitedly when she saw it was me, and I felt a pang of guilt. All of our horses got plenty of exercise, but I hadn't ridden her myself in quite a while. I made a mental resolution to do this more often—now that I had the time.

The sun was climbing slowly from the horizon as I loped the mare across our fields. It wasn't a lot of land, not by Texas standards, but it was home. Even though I believed with every fiber of my being that there was more life for me outside of Brancher, I knew I'd miss this place.

I drew the horse to a stop at the top of the only small ridge on the property—my favorite spot because I could see for miles. When I was younger I'd come to this place all the time, mostly just to think. The world seemed really big from this vantage point, full of possibilities.

And now… I had the chance for everything I'd ever wanted and more. Things had shifted, but I still had so much. And whether I liked it or not, tragedy was a part of life. But that didn't mean it had to be the final answer.

I slowed the mare to an easy walk to cool her down once we were in sight of the barn. The porch was empty and my parents' SUV missing from its usual spot, which probably meant they'd driven into town. That was okay with me because it meant fewer ears to hear me as I half-hummed, half-sang a tuneless melody to the horses while I got the mare brushed out and re-situated in her stall.

Lobo perked up at the sound of my voice, popping his head over his stall door to regard me curiously.

"Still just me," I told him when he huffed. "I know you were hoping for Annabelle since you heard the song, but who do you think she learned it from?"

After accepting the apple I offered him, he pulled his head back into the stall with another disgruntled snort and I laughed.

"Sorry, buddy. I'll bring her over another day, I promise."

No one would ever replace Annabelle as Lobo's favorite person. That bond had cemented itself when she was two years old and let him eat her cinnamon applesauce, and it refused to be broken. I knew without a doubt that Annabelle would miss parts of Texas just as much as I did—but I also knew she was up for an adventure.

And if I could keep my head in the right space, so was I.

I turned the radio up when I pulled the car onto the highway and headed back home. With the windows down and P!nk blaring from my speakers, I almost didn't hear the unmistakable clunk of my engine, but there was no denying the immediate plume of black smoke that started billowing from under the hood.

"Shit!" I glanced over my shoulder quickly before pulling to the side of the road. "And today was going so well," I muttered as the car coasted to a stop.

I unbuckled my seatbelt and climbed out of the driver's seat, cautiously approaching the front to assess the damage.

"Ouch! Shit!" I said again, jumping back when a huge gust of steam and smoke swirled out from under the hood as I lifted it. The hood clanged down with a loud crash, startling the birds on the wire overhead, and I started to laugh.

"Well, Avery, at least it's not raining," I mumbled, still laughing as I pulled out my cell phone. The last time I'd been stuck on this road wasn't nearly as amusing.

"Hey, sunshine," Fox said when he answered. Would the deep, warm timbre of that man's voice ever fail to make my heart flip-flop? *Not likely, especially after last night.* "Did you have a good ride?"

I leaned against my traitor car and tipped my head back, remembering the feel of the wind in my hair as I galloped through the pastures. "Yes. Thanks for getting Annabelle to school. Did she give you a hard time?"

"She was fine—really excited to see her friends. And Avery, you don't have to thank me for taking care of our daughter."

I could perfectly picture Fox's exasperated expression, but my heart was doing that weird thing again because he'd referred to Annabelle as "ours." I was so ready for that to be a given instead of a work in progress. I also didn't want to pop the bubble of intimacy we'd achieved last night, and Fox was right. We were a family. Taking care of each other was what we did.

"I know," I said, glad he couldn't see the goofy grin on my face. "So, she was excited, huh? Meaning she talked incessantly until you gave up on getting a word in, and then you let her have one of Heather's doughnuts for breakfast?"

"Pretty much," Fox laughed. "But we had a good time. Are you on your way back?"

"Not exactly," I said, scuffing my boot on the sedan's tire. "I've had a small mishap. Can you come and pick me up?" I looked around. "You'll never guess where I am."

Twenty minutes later I was admiring my husband's backside as he bent over the car's engine. Mechanical trouble aside, as far as mornings went this was turning out to be a fairly good one when it came to scenery.

"I hate to say it, but I think it's the end of the road for this guy." Fox closed the hood of my sedan with a hard clunk.

I jumped down from my perch on the truck's tailgate. "I was

afraid of that."

He wiped his hands on a rag that he pulled from his back pocket. "Sorry. Want to say your goodbyes? I'll get Annabelle's car seat and we can call for a tow later."

With the car mostly cleared out, Fox and I climbed into his truck and turned toward home. "There's something about you and that little patch of highway," he teased me.

"Hey," I exclaimed. "Don't blame me, blame the car. And aren't you glad it was so much less dramatic than last time?"

"I'm glad about a lot of things, Avery, namely that you're okay."

I leaned forward and kissed his cheek. "Thanks for coming to get me."

"Anytime, Mrs. Fox." He slid one of his big hands over my knee and squeezed, keeping his eyes on the road. "Actually, there's something I wanted to tell you—or ask you."

The tone of his voice had me turning my body toward him in interest. "What is it?"

Fox surprised me when he pulled the truck over to the side of the road. He turned the engine off and pushed his sunglasses to the top of his head, his face serious.

"I've been thinking a lot about the insurance meeting," he began.

Not what I was anticipating, but a wave of dread still swept over me. I hadn't forgotten about any of my problems, but they seemed a little farther away when I was on the back of a horse with the wind in my hair. "Okay…?"

"I have an idea, but I wanted to run it by you first."

When I nodded, he continued.

"None of us are very good at sitting around. I think the last couple of weeks have made that evident. I don't like the fact that the insurance company—or anyone else—gets to dictate our lives. Then I realized it didn't have to be that way."

"What are you saying?" I asked cautiously.

"I'm saying that we can rebuild the Kitchen, and we can start now. We have the cash to make a sizable dent in the cost, and I'll figure out the rest. What do you think?"

I just stared at him. "What—shouldn't I know that you have that kind of money?"

Fox laughed. "First of all, it's *our* money." He raised an eyebrow at me. "You signed all of the joint account contracts—did you even read them?"

"Probably," I said. "Well, maybe not. But Fox... are you sure?"

"There's no way I'm letting the Kitchen just fade away without a fight. That's not how this story is supposed to go, Avery. *We* write it. No one else gets to." His eyes flashed, and I knew he was thinking about the fire. "We'll get something from the insurance company, a partial reimbursement—but Brancher needs the Kitchen. Our family—the town—needs the morale boost. What do you say?"

I saw the truth in his words immediately. But the idea of Fox paying for the rebuild seemed like way more than his usual style of grand gestures... it was unbelievable.

"My dad won't want you to spend all of your money on the diner, Fox. He won't take a handout. You know how he is."

"That's why I'm going to offer to be his partner in a strictly business relationship. I'll work out the details and give him a proposal. And don't worry about the money, okay? I have a bit set aside for a rainy day, promise." The amused look on his face held a hint of dimple.

I wanted to think that this could all be solved so easily, but the simplicity of Fox's idea seemed too good to be true. Could we really rebuild the diner, use money I wasn't even aware we had, and erase all of this like it had just been one big bad dream? I loved Fox intensely for wanting to fix everything—but could he? I hoped like hell that he was right.

"I don't give a shit about your money, Fox. I never did. The reason I fell for you is the same reason that you're sitting here and offering to do this for my family." I took a deep breath, trying to hold in my tears. "You're good, and you're kind—and when you love, you love with your entire heart. And I'm really lucky to be able to love you back."

Fox caught my chin in his fingers, tipping my face up so he could look directly into my eyes. "It's up for debate who the lucky one is."

His lips were too close to resist. When we came up for air, he was grinning at me with that perfect Fox grin that I loved—full dimple, green eyes bright. "Are you ready to go home now?" he asked.

The look in his eyes told me that it was still an option to push all of my nagging doubts aside for the time being. "Yes," I said finally. "Or wait, no. I'm supposed to volunteer at preschool this afternoon, and I've suddenly found myself without transportation. Can I bum a ride?"

"It'll cost you." He raised an eyebrow and I shivered.

Oh boy. "I'm looking forward to it."

※

I had to admit that my thoughts were still slightly distracted when Fox dropped me off at the preschool and I greeted Annabelle in her classroom.

"Hi, Mama! Are you here to read to us again?" Annabelle grabbed my hand and tugged me through the doorway.

Her teacher waved to me. "If you want to get them started on a story, I'll prep the next activity."

Grouping the preschoolers together was a bit like herding cats, but I got them all settled on the carpet and opened the book that one little boy handed to me. It was a picture book about families, and after I'd finished reading, we went around in a circle so all the kids could share something about their own families.

"I have a Mama and a Fox," Annabelle said thoughtfully when it was her turn. "But I think I'd like a puppy too!"

"A puppy?"

"Yes!" She nodded for emphasis. "One with gold fur."

I smiled. This was the first I'd heard about Annabelle wanting a dog, but I thought she was definitely old enough to appreciate a pet and even help care for it. We could get a puppy now—though it might be a full grown dog by the time we actually made it to Seattle. The condo lacked a yard, but I wouldn't have to worry about a dog getting enough exercise with the number of miles Fox ran in a week.

"You have a fox?" The little boy next to her looked impressed. "A real one?"

Annabelle considered for a second. "He's real, but he's not furry. He gave my mama a ring and we went to the snow!"

"Is he your daddy?"

Annabelle scrunched up her brow and looked to me for help. "Mama?"

This was *so* not where I expected this storytime to lead. "Well, Fox is Mama's husband, so that makes him your step-daddy, and he loves you very much."

"I have a step-daddy, too," the little boy said. "He takes me to t-ball. My other daddy lives in Corpus Christi, and my mama says he can stay put right there."

"That's nice," I told him, trying not to laugh. "Would anyone else like to share about their families?"

We started an art project next, and while the kids were busy with their crayons I thought about what Annabelle said in the circle. I hadn't yet bothered to define what Fox was to her, and maybe that was a mistake, but she seemed to accept my explanation readily enough. I think I was still holding out for simplicity, but we hadn't managed to clear the way for that quite yet so step-daddy it was.

And honestly, that was just one of the obstacles we currently faced. More than ever, leaving Brancher felt like an impossible dream, one that I'd never attain because motorcycle accidents happen and fucking buildings were always burning down.

But after my introspective horseback ride today, I knew I couldn't give up on that dream, no matter what. I'd sat around for the past few weeks and felt sorry for our situation in general, and now was the time to be proactive. There were circumstances that I couldn't do anything about, but there were plenty of other areas where I *could.* And I hadn't come this far to just give up now.

I sent Fox a quick text—*READY TO GO IN TEN. COME GET US?* ♥

Annabelle was gathering her things while she talked to her classmates when I felt my phone vibrate in my pocket. I pulled it out, expecting a quick *OK* from Fox, but instead saw the little box indicating a video.

Well, now I was curious. I stepped to one side of the room, still in Annabelle's eyesight as she chatted to her friends, and opened Fox's message.

Even on the tiny screen of my phone, his photojournalistic style jumped right out from the first scene—a long stretch of highway set against a cloudy, stormy sky. The camera turned upward just as drops of rain began to fall, striking the lens and puddling there. As the rain began to fall harder, the screen blurred out altogether, clearing to reveal a darker night with hazard lights blinking through a windshield pelted by rain. A crack of lightning split the sky and then the video blacked out.

I cocked my head in confusion, wondering what Fox was trying to show me. But the clip wasn't over—the sky cleared and the camera swept a meandering, panoramic 360 over an old car junkyard. I laughed out loud when the faint strains of "End of the Road" by Boyz II Men could be heard through my phone's speakers. "Very funny, Fox," I murmured, getting ready to click back over to my messages and tell him so.

But the final scene in the video stopped my finger right where it hovered above the X. It was the parking lot at the school, just yards away from where I stood in Annabelle's classroom. The camera zoomed in on one car in particular—a brand-new, shiny black SUV with a small red bow on the driver's side window.

He didn't... Did he?

My phone buzzed again, a text breaking through the picture of the car still on my screen.

KEYS ON THE TIRE. DON'T GET MAD.

He knew me so well, even without all of his memories.

And then another text—*LOVE YOU. #SORRYNOTSORRY.*

And that hashtag! In spite of myself, I grinned all the way out to the parking lot.

CHAPTER SIX

FOX

The smile on my wife's face, along with her good-natured protesting that eventually just led to me carrying her to bed again after Annabelle had fallen asleep, made me regret that I hadn't upgraded her car sooner.

But you know her, I reminded myself. *And you're lucky she's allowed you two grand gestures—the rebuild and a new car—in such a short time span.* Avery would probably never just easily accept things that I tried to give her, but it wouldn't stop me from giving them.

I'd actually ordered the SUV weeks ago, way before the diner fire—but the delivery couldn't have come at a more perfect time. The old sedan might've been safe, but it certainly wasn't reliable. And now instead of the everyday dance of trying to get Avery to take my truck, I no longer had to worry about her getting stranded out on the highway somewhere.

That checked one box off my list of concerns, but I still had plenty to keep me going—namely what I was going to present and attempt to accomplish this afternoon. It had been days of long conversations with all of my consultants, but we'd finally ironed out a contract and now the rest was up to me.

I printed out the last of the papers the lawyer emailed me and gathered them into a tidy stack. Jim wasn't going to take anything resembling charity, even from his son-in-law, and that was no surprise. But he was a businessman with a lifetime of ranching and over two decades of running a successful restaurant under his belt, and now life had dealt him an unexpected and devastating blow— so maybe he'd take a *partner*.

It was all there, all outlined in clear terms—a great deal for him and a fairly shitty one for me. No escape clause, no guaranteed return on my cash, and a slow repayment plan that might never see fruition. All of that aside, it was the best idea I'd come up with in the past month, and even my financial advisors didn't balk too much at the idea once they'd limited my budget and fully explained the consequences to me.

Even if they'd objected, I had to do it. For Avery, for her parents, and for me. I never anticipated what the loss of Kent's Kitchen would do to Brancher, but I saw it every day, every time we drove past what used to be the busiest storefront in our little town and smelled the smoke, saw the charred beams and the chain link fence surrounding the site.

Brancher needed Kent's Kitchen. The Kents needed it to keep the ranch. And I'd be damned if I couldn't do something to bring it back.

I slid the paperwork into an envelope and tucked it into my messenger bag, slinging it over my shoulder as I walked out the front door to where my truck waited in the driveway.

Possible scenarios ran through my mind during the entire drive out to the Kents' spread, but when I pulled up in front of the house I mentally shoved everything aside. Either Jim would want to do this with me or he wouldn't, and whichever way the dice rolled, I wouldn't regret asking.

"Mornin', Fox," Jim said when he answered the door. "C'mon in."

Unlike when I'd shown up on his porch to apologize for my

reckless and selfish behavior in Seattle, this time I'd actually called and asked if I could come by. I knew Jim probably had to be at least a little curious, but his measured, steady amble into the kitchen gave nothing away.

"Coffee?"

"No thanks," I said. I'd had about a pot and a half already while I finalized the proposal.

He nodded. "Have a seat. Got somethin' on your mind?"

Jim and I were the same in a few ways, and one of those was a low tolerance for bullshit. So I decided to do us both a favor and just come out with it. "I want to help you rebuild the Kitchen."

Jim set his cup on the table and sat back in his chair, his gaze steady. "Not sure I'm followin'."

I slipped the contract out of my bag and set it in front of him. "I have the money and you have the legacy. We can make the new building more modern and efficient, but keep it the same Kitchen style and menu that everyone loved."

He picked up the papers and started to read. "That's all in here?"

"I'll put up the money in return for a forty-nine percent share. When everything is up and running, I won't recoup until debts are settled and the Kitchen turns a profit."

"And then?" Jim didn't look up.

"And then—" This was where I didn't know how he'd feel. "Then you decide. You can buy me out in installments, or we can stay partners."

He said nothing, just kept reading.

And because we were alike in that way, I gave him the time he needed.

"Why do you want to do this, Fox?" he asked finally.

It wasn't a no. Not yet. "Because I'm fucking tired of letting other people dictate my family—our family's—future." The words came out in a rush, and Jim looked up from the contract. "Let's end it now."

Everything we weren't saying flashed across Jim's face—the

financial strain, the family's legacy, the heartache of our wives and the frustration we felt on the daily, sitting by and letting things happen instead of making them the way we wanted. It wasn't like us. Jim and I were similar, yes, especially in the way I'd banked on —we took matters into our own hands to accomplish what needed to be done.

"You sure?"

I nodded. "We can do this, Jim. Together. What do you say?"

Avery's dad was silent for another long moment, enough time to make me sweat, wondering if I'd read this situation all wrong.

"I've got some money, too," he said. "Rainy day and whatnot. I knew it was nowhere near enough—but now it doesn't have to be." He put out his hand.

I shook it, relief bringing a grin to my face. "Partners?"

"Partners."

↘↙

My relief was short lived.

"I'm sorry, Mr. Fox, but I just ain't got time to take on another build."

"I understand. Thanks."

I ended the call and dropped my phone onto the table where I sat outside a little coffee shop in Midland. The wind had kicked up a bit, resulting in a dry, heavy breeze that did nothing to alleviate the headache I'd gotten this morning. The side effects of my bike accident were still real and still prevalent, but I was fairly certain that this particular pounding in my head came mostly from frustration. Scrubbing a hand roughly through my hair, I considered my options.

With Jim on board, the next step was to find a contractor. Over the past few days I'd gotten a few names, but so far nothing was panning out. Everyone was either too busy or short on crew. I was at the bottom of my list without a single lead—four rejections including one man who'd hung up on me as soon as I'd told him the project, plus messages left for two other contractors who hadn't yet returned my calls.

"You'd think I was trying to get people to work for free," I muttered.

My empty coffee cup wasn't helping any of my current problems, and I was just about to rise and go inside for a refill when my phone buzzed from its facedown spot on the table.

"This is Beckett Fox."

"Hello, Fox," a deep drawl came from the speaker. "Got your message about the Kents' diner—mighty ambitious build you got yourself into there, son. Any takers yet?"

"Not yet," I said slowly, trying to place the voice with a face. "Tripp?"

"That's right."

Tripp Mason was an old friend of Jim's and his first choice when we'd discussed who our contractor would be. *"Tripp's a tough old bastard, but he's fair. If we can get him, he'll do a good job for us."*

"Thanks for calling me back," I said, flipping open my notebook. "Are you available for the project?"

He let out a rusty chuckle. "Private build with a shit budget and no timeline? Sounds terrible."

I felt like banging my head against the table. "Okay then. Sorry to waste your time."

"Wait a second there, Fox." Tripp's voice held a faint amount of amusement. "Y'all are serious about this?"

I couldn't get a good read on this guy. "Have you ever known Jim Kent to make jokes?"

Tripp snorted. "All right then. Let's meet next week to talk about the plans. Monday work for you?"

"Absolutely. I'll see you then." I felt a weight lift off my chest. "Thanks, Tripp."

"Don't thank me yet," he grunted. "And Fox? It's going to be hell getting a crew on short notice. All of my regulars are on builds and it's slim pickings already. The whole county is torn apart and there ain't enough guys to put it back together."

The weight that I'd just shoved off of me threatened to pile itself back on. "I get it. But don't worry. I'll start looking right away."

This was good. This was progress. Tripp had a slightly pessimistic attitude about rounding up a crew, but I wasn't going to let that stop our forward momentum. I gathered up all of my paperwork and hopped into the truck to head home to Avery. I finally had some good news for her—the rebuild of the Kitchen was officially underway.

"Avery?"

I came into the house quickly, tossing my messenger bag and jacket on the bench we used as a catchall by the front door. I'd made good time coming home from Midland, and seeing as the SUV was still in the driveway I knew Avery hadn't left yet to pick up Annabelle.

"In here!" Her voice coming from the living room made me change course just as I was about to head into the kitchen.

"We're all set with—" I stopped short when I saw her sitting solemnly on the couch, a stack of mail clutched in her hands. "What are you doing?"

"Hi," Avery said slowly. "I'm glad you're home."

I ran my eyes over every part of her, searching for a clue to her behavior. Same bright eyes, same wild hair, but different—I paid attention to subtleties and hers were all but screaming at me. *What was up with my wife?* "I'm missing something here."

"Will you sit, please?" she asked.

My body's response was automatic and I lowered myself to the couch even as I continued to study her. "Avery? What is it?"

Her smile was hesitant as she held up two envelopes. "Our letters came today."

Letters. College. Fuck. With everything that had happened in the past few months, I hadn't given it much thought. Well, that wasn't entirely accurate. I'd thought about it as far as Avery was concerned, whether or not she'd be granted deferred admission to the grad program at the University of Washington, how she and

Annabelle would adjust to living in Seattle, and now the concrete knowledge that Avery and I needed to make sure her family in Brancher was absolved before we could leave.

But as far as my own acceptance to the filmmaking program that I'd queried... now my beautiful wife was in possession of the envelope that could dictate my next career path, and I didn't know how I would feel about the contents.

"Before we open these, Fox..." Avery paused. "I want to talk to you about something else."

Every possible scenario came and went through my head as I processed her words—from her changing her mind again to contingency plans in case one or both of us didn't get accepted. But I just nodded. "Okay."

"I've been thinking a lot about what you said the other day, about letting the insurance company decide where we go from here. And not just them, but J.D. too." She took a deep breath. "I don't want to do that anymore. I'm so glad you want to rebuild the Kitchen, and I want to do the same. I want to rebuild our family and that means pushing forward with the adoption. With or without J.D.," she added.

I stared at her. The look on her face reminded me uncomfortably of the time just following my accident, when her nightmares had come to life and she was fighting to keep our family together. If this was worse than that... I wasn't doing my job as her husband and her partner to reassure her that everything would be okay.

"Avery, we're fine," I said gently, putting my arm around her. "Nothing can break us, not even close."

She shook her head. "I know we're not broken," she insisted. "But that doesn't mean we can't be even stronger."

This obviously mattered a lot to her. Hell, it mattered to me, a ridiculous amount, even though in my gut I knew it was only a piece of paper. But after piecing together a million film clips I knew a thing or two about symbolism, and this was a big one.

"If it's important to you, it's important to me. I'll call the lawyer in the morning, see what our next steps should be."

"No. I'm going to handle this, Fox. I'm going to make us a real family, on paper, forever."

"Are you sure? If you need anything from me—"

She interrupted me with a kiss. "I know."

I wanted to do everything for Avery, to be everything for her that she'd ever need. But I wasn't such a conceited ass that I couldn't recognize the fact that my wife was a force to be reckoned with. It was what had attracted to me to her in the first place—she didn't need me, and every day she let me in was a day I felt I'd won the best prize ever.

"So should we open them?" I gestured to the envelopes in her hand. "You first."

Avery set my letter aside and slowly slid a finger under the flap to open her envelope. Halfway through she stopped and shoved it into my chest. "Nope. I can't. You read it."

"We both know what it's going to say," I assured her, but I pulled the letter out with a little trepidation just the same.

If Avery wasn't granted her deferred admission, we weren't going to Seattle. That would be okay with me, but she'd have to scramble to contact the other universities and see if anyone would take her this late in the admission process. New York was probably still an option, but I didn't think she wanted that anymore.

"You ready?" I asked, and she nodded. The first words I read when I unfolded the paper made me smile. "Congratulations."

Avery's grin lit up the entire room. "That's a sign, right? That everything is going to work out?"

"I think so." I held up the other envelope. "Here goes nothing."

There was no question that my late application to the undergrad film program was a long shot. I hadn't been to college in years, and when I'd finally decided to apply I only had a very short time to put it all together. I wasn't even sure if I met all the prerequisites for admission, but it was worth a try.

Avery took the letter out of my hands gently. "Let me do it." She opened the envelope and scanned the contents, a puzzled expression on her face. "I don't understand."

I felt a small twinge of disappointment. "It's okay, Avery," I began. "We both knew it was only a maybe."

Honestly, I wasn't surprised. If my submission wasn't what they were looking for, I had months to hone my application for next year. But I still hated to fail, even at something far-fetched and redeemable.

"But…" she looked up at me, her eyes filling with tears. "This isn't how it was supposed to go."

"Yes, it is," I said gently. "You got in. That's the most important thing. We're going to Seattle." There were a million contingencies to that statement that I knew she'd try to bring up, but I wasn't going to focus on them now.

"We can't go if you—"

"Yes, we can. We already talked about this." Life had taught me to prepare for more than one reality, and these past few months qualified for that in spades. "Lucas isn't in one place long enough anymore to be the lead monitor of his security mainframe, and it'll be simple to move it to Seattle where I can be in charge of the new branch of the company. School will always be there, Avery. I promise you—it's going to be fine. Let's focus on what we need to do before we leave, okay?"

Avery was quiet for a long moment, so long that I thought she might continue her protest when she finally spoke. "Okay," she said, and I felt myself relax a bit when she rested her head on my shoulder. "What was it you wanted to tell me when you first came in?"

I'd almost forgotten why I'd rushed home. "I'm unbelievably happy that you got into your program, Avery. And I'm not worried about school—not right now. I'll reapply, and before that, I have plenty to do here."

"Plenty to do?" she repeated.

I tipped her face up, kissing her lips once before I spoke again. "Yep. I found a contractor for the rebuild. We start on Monday."

CHAPTER SEVEN

AVERY

I didn't realize how much I enjoyed staying busy until I found myself looking for ways to occupy my time. Having a small child, free hours during the day were a luxury I was unfamiliar with —until I didn't have a day job anymore. And because Fox was busy trying to start the rebuild, I actually volunteered to drive out to the police station for an insurance errand. I wished I was going to Midland for nearly *any* other reason, including getting a cavity filled or maybe a three-hour final exam in a subject I hadn't studied— pretty much anything except my current reality.

Yes, hi, I'm here to file papers about the arson at my family's diner? The one that my baby daddy burned down. Yes, I'll take a number. Yep, totally normal. And tomorrow I was coming back this way to go meet with our lawyer. What was my life now?

It was a very boring drive, but at least I had my new car to keep my company. I couldn't get over it—this car had every feature available. I was pretty sure it could wash a load of clothes and maybe even proofread my term papers if I needed it. The convenience of having my own reliable ride also cut the time on this errand in half because I ordinarily would have borrowed my parents' SUV, and the ranch was in the complete opposite direction. So even though overall I was losing, the travel mode and time efficiency was still a win.

It also made me feel slightly better to plan on hitting a couple of my favorite thrift shops on my way out of town. I rushed through dropping off the inspection paperwork with the officer at the front desk, my mind on antique glass bottles for my fireplace mantel and maybe even a cool leather jacket for me if I was lucky, when I heard someone calling my name.

"Mrs. Fox! Avery! Wait up!" Detective London jogged down the sidewalk toward me. "Do you have a minute?" she asked.

"Sure," I said slowly. "What's going on?"

I thought I was only supposed to drop off papers—if they wanted me to speak with someone surely they'd have asked?

Unless…

Shut up, Avery. I'd been thinking about this since the last time we'd spoken. They'd never find J.D. unless he wanted to be found, and he would never want to be found unless they offered him something he wanted. Something he felt he was owed.

Detective London didn't hesitate. "I watched you in that meeting the other day. You think we're going about this the wrong way."

Shit. I surveyed her with what I hoped was a skeptical look even as my heart raced. *Damn me and my telltale facial expressions.* I prayed Fox hadn't noticed.

"You're a mind reader, now?" It came out more sarcastic than I intended, but the escalating situation was starting to weigh more heavily on me.

"No." She crossed her arms. "Just a detective."

And apparently a decent one, the current state of our case notwithstanding. "I don't know what you're talking about."

"You say you know who set fire to your diner. But no one can find your ex. Can you?" She narrowed her eyes at me. "Do you think you can?"

"No," I said quickly. "I have to go." I turned on my heel to walk away, but then stopped abruptly a beat later. *We need this.* "Maybe. Yes. Just an idea."

The detective hadn't moved. "I think we had the same idea, and my partner shot it down." She smirked at me when our eyes met. "Your husband scares him a little."

"It doesn't matter," I told her. "I can't. Fox would lose his shit, and we've been through enough already."

Her expression sobered. "I get that, Avery. I do. But you know as well as I do that we're running out of time, and each day that goes by exponentially increases the chances that we'll never find him. You don't want that, do you? Of course you don't." She paused. "You want your adoption settled. You want your family to be able to move on. And you need this resolved to do that, right?"

I nodded slowly. I hadn't agreed to anything, and yet I already felt like I'd sold my soul. This wasn't Fox's fault or his responsibility, no matter what he thought. It was mine.

"Then help me find him. Help me put him away where he can't hurt your family—or anyone else."

The events of the past couple months swirled through my brain, from the break-in to the diner fire to the sad look on my mom's face and the frustrated look on my dad's. I thought about the insurance adjuster's grim words and the reality of our adoption case. I thought about Annabelle, the worried look I sometimes caught in her big eyes, and how she knew something was wrong even if no one told her directly.

And I thought about my husband, the best man I'd ever known, and the guilt and anger he carried with him that he tried to tamp down for my benefit. We'd weathered a storm in Seattle only come back to Texas for another. And maybe, just maybe, I could do something about it.

But at what cost? "I can't."

Something flickered in Detective London's eyes, but she nodded. "Here's my card. If you change your mind, give me a call."

~\!/~

"Avery? You're not listening to a single thing I'm saying, are you?" Heather waved a hand in front of my face. "Hello?"

Her voice startled me and I blinked. "I'm sorry, Heather. Really."

"What's up with you today?" she asked. "What are you thinking about? You hardly said a word at lunch."

I randomly grabbed a shirt off the rack and held it up to myself. "Do you like this?" When she just stared at me I continued. "I'm having fun, I swear! How often do we get to go shopping together? This is great!"

"First of all, that shirt is hideous. Second, you are *not* having fun. C'mon." She jammed the hanger back on the rack and pulled me out of the store and down the promenade to the food court. "Sit here. I'm getting us a cinnamon roll and then you're telling me what's going on."

As if I could think of anything besides the disappointment of my lawyer meeting this morning. As if I could think of anything but my very strange conversation with Detective London. There was basically a cacophony of doom in my head, and it was definitely getting me down. I was surprised it had taken Heather two whole hours to demand answers.

Answers, indeed—that's what everyone wanted. I knew the real key to get J.D. out of hiding, and it was the same way we'd managed to contact him in the first place—money. Always money. Offer him the right number and he'd come running, that much I was still sure. It was everything else that went along with that idea that I hadn't quite figured out yet.

I felt a little guilty about speaking with London even though I hadn't been the one to initiate it. I'd made Fox promise not to do anything reckless, essentially hobbling him and his connections, including Lucas. But if I helped Detective London... I was actually working *with* the police, so it wouldn't be the same thing at all. Right?

No, Avery. Keeping anything from Fox was a terrible mistake, and I knew it. But a huge part of me was afraid, terrified, of what would happen if J.D. and Fox ever came face to face again. Who could blame me for wanting to avoid that at all costs? The important thing would be for J.D. to pay for his crime. How that came about didn't really matter so much, right? My guilty conscience said no, but I pushed it aside for now.

I twisted my hands nervously while I waited. What was I supposed to tell Heather? That I'd decided to try and find J.D. on my own, with a little help from the local detective force? It sounded unbelievable even to me, and I was the one who came up with the idea. If I could just get J.D. to trust me again, to call me and say he'd meet up somewhere—that would be all we needed. Then I could tell Fox, and this huge terrible weight would finally be lifted from me.

Because that's what was really weighing, more than anything. Not telling Fox.

Heather came back to the table with two cups of coffee and a cinnamon roll, which she slid in front of me as she sat down.

"Okay. I'm ready."

"I don't know where to start," I admitted. "It's… a lot."

She raised an eyebrow. "I can always get another cinnamon roll."

"I went to see our lawyer this morning."

Heather made a face. "It didn't go well? What did he say?"

I sighed. "He's nice, but not nice enough to just tell me what I wanted to hear about the adoption. Basically, J.D. has surfaced, and that means he has rights."

"He burned down the diner!" Heather exclaimed. "What do you mean, he has *rights*?"

"No conviction as of yet." I rubbed my temple. "Hasn't been found or accused of anything."

"And no sign of him anywhere, either." Heather frowned. "Ugh. I'm sorry. I thought at least now you could get the adoption settled."

"Me too. But when Fox and I had the last meeting a couple weeks ago with the detectives, I spent the entire time thinking that we weren't ever going to find J.D. this way."

"What do you mean? I know I told you what Lucas and Fox want to do—are you finally okay with it?"

"Not exactly." I took a sip of my coffee, the scalding temperature doing nothing to calm my nerves. "Fox and Lucas pissed him off, he's assuming the cops are looking for him, and he doesn't care about Annabelle. He could easily ghost forever—these are small towns with the same rodeo circuit always passing through and I still haven't seen him in years. Who's to say he wouldn't disappear indefinitely this time?"

"Good point. So what was the detectives' plan?"

"They don't have one," I said, shifting uncomfortably. "I do."

"You—what?" Heather stared at me. "What are you talking about?"

"Not a single person he knows is going to give him up to the cops. He's so insulated that they'll never even get close. But what if… what if I contacted him, and pretended like he wasn't a suspect in the fire? Like we thought it was an accident, things are business as usual, and offered him his check?"

All of the blood drained out of Heather's face. "No way. You're using yourself as bait? What the hell is Fox thinking? I can't believe Lucas didn't tell me about this!"

I didn't say anything, just looked down as I turned the coffee cup in my hands. This was the biggest load of guilt I'd ever carried, especially when I remembered pleading with Fox to let me in, and to tell the truth. It was what our foundation was built on, and he'd needed me to remind him in those days after the accident. Now I was going back on everything I'd insisted on.

I could argue that it was for the greater good, that keeping him in the dark about these plans would ultimately right a thousand wrongs, but it still didn't change the core. I was lying to my husband about something incredibly important, something he'd promised never to do.

And it made me feel terrible.

And yet.

"Fox doesn't know. Oh my god, Avery, he doesn't know?" Heather's volume increased over her last words and she ducked her head when a couple from the table nearby turned to stare at us.

"What are you thinking?" she whispered furiously.

When the couple kept staring, she raised her voice again, this time in their direction. "What are y'all looking at? Back to your fro-yo, please and thank you!"

"I'm thinking we've been through enough—I need to end this, once and for all." My gaze was steady as I looked at her. "None of us knew how this would turn out, but we had the best intentions up until the last straw. That's over now, it ended the day the Kitchen went up in flames."

Heather's eyes softened. "I get it, Avery. I really do. But are you sure about this? Fox will lose it when he finds out, and what if you get hurt, or—I don't know! Anything could happen!"

"J.D. doesn't decide how I live my life anymore. He has too much power, and that's why I'm doing this—to take it back."

She nodded slowly. "Fine. What *exactly* is the plan?"

"I haven't worked out all the details yet. But essentially—I reach out to J.D. and wait for him to confirm that he's gotten my messages. Probably a phone call, though it may not even be from him. From there, we'll set up a meeting."

"But what about Fox? Why would J.D. think talking with you would be any different from when he's dealt with him?"

"I still have to lay the groundwork—I didn't know about his deal with Fox, I don't blame him for anything, and I want to help Annabelle's father out of the jam he's gotten himself into."

"And he's supposed to buy that?" Heather asked dubiously.

"What are his choices, really? He doesn't rodeo anymore, and he's built himself up a high tolerance to whiskey and God knows what else. He needs money. I'm his only option."

"Shit."

"Pretty much."

"He's unpredictable, Avery. I don't like it. He set the diner *on fire!*"

This was the part I didn't even want to think about myself. I wasn't afraid of J.D.—not really. But when he was backed into a corner all bets were off and I had no idea what to expect.

"I'll deal with it."

"You'll *deal* with it?" Heather asked incredulously.

"I'll have backup," I said lightly, shrugging.

"You've got to be fucking kidding me, Avery. Did you turn into some sort of a spy when I wasn't looking? This is nuts! It doesn't even seem like real life."

For this, I had an answer.

"From the minute I met Fox it hasn't seemed like real life to me, Heather. It was too good to last without complications, and when they came I wasn't surprised. Ripped in two, but not surprised. The last two years of my life have been extraordinary and terrible at the same time. And I'm tired of waiting for the other shoe to drop. We've come so far and I won't let this derail my happiness." I paused. "That's how I know this is what I have to do. This was never Fox's battle, it was always mine."

"I don't think—"

"No. I should've put on my fucking big girl pants, gotten a lawyer, and handled this a long time ago, but I was too busy and put it aside. That was my mistake, and one I won't make again. How am I supposed to teach Annabelle that she can overcome anything if I can't show her?" Tears welled in my eyes but I blinked them back. "Fox wants to save us from everything and I love him for it. But I have to remember that I am fully capable of saving myself."

Heather sat back, absorbing my words. "Okay."

"Okay?"

She nodded. "I don't like it, but I get it."

"Thanks."

We looked at each other for a moment, the years of our friendship history mixing together and fusing into today. I felt right on the edge lately, right on the edge of words and tears and feelings and the precipice that would change everything forever. My choices were to fall or to jump and I preferred to be in control of my own destiny.

"You'll be careful, right?"

"Of course, Heather."

"All right then. Go kick some ass."

CHAPTER EIGHT

FOX

You could have all the money in the world, but when it came down to a lack of manpower, it didn't mean shit. I'd spent days on the phone, trying to find a crew that could come and work on the diner rebuild. But unless I wanted to ship in a group of workers from another state at an exorbitant cost—far beyond our budget because wages would have to include overtime, travel, lodging, and a per diem—there were no able bodies to be had.

The oil fields had lured many of the construction workers away with promises of big money for hard labor, and some were riding ranges with cattle herds for seasonal work. Everyone else within four hundred miles was already on a job, repairing buildings damaged in the slew of recent tornados.

Jim Kent was a proud man. I understood that. For as readily as he'd agreed to our partnership, I knew it was hard for him to need anything from anyone. We'd come so far, and I wasn't willing to give up now. The plans were drawn and approved, the equipment rented, the lumber and supplies ordered. The only thing we were missing was a crew to build it.

Aside from that, I was preoccupied about Avery. After she'd gotten her acceptance letter, I thought we were in a good place, on the same page about moving forward. I allowed myself about three minutes of self-pity, and then it was back to business as usual.

Her focus was zeroed in on the adoption, as mine was on the rebuild. But after her meeting with the lawyer, I felt like things had shifted yet again. She'd been so upset when she came home, and it killed me. I'd never felt so fucking helpless in my life, but I'd promised her that I'd stay out of it and therefore my hands were tied—the ever-present problem of J.D.

One thing at a time, I told myself. *First, we start the build.* Sure, I'd promised Avery I'd stay out of it, but that didn't mean I couldn't dispatch a few select people on my behalf.

"Any luck with a crew?" Tripp asked when I met him at our usual Midland coffee shop.

"No," I admitted, shoving the lid down on my to-go cup. "There's no one."

"I told you, kid." He took a long pull from his drink. "Not much else we can do."

I flexed my shoulders in irritation—not so much at Tripp, although he wasn't helping with his less-than-chipper attitude. "You were right, okay? Too many disasters, not enough people."

He coughed. "Mother Nature can really fuck up your plans, can't she?"

He didn't know the half of it. She and I had a tenuous relationship at best. "I can get a couple guys. Henry and Jim, maybe my brother. We can start to frame it at least, see what happens." I wasn't going to give up so easily, no matter what Tripp said.

"A build like this, we need a crew of at least ten or so. Otherwise, we'll make no progress before the weather turns." He gave me a long look. "It's not too late to postpone."

"I'll get them," I said, draining my cup and tossing it into the trash can. "You show up with the plans, and we'll get it done."

We said goodbye, and I walked down to my truck parked on

the next block. Every time I felt like we'd taken one step forward, we got knocked back. I wasn't one to admit defeat, not until it was completely out of my hands. That was something ingrained in me as a paramedic—you kept administering CPR, no matter what, until the patient disappeared into the operating room.

The screen on the truck's dashboard showed Lucas' name a split second before I heard the ringing come through my speakers.

"Hey, Luke." I put the truck in reverse to pull out of my parking spot. "What's up?"

"You sound like hell," he said bluntly.

I grinned in spite of myself. "Thanks, asshole."

"What happened?"

"Where do I begin? Still no crew, Tripp wants to bail on me, and we're supposed to start building next week." I picked up the water bottle from my cupholder and frowned at it. "Plus I'm out of coffee."

"Well, it's your lucky day then, because I happen to have a fresh cup in my hand with your name on it. Come pick me up."

"Come pick—" My brain took a second to register his words. "Are you in Texas?"

"I sure as fuck hope so, because otherwise you're shit out of luck with the coffee." He laughed. "C'mon, I'm at the airport and your latte is getting cold."

Fucking Lucas. He was the only person on the planet who could supremely irritate me and make me want to hug him at the same time. He'd really come through for me this past year, and I'd never forget it—not like he'd ever let me.

"I don't drink lattes," I told him.

"I'm trying to bring a little refinement into your life."

"I hope you also brought a tool belt."

"Just come get me, B."

⁓⟋⟍⁓

"You need to expand your reach if you're going to bring some guys in," Lucas said, gesturing with his wine glass. "What we're missing here is *marketing*."

I raised an eyebrow at him as I stood to clear the dinner dishes. "What we're missing here is a crew of able-bodied individuals who want to build a diner."

Lucas shrugged. "Okay, whatever. So we've got you, me, Jim... who else?"

"Henry," Heather supplied, setting one of her homemade pies on the table.

"Definitely Henry," Avery said as she walked back into the room from putting Annabelle to bed. "He's retired and bored. Joy says he's driving her crazy since they're both home all day now."

It was difficult for me to imagine the quiet, gruff older man being anything but a statue of solemn silence. But then I added Joy to the mix, with her no-nonsense personality and eagle eye, and understood. What was that quote? Something about space in your togetherness? Any couple could probably benefit from that now and again.

I glanced over at my wife, fighting the urge to kick Lucas and Heather out the door so I could be alone with her, feel her skin, touch her face, make her laugh. *Okay, any couple could benefit from it except for us.* I wasn't good at separation from Avery.

"I've been all over Midland and Odessa, to the unemployment offices, the lumber yards, the temp agencies, anything I could think of," I told Lucas. "My next option is just to put up flyers and hope we have a turnout."

"Marketing," Lucas repeated. "Supply and demand. Textbook economics. Taking need and turning it into opportunity."

"Now you're just saying random shit."

Avery and Heather laughed, but Lucas was undeterred.

"I pride myself on knowing a little bit of everything," he said, stretching. "Makes me more versatile."

"Makes you just shy of useless," I grumbled, but I didn't mean it. It wasn't fair of me to take my frustration out on my brother, not when he'd flown two thousand miles to help. But with the start of the diner build looming before me, I was cutting it close when it came to crew—way too close. And if I couldn't get it done, I wasn't just letting Tripp down, I was disappointing my wife, my in-laws, and the entire town of Brancher. *No pressure, Fox.*

Lucas ignored my crappy attitude, like I knew he would. The look in his eyes told me that for all of his superfluous talk, he was aware that this was a serious problem. "Tomorrow, B. You and I will paint the town with flyers. Yeah?"

I nodded. "Thanks, Luke."

The four of us sat in reserved silence for a moment before Heather spoke. "I think we'll let y'all get turned in for the night," she said. "Fox, you enjoy the rest of that pie, okay?"

Avery and I walked them to the door, the girls discussing their plans for the following day—something about preparing for a craft fair at Annabelle's school. I was glad Avery was keeping herself busy, but I knew I was out of the loop with her because I'd been so busy trying to get the build started.

The weight of my guilt hung heavy over our goodbyes. I took this project on not to be a hero, but to reassure my family that we could move on from anything that was thrown at us. I had to get it done—but I didn't want to alienate anyone in the process. Avery was keeping herself busy with volunteering, Annabelle's daily needs, hopefully still planning for grad school—I knew she could handle all of that and much more, but I still wanted to be there for her. My brother was using his entire hiatus vacation from High Road Divide's tour to help me, and I owed him already for the reality check he'd provided me in Seattle.

There was a lot on my plate but I did better that way—time for calculated moves only and zero speculation. If it was time for me to fall back on the Hotshot work ethic that had gotten me through hundreds of fires and other disasters—I was up for the challenge.

Lucas was too, even though he complained bitterly when I picked him up the next morning just before dawn.

"Are you fucking serious, B.? I'm jet-lagged and a little

hungover. The sun isn't even up. As far as I'm concerned this still counts as the night before."

I'd been up for two hours already, watering a lawn that didn't need it and making sure Annabelle's lunch was all packed and ready to go. After that, I tried to read a little before the girls woke up, but when that didn't calm my racing thoughts I decided to just go grab Lucas.

"Stop complaining and get in," I said.

"Coffee," he mumbled. "I'm in it for the coffee."

"I'm in it for the idea of actually getting this build off the ground, but yeah, I could go for some more coffee too."

Some of the businesses were just starting to open their doors as we began to check all of the places I'd been advised to visit. Our last stop was a home improvement store, which usually would have a line on available workers, but I hadn't had much luck. In one way that was a good thing, because it meant that everyone who could or wanted to work actually had a job. But for me, more immediately, it was fucking terrible.

After thoroughly checking the job board on the side of the building, Lucas shrugged, shaking his head in disbelief. "I thought you were exaggerating, but this is the third place we've tried. What now?"

"Told you," I said. "More coffee?"

If there was one thing I could count on in Texas, it was strong coffee and plenty of it. The donut shop by the home improvement store was calling my name with that plus the promise of an apple cruller, and Lucas followed me across the two-lane street into the sugar-filled air of the tiny store.

"Two coffees please," I told the woman behind the counter. "And a half dozen of the crullers."

"I can't eat any of those," Lucas said in a low voice. "Heather will smell them on me and know I cheated."

"Thank you," I said, collecting my coffee cup and the pastry box. I rolled my eyes at Lucas. "You're kidding, right?"

Before he could answer, I heard someone calling my name.

"Fox, ain't it?" I turned to see a short, stocky, gray-haired man standing there, arms crossed over a barrel chest. He looked me and Lucas up and down quickly. "Jim Kent's son-in-law?"

"That's me," I said cautiously. One of the many incredible drawbacks of my amnesia was the uncertainty of introductions—had I met this man before but just didn't remember? I glanced to Lucas for help but he seemed just as confused as I was.

"If you're out lookin' for help to rebuild that diner, you might as well look elsewhere," the man said gruffly. "Nothing for you here."

"I see that—we haven't had much luck," I said cautiously. "The lack of labor is really putting us in a bind. If you know anyone who needs a job, I'd be grateful if you'd pass the word along."

He regarded us for a moment. "Any truth in the stories goin' round out there?"

Lucas cocked his head and surveyed the man. "I'm not sure what you've heard."

"Oh, I heard plenty. One of the local boys come back to haunt his daughter, is that right? Hotheaded rodeo type, never had much sense. And now Jim Kent may have to sell his family spread. A shame is what it is." A couple of the men standing behind him nodded in agreement.

My frustration with the situation threatened to boil over as I stared at him, my hands tensing and threatening to crush the box of crullers. "Something like that."

Not everyone had all the facts, but it didn't stop them from forming their own opinions—largely accurate but still clouded by preconceived notions. Avery could never know about this.

The old man frowned, shaking his head. "Damn shame."

"Agreed." Lucas turned to the small group that had gathered. "We're serious about needing workers. If anyone is available, it's an honest job. Let's go, B."

I kept my face completely blank until we got back into the truck. "*FUUUUCK.*"

"Heather told me people were talking." Lucas shook his head.

"At least they've got the story mostly straight."

"Small victories." I scrubbed my hands through my hair. "I just feel so fucking bad about all of this."

"Of course you do." Lucas snorted. "You're a fixer. You always have been. It's exhausting, have I mentioned that? And I think some of it's rubbing off on me."

"I guess we'll find out." I started the truck's engine. "Hey, Luke? Don't tell Avery, okay? She's already all torn up about the plans to move to Seattle and worrying about her parents. I don't want her to feel worse."

Lucas was silent for a moment. "I know we talked about you heading up a Seattle branch when you move, B. I want you to, but I also want you to know there's no pressure. Whatever you need to do for your family—do it."

"The worst thing I could do for my wife is let her guilt hold her back. We're going to Seattle, Luke. I don't know exactly when, but we'll get there."

He nodded. "And B.? I know you want to let the police handle things, but—"

I cut him off. "You'll be the first to know."

―✶―

How the fuck am I going to pull this off?

That was the first conscious thought in my mind when I opened my eyes the next morning. It was followed closely by *Avery's naked,* but I didn't even get to act on that one before I made myself roll out from under the covers and start to get dressed. *Sometimes being an adult really sucked.*

"Fox?" Her drowsy voice permeated my thoughts. "What time is it?"

"Too early, sunshine," I told her, coming to sit on the edge of the bed where at least I could appreciate her sleep-tumbled hair and smooth skin, even if I didn't have time to touch her the way I wanted to. "Too fucking early."

She frowned a bit at my words. "Are you ready?"

No. "Yeah." When she didn't look convinced, I continued. "It'll be okay. Maybe a little on the slow side for a build, but we'll work it out."

By Tripp's estimation, we didn't have much time before the weather started to take a shit on us, bringing everything from scattered showers to electrical storms and the occasional tornado. The Texas heat was always a constant, but every now and again Mother Nature liked to make things interesting. If we factored in potential delays, this build could stretch out indefinitely, especially considering our small crew.

"This is more than just for us—I know you understand what the Kitchen means to this town. You have the biggest heart, Fox." Avery reached up, wrapping her arms around my neck and pulling me down to her warmth. "I love you."

I kissed her, wishing again I had all of our memories intact, wishing I could use my words the way she did so I'd be able to tell her that regardless I still understood all of her, every whisper and sigh, every gentle way her body gave, and most of all how her voice changed when she was sad.

I couldn't fix everything for Avery no matter how much I tried and no matter how much I would always want to, but I'd do the best I could for her and for Annabelle until I could do no more. I guess Lucas was right—it was in my nature to help, and that tendency was magnified tenfold when it came to my family.

"I have to go," I said when we broke apart, kissing her fingers as they trailed across my jaw. "Go back to sleep."

She nodded drowsily. "Annabelle and I will come by after school."

The streets were quiet and still as I drove my truck toward the town center. It was early, but more than that, there was a distinct part of Brancher that was missing without The Kitchen. Normally at this time we'd be starting breakfast for some of the early-rising ranchers and catching up with some of the other local business owners as they stopped in for coffee before starting their own work days. Even the owners of the little espresso stand were overwhelmed, hiring Claire on temporarily to help them with the extra demand.

"We're grateful for the business, Fox, but not at y'all's expense," Gladys behind the counter told me the day I'd met with Tripp.

I slowly eased the truck into a parking spot across the street from the remains of the diner and slid out of the cab.

"This is it," I said, my voice clearer than my thoughts as I used my camera to pan the scene and record the magnitude of what lay in front of me. "Day one of The Great Kitchen build." I turned the lens to my face. "So far, it's just me. And it'll probably end with just me. But eventually, it'll be done."

The demolition was finished, and what was left included a few dumpsters of salvage and all of the fresh materials. Tripp's plans kept the same square footage, but utilized the space much more efficiently, giving us room for more tables and better pantry storage. I could see the new restaurant keeping the charm of the old building with ease, but integrating modern conveniences such as central air as opposed to the window units we'd used previously.

I was itching to start, to see the new walls go up and the plans take shape. But with the size of our crew, I knew I had to be realistic. There was a chance that the flyers I'd distributed would yield a few day workers here and there, but with the lack of available bodies, it could very well be a skeleton crew the whole way.

I was sitting on the tailgate of my truck when Jim pulled up with Henry in his passenger seat.

"Mornin'," he said, getting out and coming around the side to greet me. "Been waiting long?"

"Just a few minutes," I answered, shaking Henry's hand when he joined us. "The others should be here soon."

I'd tried to get Lucas to stay at the house with us, but he'd opted for a short-term lease in Midland instead, saying he could bring in supplies on his way into town if needed. I was sure this arrangement was made with Heather in mind as well, who was now having to reach further out with her business after she'd lost the Kitchen's orders and probably appreciated the ability to work out of his place in Midland.

When Tripp and Lucas arrived, we started to walk the site.

"The foundation is fine, so first we clear out whatever was left by demo, and then we frame." He pulled on his work gloves. "Ready?"

Lucas and I did most of the grunt work through the morning, letting Tripp, Jim, and Henry organize the lumber and start to prep for framing. By lunchtime, I'd worked up a sweat and an appetite, and Lucas slapped my back when we parked ourselves by the water cooler to take a break.

"Fuck," he groaned, stretching his back. "I'm a good brother, B. Don't forget this, okay?"

I smirked at him. "Wishing you were on a private plane right now, Luke? Or relaxing in a five-star hotel suite in Europe?"

Lucas took a long drink from his cup, holding his middle finger up while he swallowed. "You have an extremely warped view of what I do for a living. But honestly, yeah."

I was about to bust his balls a little more when another truck pulled up across the street. Since our part of the block was largely deserted due to the construction, I hoped it wasn't an inspector or someone else coming to deliver bad news. My own recently separated shoulder wasn't feeling great, but it was infinitely more bearable than another setback.

"Who is that?" Lucas stood up, trying to get a better look.

When the first man stepped out of the truck's cab, I felt my face stretch into a grin. "Derek."

Kyle hopped out next, and for the first time in weeks, the idea of this build was looking doable. But nothing could've prepared me for the third person Derek had in his truck. I blinked twice, squinting through my sunglasses.

"Is that... Chase?" Lucas's voice was incredulous.

"Yep," I said, draining my water cup and getting to my feet.

"I'll be damned."

"You probably will, Luke, but it'll be for something much more interesting than this."

The three men crossed the street, looking ready to work in old jeans and construction belts. I met them at the edge of the street.

"Hey Fox," Derek said easily. "Heard you needed a little help. Kyle and I decided we'd cut down to half days on our other sites and get this thing moving. You got room on your crew?"

I laughed, glancing around. "Yeah, I think I can squeeze you in the rotation."

Kyle grinned. "You got ol' Tripp leading this build? I haven't seen that guy in a minute. C'mon," he said to Derek, and with Lucas, they headed over to where the other men were standing.

"And you?" I said to Chase. I didn't have memories of the last time I'd seen him, but I knew enough to realize that he'd made a big effort coming back to Brancher, especially with everything that had happened.

"I'm here as long as you need me," he replied, meeting my gaze steadily. "That's what we do, right?"

I nodded at his reference to our Hotshot firefighting days. To that one specific day, the one when everything changed. "Yeah. Thanks, man."

"I got you, Fox. For you and Avery, and the Kents... it's the least I can do. I mean it."

I slung an arm around his shoulders as we walked back to Tripp's layout table. "Remember that when your blisters have blisters."

The eight of us worked through the rest of midday, making more progress than I could've hoped without the inclusion of Derek, Kyle, and Chase. When Avery's SUV pulled up, I saw the shock register on her face when she spotted Chase, but he respectfully kept his distance until she approached and gave him a quick wave before greeting the rest of my motley crew.

"This is... a day for surprises," she said, amusement clear in her voice.

I studied her closely, cautiously pleased with her reaction to

Chase's presence. There was a lot of history there, some not so ancient, but she seemed happy that he'd come home to help us. I'd let it ride for now. "No kidding. Where's Annabelle?"

"I'm on my way to get her now. Just wanted to drop a couple things off with you first." She stretched on her toes to kiss me.

"What is it? Is it cake? Did Heather send cupcakes?" The barbecue sandwich I'd eaten at lunch was a distant memory.

Avery laughed. "No, but if you ask, I'm sure she'd be happy to. You know how she feels about your face."

"I'm standing *right here*," Lucas called from a few feet away.

Avery waved her hand at him dismissively. "Anyway, can you help me?"

Dutifully I followed her to the SUV, but before we reached the rear passenger door, it opened. I took a step back as two men slid out of the backseat and grinned at me.

"Surprise," Avery said softly. "Look who showed up at our door."

If I was shocked when Chase showed up, it was nothing compared to seeing my two best friends standing before me.

"What the hell are you guys doing here? You're a long way from the Oka-Wen." I slapped McDaniels' outstretched hand with a grin.

"You thought we were gonna let you play home-on-the-range out here all by yourself? I see enough of Sloane's ugly face on the fire line, I don't need to take vacations with him for quality time," McDaniels smirked.

Sloane rolled his eyes at McDaniels before turning to me. "Your mom called, told us what happened. We're here to help you, man. Put us to work."

I didn't know what to say. I looked back and forth between the two of them. Seeing them here in Texas was the last thing I expected but again—I should've known better. If there was a way, any way, they could come through for me, they probably always would. Just like I did for Chase, and now Chase did for me. Somehow, it always came full circle.

"I have to pay you mostly in beer," I said finally, and McDaniels laughed.

"Don't need the money but we'll take the beer. We cashed in—sick days, vacation, all of it. You got us for six weeks, Foxy. Let's build some shit."

CHAPTER NINE

AVERY

"Okay, we've narrowed it down to three. What's your final decision?" I held the costumes out in front of me. "You have to choose one, baby."

Annabelle cocked her head to one side, considering. I mean, I understood her dilemma. Trying to pick between Alice in Wonderland, a fairy queen, and Wonder Woman was probably the toughest decision of her life thus far. But Halloween was tonight, and we'd been in the party store for an hour and a half. I was already verging on a mom-fail by waiting until the last minute—luckily there were still plenty of costumes to choose from.

"I want..." She stepped back and surveyed them all again. "Alice."

Sweet relief. "Great! Let's go."

"Wait, Mama!" Annabelle tugged on my hand as I started to head to the register. "What about you? And Fox?"

I wasn't planning on dressing up this year, but what the hell. Quickly I grabbed an adult-size Cheshire Cat costume for me and just the hat from the Mad Hatter's ensemble for Fox. "Okay! All set."

It was imperative to make retail decisions quickly when you had a preschooler and so far we'd failed spectacularly at that, so I wasn't going to add any more time picking a costume for myself. I figured I had about another thirty minutes before she would either need a snack, a nap, or the potty—and I still had to stop at the grocery store and the post office.

These last couple of weeks had been incredibly busy for Fox, but I was more than happy to hold things down on the home front. *My husband was rebuilding the Kitchen.* Even though I'd seen the site with my own eyes, I still couldn't believe it. Not that I didn't believe Fox could do it—I was fairly certain that he could do anything. But the fact that he wanted to, that he felt so strongly about family that he would take this on. That was the unbelievable part, just like so many of his grand gestures. Being loved by Fox was surreal in the very best way.

And the fact that he loved me so much—it just strengthened my resolve to find J.D. and end the legal part of this nightmare. Fox was rebuilding what we'd lost, healing us in his way. I would do my part and make sure that man could never hurt our family again.

But before that, I was going to take my kid trick-or-treating. While Annabelle went down for a late nap, I put the taco casserole Fox prepped into the oven and tidied up the house a bit. With any luck, the casserole would be done, Annabelle would awaken, and Fox would come home from the construction site all at the same time.

I called Heather while I chopped lettuce for a salad. "We're coming by after dinner, okay?"

"Perfect." Heather sounded distracted. "Just trying to finish up these treats before sundown. I swear, the kids start ringing the doorbell earlier and earlier every year."

"Well, not everyone makes homemade candy like they're the Southern belle version of Willy Wonka," I told her. "You'd be less stressed if you bought a few bags of lollipops like I did."

"Not everyone wins the State Fair contest for confections three years in a row, either," Heather said smugly. "Give out store-bought candy? I'd rather cut the lights and sit in the dark all night."

I laughed. "Your 'too much' gene is showing again."

"Loud and proud," she said. There was a clatter in the background. "Dang it! I gotta go. I'll see y'all in a bit!"

I hung up the phone just as Fox walked through the door. "Something smells good," he said, pulling me in for a kiss.

I came up breathless. "It better—you made it. I just wished it well when I slid it into the oven."

"Where's Annabelle?"

"Napping," I said, kissing him again. "I want to let her sleep as long as possible because we'll probably be out late tonight." I slid my arms around his neck. "The casserole still has fifteen minutes."

Fox put his lips to my throat. "How should we pass the time?" he murmured, sending a chill up my spine. Fifteen minutes with Fox had endless possibilities, and I liked all of them.

"How about you put your hand here," I said softly, sliding Fox's hand up under my shirt. "I'll put mine here." My fingers delved into the waistband of his boxer briefs. "And we'll see how it goes from there."

Fox's eyes were deep green pools. "I know exactly how it'll go." In one quick movement, he boosted me up with his free arm, turning to look at the oven timer. "Only fourteen minutes now, sunshine. Better hold on tight."

⁓⁄⁓

"Wow." I hadn't looked closely at the package when I bought the costume, and there was no turning back now.

"What's wrong?" Fox asked immediately from behind the closed door. *Can't trust myself in there with you right now,* he'd said. *Not if you're naked.* I felt the same way. It was never enough.

"Nothing!" I came out of the bedroom with a flourish. "Ta-da! These are just like pajamas! This is amazing!"

He took one look at me and started laughing. "Is that a onesie?"

I nodded. "Yup. Goodbye, sexy Halloween costumes! I'm only wearing onesies forever. Gender-neutral is the way to go."

Fox's dimple made an appearance as I twirled around in the hallway. "You look real cute, sunshine." He reached for my striped furry waist. "Let me see a big Cheshire Cat smile."

I grinned at him, and he quickly covered my mouth with his own. *I could really use another fourteen minutes with this man right now.* The costume was comfortable, but there sure was a lot of material between me and my husband. I'd have to think about that for next year.

"Mama!" Annabelle called from her room. "Is it time to go?"

Fox and I broke apart just as she came out wearing her Alice dress, plastic pumpkin in one hand. Admittedly, this was the costume I wanted for her all along, because I knew she'd be perfect as Alice with her long blond hair. But Annabelle was starting to become her own person, and I tried to let her make decisions when I could. You know, unless that decision was to try and eat her body weight in cookies or tickle rattlesnakes or something.

"Hi, Alice. Have you seen my daughter Annabelle?" I asked. "We're going trick-or-treating and I can't find her anywhere."

Annabelle burst into giggles. "Mama, it's me! Annabelle! I'm just wearing my costume!"

I feigned relief. "Oh, Annabelle. Thank goodness. I didn't even recognize you!" I loved that she was still little enough to play like this. I knew someday she'd be rolling her eyes and running off with her friends, but for now, she thought I was hilarious.

"You look exactly like the kitty, Mama." She turned to look at Fox. "Where is your costume?"

"Oh, sorry." Fox perched the Mad Hatter's top hat on his head. "Right here."

"Hmm." Annabelle surveyed him. "Okay."

"I feel as though I've disappointed her," Fox whispered in my ear as we walked down the hallway to the front door. "Where's the rest of the costume?"

"I didn't get it," I whispered back. "We were in a hurry and I also didn't think you'd want to wear a strange little suit all night."

"Point taken." He paused as Annabelle found her cardigan sweater. "I do have a couple suits but none of them are little and strange. Should I put one on?"

"Mama! Fox! I'm ready!"

I shook my head at him minutely. "She's over it. Let's go!"

Annabelle took Halloween very seriously. This was only the second year that she'd really grasped the concept, but once she had, it was like getting candy became the mission she'd been born to lead. Only the fact that I imposed an ironclad rule of hand-holding kept her from speeding down the block and leaving me and Fox in the dust.

"C'mon, Fox," she cried, dragging him up the porch steps to our neighbors' house. "Mrs. Vancity is waiting for me!"

The thing was, she wasn't wrong. The Vancitys loved Annabelle like a granddaughter. In fact, nearly all of our neighbors had a soft spot for my little girl, and that was evident when I weighed her stash in my hands after just a couple blocks.

"Annabelle, we aren't even halfway to Auntie Heather's and your pumpkin is almost full!"

Her grin flickered just a tiny bit. "It's getting heavy, Mama."

Fox pulled something out of his back pocket. "Let me see." He unfolded a reusable grocery bag and dumped Annabelle's candy into it, then handed the empty pumpkin back to her. "Ready for round two?"

"Yay!" she cried.

I just looked at him. "You were a Boy Scout, right? Because if not, this just isn't normal." I thought *I* was overly prepared for things, as my alter-ego "Most Organized." But I'd met my match in my husband.

He shrugged. "You gotta step up the candy game once they get a little older. Lucas and I used to have a secret stash spot that we'd revisit three times, just to leave off candy and keep our bags from filling up before the night was over."

"How much candy could two kids possibly need?" I asked.

"Don't let Heather hear you say that," he whispered to me as we rang her doorbell.

The door swung wide open and Heather appeared, wearing a Glinda the Good Witch costume. "Finally! Come in, come in! Welcome to the wonderful land of Oz!"

If my best friend was surprised to see me in a Cheshire Cat onesie, she didn't bat an eye. But when Lucas appeared next to her in a full-fledged scarecrow costume, Fox couldn't contain his glee.

"You've never looked better, Luke."

I had to admit, they'd both committed admirably to their theme. Heather's dress was gorgeous—poufy, spangled, and the perfect shade of Glinda pink. And Lucas—he was the most muscular scarecrow I'd ever seen, but his patched shirt and pants just the right level of threadbare, with errant pieces of hay sticking out from every seam.

Lucas sneezed. "Shut up, B."

Heather ignored them. "Are you a good witch, or a bad witch?" she asked, waving her wand at Annabelle.

Annabelle looked at her blankly. "A good witch?"

"Of course you are!" Heather plunked what sounded like two pounds of candy into Annabelle's bucket. "My favorite!"

"You guys really do look great," I said. "Where did you get the costumes?"

"Lucas ordered them from someplace in L.A.," Heather twirled, her full skirt twinkling. "Isn't this dress beautiful? I miss pageants. Do you?"

I decidedly did not. But that was probably because I never won.

"I wanted us to be Frankenstein and his bride," Lucas said, hefting the tub of festively wrapped candy he held in his arms. "But I got outvoted."

I caught Heather's eye. *Bride?* I mouthed at her, but she just shrugged. "Frankenstein was the doctor," I said. "You'd be Frankenstein's *monster.*"

"Whatever." Lucas scratched at the hay sewn to the collar of his shirt. "This is itchy. How'd you get away with just a hat?" he asked Fox.

"I'm already married," Fox joked with a grin and I snickered.

Annabelle pulled on my sleeve. "Mama, are we getting more candy?"

"How about a caramel apple?" Heather asked, waving her wand around a little more for emphasis.

"Okay!" Annabelle dropped her pumpkin like it was old news and started to follow her into the kitchen.

Of course, with Heather, it was never *just* candy. I should know that by now. "Wait for me! I want one too."

"Next year, I'm thinking Flintstones," Heather was saying as she walked. "Lucas can be Fred, I guess, but I feel like he's more of a Barney."

Next year... next year we'd be in Seattle, Heather and Lucas would be in Los Angeles, and there would be no over-the-top treats or best friends just down the street. These moments were slipping by more quickly than I'd anticipated—too quickly.

"Something wrong?" Fox asked as we walked home.

Annabelle snored softly on his shoulder, and I tucked her sweater in a little tighter. She was the proudly tired recipient of probably a zillion pieces of candy, but not even the sugar from Heather's gourmet caramel apple could keep her awake when she was ready to crash.

"No," I said. "Just feeling a little nostalgic, I guess." The idea of missing Texas was abstract for me—I hadn't ever left long enough to really feel like I was gone. Even when we were in Seattle after Fox's accident, I was too focused on his health and rehabilitation to be homesick.

But now... I'd allowed myself to think about leaving again, now that the Kitchen project was underway. Everything was about to change much more permanently. Next Halloween... well, I wasn't sure what would happen. Did the condo complex get many trick-or-treaters? Maybe there would be a carnival at Annabelle's new school.

"You've built a great life here, Avery." He shifted Annabelle to one arm and slipped the other around my shoulders. "Thanks for letting me be part of it."

"Don't be ridiculous. You made it even better," I told him. Fox was the icing on every cake for the rest of my life, and I wasn't mad about it.

But when I thought about it, I knew he was right. I'd built myself a strong foundation here—but soon it would be time to go.

CHAPTER TEN

FOX

Something was bothering Avery, and she didn't want to tell me about it. I might've been preoccupied with the diner, but I wasn't completely oblivious. She was different lately—distracted. At first, I'd chalked it up to residual emotion, or maybe even exhaustion, but now I was sure it was more than that. But every time I brought it up, I got the same answer.

"Don't worry, Fox. I'm fine—and you've got enough on your mind."

"I'm never too busy for you, or for Annabelle." I grasped both of her hands in mine. "Nothing else even comes close."

For Avery to tell me not to worry about her—it was laughable. I might not have had as much time to focus as I'd have liked, but she was still at the forefront of my mind every minute of every day, no matter what I was doing.

Even when working with power tools. I looked down at the two-by-four as I slid the saw blade through on the diagonal. My preoccupation with my wife could very well result in the loss of a finger if I wasn't careful. Being unable to directly fix whatever was bothering Avery was incredibly annoying, but working with my hands helped a little—at least I was doing something constructive.

"C'mon, Foxy," McDaniels said, coming up next to me. "Lunchtime. Let's go get a steak or something."

I shook my head, pushing my hair out of my face when it fell down in front of my safety glasses. "I'm good. You guys go ahead."

"Nope." McDaniels reached down and pulled the plug on my saw. "You're coming. You've been here fourteen hours a day for the past week, and that's just fucking ridiculous, even for you." His lips twisted into a wry smirk. "We're gonna go offsite and eat some food that didn't come in a paper bag."

"Can't," I said. "I need to finish this."

"It'll keep, B." Lucas appeared on my other side. "Don't make us drag you out of here. Even Tripp is coming."

I looked at the two of them. I didn't want to go, but at the same time, I knew I needed to. It was important that the crew behaved like a unit so we could work together smoothly. "Okay."

Lunch choices were severely limited without the Kitchen, but we were working to remedy that. Once we were all sitting at a table near the dark bar at Lucky's I remembered exactly why.

"What's good here?" Sloane asked.

I glanced up from my menu. "Not much."

"I heard that," Janie said, coming over to take our order. "Don't care, though." She clicked her pen. "Hi, Mr. Kent, Tripp, Henry, Derek, Kyle… Lucas. Welcome home, Chase. Who are your friends?"

If I was wondering if Janie was still pissed at me for not remembering her at first, the answer to that was apparently yes— she wasn't even acknowledging me now. I'd have to ask Avery about Janie's status quo for grudge-holding.

"Sloane, McDaniels, this is Janie," Lucas said. "Janie, this is Jeremy and Trey."

"Hel-lo Janie," McDaniels said, looking up from his menu with a grin. "Where have you been all my life?"

Janie stared at him, still clicking her pen. "Does that line, like, work for you? Ever?"

McDaniels, that fucker, was not fazed in the slightest. "You could let me know while I cook you breakfast."

"Gross." She clicked her pen again. "But maybe."

I tried really damn hard to keep a straight face while Janie took everyone's order, but it was difficult between McDaniels' shit-eating grin and Janie's blatant refusal to look at anyone other than him. When she'd finally walked away, Kyle thumped McDaniels on the back.

"Congratulations, McD," Derek said. "I think she likes you— and that's saying something, because she's shot down everyone except your boy Fox here."

McDaniels looked up at me in alarm. "Did you—"

"No," I said quickly. "Never. Not even close. And she hates me now because my amnesia erased her from my brain, so your path is clear. I wish you the best of luck."

"She thinks you're a dick." McDaniels' voice was thoughtful. "One of the few and proud unaffected by the Fox. I knew that girl was a rare gem."

For fuck's sake. "Shut up, McD."

"You're going to crash and burn," Sloane said to him gleefully. "I can't wait to see it."

Henry, Tripp, and my father-in-law were sitting on the other end of the table, blissfully unaware—in my opinion—of everything that was happening at our end. We were an interesting group, spanning a couple of generations and about a million years of life experience.

At this point, any sage wisdom was definitely concentrated at the opposite end of wherever McDaniels was sitting. But in spite of his somewhat inflated and definitely misplaced bravado, I had to hand it to the guy. He diffused any situation with humor in the same easy way he wielded his Pulaski ax in the middle of a firestorm—everything came naturally to McD.

"She loves me already." McDaniels pointed to the extra pickle on his plate after Janie deposited his burger.

Amended: everything came naturally to him—except maybe humility.

~\l/~

"What do you have there?" It was dark outside when Avery came up behind me where I sat at the kitchen table in front of my laptop. "Is that from today?" she asked, draping her arms around my neck and resting her chin on my shoulder.

"From this week, mostly."

I'd uploaded some of my GoPro and iPhone videos onto my computer and started to sift through them. We were making progress, but I felt like we could be more efficient and I was hoping that watching the tripod footage would give me some ideas on how to work smarter.

I was also betting on the chance that Avery would want to watch the clips with me, and that it would make her feel better, feel more included, to see the Kitchen being reconstructed right before her eyes. She'd been by the site, but she hadn't really ventured inside the gate. Now she could see exactly what we'd been doing and seeing that her interest was piqued immediately, I knew I wasn't far off in my estimation.

In my eternal quest to be the one who took care of everything, was I unintentionally keeping my wife out of the loop? I'd had this same feeling when the J.D. shit hit the fan, and I didn't want to inadvertently exclude her again, especially when this was such a different situation—every day was its own small victory.

"Is that Gladys from the espresso cart?" Avery untangled herself from around my neck and pulled up a chair so she could sit down.

Yep, definitely interested. I knew it.

"Yeah," I said. "She comes by sometimes and brings us a fresh pot of coffee."

"That's nice of her," Avery said slowly, still watching the screen. "Feeding your addiction."

"Yep. Sometimes I even let the rest of the guys have some."

I fast-forwarded through the next bit, some framing work that we were completing much faster now. I started filming all of this on a whim, but now I was seeing that it was actually helpful—and humbling—to see our mistakes. But mostly helpful.

"I wanted to ask you about something," Avery said. Annabelle was in bed, I'd made my own version of kettle corn in anticipation of a Jason Bourne marathon, and my body was aching in places I'd previously felt strong. *Maybe Avery would want to take a hot shower together later.*

"What's up?" I made a conscious effort to bring my thoughts back to the present.

"I got an email from my undergrad advisor," she began. "There's a seminar on grad school preparation in Abilene next weekend, and I want to go. What do you think?"

"First, I think that you don't need my permission." I tossed a handful of popcorn into my mouth. "And second, of course you should go. I'll miss you, but luckily I have a crew full of jackasses to keep me company."

All of that was true, but there was more. No, I didn't love the idea of Avery traveling without me. But Abilene wasn't that far, and Avery needed a break. I could see it on her face, the daily strain of everything we had on our plate taking its toll. It would be good for her to get out of Brancher, focus on grad school and the future a bit.

I told myself that setting Lucas and Rambo Garrett on J.D.'s tail wasn't a violation of the promise I'd made to her, but that was a very subjective opinion, one that I wasn't sure my wife would share. So far they'd only followed a few leads, but I knew J.D. was around somewhere, and I couldn't make sure he stayed far away from my girls unless they stayed close to me. But that was my own paranoid bullshit, and there was no reason to stop or alter the way we were living our lives. It didn't really matter when or where she was going

—I didn't make a habit of standing in Avery's way.

"Okay, great." There was something in her eyes I didn't recognize when she smiled at me, but it passed quickly. "I'll book it."

"Good. Ready for the movie?" I asked, getting up from the table.

Part of me wondered if she was a little apprehensive about the trip herself, but any coherent thought ran right out of my head when she all but laid on top of me on the couch. *Movie? What movie?*

She buried her head in my neck. "You're comfy."

"You're gorgeous," I replied as I kissed her temple.

I held her in my arms, tucking her head under my chin before I grabbed the remote to start the movie. It was moments like these that I could scarcely believe I'd gone back to the Hotshots so soon after our wedding. Who wanted to freeze their ass off listening to Sloane talk in his sleep when they could spend the night wrapped up with the most beautiful girl in the world?

I knew *why* I'd done it, of course. Even without my full recollection, it was very true to form for me to deny myself something I wanted and use honor and closure as penance for happiness. Almost scrambling my brain on the highway hadn't completely altered that tendency, but I was working on it.

We watched the opening scenes, but I could feel Avery getting restless. She shifted, rolling from her back to her side, tucking herself in tighter to me. I wasn't complaining, but it was obvious that she didn't want to watch the film I'd picked. It wasn't until I paid more attention to the plot than my wife's body that I realized why—Jason Bourne was suffering from an intense bout of amnesia. His entire world was turned upside down, and he had no idea who he truly was.

It wasn't exactly art mirroring life, but it was clearly too damn close for Avery's comfort. I opened my mouth to tell her we could watch something else, but she surprised me by rising to her elbows and pressing her lips to mine. *Or we could get naked. I'm adaptable.*

The kiss she gave me was lingering, but she slid her body from the couch and stood up. "I think I'm going to take a bath."

Damn. I understood she wanted to relax, but I was hoping maybe we could achieve that together. "Okay."

I watched her walk away, her soft footsteps heading down the hall. But instead of the telltale creak of the bathroom door, she paused. "Want to come with me?"

I'd never gotten to my feet faster.

Our bathroom was on the small side, just another project I was planning before I decided to rebuild a diner instead. Avery sat on the edge of the tub, testing the water as it poured from the spout. Her gaze locked with mine as I unbuttoned my jeans, kicking them to the side. I watched her face as I reached behind me to pull off my shirt, her eyes raking over my chest.

I cared about being fit and healthy, but I'd never really given a damn about how I looked until she saw me. I knew I was in good shape, that I looked okay in a mirror, that I never had much of a problem with women. But that was superficial. When Avery looked at me I knew she saw those things, but she also saw my scars—the vicious white markings on my leg, the long sweeping remnants of road rash on my arms and back, the tape I sometimes wore to keep my shoulder strong. She also saw the ones on my heart, the ones from Landry, from our lost camper, from everything I wished I could do differently but didn't have the chance. She saw all of me, and she still looked at me like *that*.

I stood motionless as she rose and slipped one shoulder out of the long shirt she wore. When it was on the floor, along with her leggings and whatever else, I finally allowed myself a breath—and it was more like a sharp inhale. How I got here, how I deserved her, deserved this—it still blew my mind sometimes.

Gingerly she put one foot in the bath, and then two, turning to offer me her hand. "Come on," she said softly.

I didn't know if we would fit, but I'd die trying.

With some careful maneuvering, the tiny bathtub was actually comfortable. Avery leaned against me, her back to my front as she sat in between my bent legs. I watched as the steam rose around us, enjoying the feel of her skin against mine.

"I'm sorry about the movie," I said, running a washcloth over her shoulders. "I didn't think about it."

"I had no idea it would bother me so much," she admitted. "But I do think this is better." She grinned at me over her shoulder.

"No contest." *Sorry, Bourne.*

I dipped my head down to breathe her in, my nose just behind her ear. Reflexively, my grip went to her waist, sliding over her smooth skin under the water. When she shuddered, I found myself pressing my lips to her neck, softly, just a taste.

Avery turned herself more gracefully than I thought possible in the small space, reaching to wind her arms around my neck, her face now just millimeters away.

"Even better," she breathed.

It was so simple, just a small movement that joined us together, but the feeling of her all around me brought a surge of energy to the base of my spine. I moved slightly, loving the way she bit her lip, her eyes hot on mine.

"Fox?" It was a half-gasp, half-moan.

"Yes?" I needed every bit of my self-control to keep my body still as she gripped me.

"Love me."

As if I could do anything but. As if I wanted anything more. I would show her that.

And later in our bed, when we finally exhausted ourselves with loving each other, I held her until I heard her breathing become even. But even physically spent, I couldn't quiet my brain. I tried, I wanted to, but there were too many moving parts that needed my attention.

Restless, I got up and went into the living room to switch on the Bourne movie again.

Life didn't have to stop, but it could proceed with caution.

AVERY OVERNIGHT IN ABILENE SOON, my text to Garrett read. *MAKE SURE SHE'S OK? DETAILS TO*

FOLLOW.

I had a response within minutes.

DONE.

⁓⁙⁓

Watching the walls go up on Kent's Kitchen was validating in a way I didn't realize I needed. Every sheet of plywood, every framed window, every nail that I hammered into solid wood symbolized the beginning of a new chapter.

I also liked the feeling of being on a crew again, that sense of camaraderie that came with all of us working toward the same goal. It was different, constructing instead of preventing destruction, but the end result was the same—the landscape would be changed by the time we were finished.

"Hey, Foxy," McDaniels called from his perch high up on a ladder where he was laying roofing paper. "You got those staples for me or what?"

I pointed my GoPro at him, capturing his grinning face silhouetted against the bright sky. "I'm coming, I'm coming."

I delivered McDaniels' supplies and was checking the plans for the electrical work when I saw Tripp's truck pull up across the street. Now that we were well underway, he'd taken some time to check on his other jobs and make sure things were still running smoothly. But every afternoon he came back again, staying until the sun went down and occasionally even joining us for a beer at Lucky's.

"Made good progress this week," Tripp said, grabbing a set of blueprints from our work table and squinting at them. "Farther than I thought. I'll be damned if we aren't almost caught up to where we should've been two weeks ago."

I smirked at him. "Don't overwhelm me with praise, Tripp. I'll start blushing."

The older man grunted. I'd learned his snorts and shrugs well enough by now, and that particular grunt usually meant he was mildly amused by whatever was said but not enough to crack a smile. I'd done some calculations of my own in regards to our schedule, and because we were no longer hemorrhaging money like we had during the first few weeks, I counted everything from this point forward as a potential win.

"We'll finish up the roof prep and get ready for siding on Monday," he said. "When we move inside, it's plumbing and wiring." He gave me a sidelong glance. "Try not to electrocute each other before the inspection."

"You have no faith, Tripp," Lucas said, coming up beside me. "None at all."

"He's seen your work," I said, earning another grunt from Tripp as he left us to check out where Jim was working.

"He's right, though. Not about that," he said when I started to laugh. "About our progress. Two weeks ago I thought we'd all lost our minds—but like Tripp said, we're catching up." He raked his hand through his hair. "Imagine what it could be if we got a few more crew members."

I shook my head. "Can't imagine," I said. "No more money for crew."

"Seriously?" Lucas stared at me. "What happened?"

"According to Tripp, we had a shit budget to start with. But in my opinion, we made necessary sacrifices in order to have the cash for the improvements we made on the design." I shrugged. "It'll pay off."

"If you need money, B.—"

"No." I cut him off. "I have room to increase the estimate, but I have to keep the budget as is. If I had my way, Jim wouldn't know a thing about how much all this costs. But Tripp's reporting directly to him so my hands are tied, and Jim insisted that we change the contract to start my reimbursement on day one of the reopening. So now we have to be realistic. It doesn't make any sense to saddle the Kents with a crazy debt. I want them to not only be able to keep the ranch but be as successful as possible. We'll get it finished on budget, it'll just take some hustle."

Lucas nodded. "I understand."

"But thanks. And really, if I'd blown through all of my trust already you should be kicking my ass, not offering to help."

Lucas laughed at my dry observation and then we were silent for a moment before he spoke.

"Do you ever think about it, B.? The money, I mean? It still seems abstract to me even after growing up the way we did."

The truth was, before Avery and Annabelle I'd thought about my money very rarely. Lucas and I weren't billionaires, but we'd each come into very substantial trusts when we turned twenty-five. That was the byproduct of having an eccentrically famous artist for a mother and a hard-ass retired general for a father—you get your inheritance, but not before you prove you can make something of yourself without it.

Following in Lucas' footsteps, I managed my trust with a complicated combination of investments, high-return savings accounts, and a bunch of other things that I pretty much let my financial advisors handle. Looking at the bottom line was much easier, and Lucas was right—the money did seem abstract.

"Sometimes. Been on my mind more lately, I guess."

One of the reoccurring thoughts I had was that maybe someday Avery and I would buy a ranch of our own out here in Texas. I wondered if she'd like that—I knew she loved her little house, but the operative word in Texas seemed to be 'acreage.' We were looking ahead to Seattle, but I found myself reaching even further than that. When it came time for her to graduate, what then?

"Me too," Lucas said. "Never thought I'd say this, but I'm getting a little tired of living out of a suitcase. Things are different now, I guess."

I wondered if he meant Heather, but I figured he'd tell me when he was ready. I'd felt the same way when it came to the choice of going back to the Forest Service or being with Avery. Was my brother considering changing his life? In spite of my mother's best efforts, we'd been conditioned by the General for living alone. Taking that plan and shoving it directly into the garbage was the best move I'd ever made.

"Different isn't a bad thing, Luke."

CHAPTER ELEVEN

AVERY

"**M**orning!" Heather breezed through my open kitchen door with a bakery box in her hands, just like she had a hundred other daybreaks in the past. She glanced around the room, which was empty aside from where I sat at our small table. "Annabelle off to school already?"

"Yeah. Fox took her."

She slid the pink carton onto the counter and flopped down in the chair across from me. "Dang it, I made a pink sprinkle doughnut just for her."

"She can have it for a snack when she gets home," I said, laughing a little at the disappointment on Heather's face.

"Oh, I suppose. But afternoon sugar just isn't the same as a first-thing-get-your-engine-roaring rush." She raised an eyebrow at me as she leaned back in her chair. "What's wrong with you? You look weird."

"Good morning to you too," I said dryly. "We don't all awaken and jump on a sugar high, you know."

"I wish, it would be good for business." She looked at me again. "But really, what's up?"

"I told Fox I needed to go to Abilene for a grad school seminar."

Heather looked at me blankly. "And?"

"And there is no grad school seminar."

Her face changed in an instant. "J.D. called you?"

"Not yet."

"Then what?" Now Heather just looked confused.

"I decided to be proactive," I said. "There's gonna be a big rodeo down in Abilene, and I'd be willing to bet that J.D. shows up."

She didn't seem convinced. "I thought he was retired?"

"Not by choice," I corrected her. "But he needs money, and he clearly has no other marketable skills. Plus, he's all about the swagger—he needs people to brag to, and what better audience than the ones who think he's all washed up? He has something to prove and the rodeo is the perfect place to do it."

"I don't think this is a very good idea, Avery. What did Detective London say?"

This was the part that I was still debating, the part that I knew would make Heather upset. "I haven't told her yet."

"No!" Heather stood up. "I do not like this at all, Avery," she said, starting to pace the kitchen. "I was going along with it when I thought you were working with the detectives, but just barely."

"I'm going to tell them," I grumbled. "I think so, anyway. She might feel like it's a waste of time if I haven't heard anything from J.D. yet. I'm so tired of all these dead ends."

"If you already think it's going to be a dead end, why would you even go?" Heather cried. "Stay home, let the detectives do their jobs."

"Fox is rebuilding the damn diner, Heather. Am I just supposed to sit around while my husband busts his ass? I can't."

"I'm not sure I'll ever agree with you on this."

"I know, Heather. But I have to do something—I have to try."

─╲╎╱─

Fox was coming home exhausted every day, but he seemed happy. In the weeks since the construction started, I'd barely seen him during daylight hours. When Sloane and McDaniels had shown up at the beginning of the build, my parents insisted they stay at the ranch instead of renting a room at the little motel just outside of town. With the rarely used bunkhouse aired out and restocked, and the guys in possession of the keys to the diner's pickup, they were comfortable, well-fed, and independent.

"Might have to extend our stay," McDaniels said to me one day with a wink. "I like ranch life."

"Fewer trees, less fire," Sloane agreed. "A nice change of pace."

Now my mother was in her element, cooking big breakfasts again and packing lunch spreads for everyone to enjoy.

"We can't fix everything with food, I know, but you can't work hard all day on an empty stomach," she told me, assembling the ingredients for ham sandwiches.

Between her and Heather, the crew was stuffed and sugared, there was no doubt about that. In my mind, the food was the least we could do—the fact that they were out there working for our family was a huge blessing that would probably never be able to be repaid.

I appreciated every single one of them, especially the ones that surprised me... like Chase. He'd shown up for my family and for me, to right a wrong and remind me of his true character that had gotten lost somewhere between his leaving and his actions when he finally came back. But he also showed up for Fox, because of their bond that could weather anything. I knew we had friends in this town, but there was no doubt about it—my husband brought out the best in people.

So when my mother suggested we put together an end-of-week barbecue for the crew and friends, I immediately agreed. It was the perfect distraction from everything that happened over the past few weeks—especially for me, as I'd rather be bagging sandwiches and delivering cupcakes than thinking about what I was attempting to pull off behind Fox's back.

My family was aware that our moving plans were still in limbo, much to my dad's dismay. But things still weren't right in Brancher, and they wouldn't be until I found J.D. I couldn't leave before then. Fox was doing his part—I had to do mine.

"Avery, are you finished shucking that corn?"

"Almost!" I called into the kitchen from my perch on the back porch. I looked down at the pile of husks at my feet. Apparently, we were feeding the whole town, because I'd shucked almost an entire field's worth of corn.

But I couldn't fault my parents for wanting to do what they always did—bring people together over a meal. I'd shuck a million ears if it meant that we could have everything back the way it was before. The guys were working to get the diner back to normal and it seemed like everything was really coming together. In my own head, I could be pessimistic as hell about the rest of it, but that was a huge load off my mind to start.

I piled up the corn ears on my tray and carried them into the kitchen, walking in just as my mother put the finishing touches on her famous potato salad. Joy was at the counter next to her, cubing a watermelon and dropping it into a bowl.

"Smells good in here," I said. "What's in the oven?"

"Rolls," my mom answered. "And three kinds of casserole."

"I'm fixin' the fruit salad, and the beans are near done," Joy said, moving over to stir a pot on the stove.

"Go out and check on them at the grill, will you, Avery?" my mother asked. "Heather will be here soon with the desserts and I sent the boys into town for more beer." She offered me three bottles. "Go give these to your father, Henry, and Fox."

I held out my hand for the beer at the same time as my cell phone buzzed in my pocket. "Fox wants to know when to start grilling the corn." I looked up from the text in dismay. "Why did you have me shuck everything if you were just going to put it on the grill?"

"Your daddy would barbecue the entire meal if I let him," my mother grumbled. "I told him a thousand times I was going to boil that corn. It's sweeter that way, but he doesn't listen. He needs to stick to his part and I'll do the rest."

This was the four thousand and seventh reason we needed the diner back—my parents couldn't agree on how to run one kitchen between them, so it was infinitely better if they had two.

"Avery? Why are you just standing there? Go check on those ribs, please."

She looked so exasperated about the corn situation that I had to hide my grin as I turned to exit through the back door. The sun was hanging low in the sky as I walked down the porch steps and crossed the yard to the barbecue. I waved to Annabelle as she ran by with the dogs trotting behind her.

"Mama!" she called. "Are the fireflies coming to our party?"

I laughed. "They'll be out soon, baby."

It was moments like these, with my family gathered around and the smell of barbecue and clean air and alfalfa all around me, with happy little girl giggles and dog grins and big open sky—these were the moments that I could almost forget about everything else. These were the Texas moments that would be prime fodder for nostalgia if and when I finally moved away, and they also served as a pretty good buffer for all of the bullshit that lurked around the edges of my life.

Most days I could push it away, especially when I had nights like these. But in the back of my mind, I was always so conscious of how quickly everything could change—in a heartbeat, in a quarter mile, in one spark of flame. Now that I knew that, there was no way to forget it. And also no way to keep from anticipating what would come next.

Fox's face lit up in a beautifully dimpled grin when I handed him the cold beer, and if the air had seemed at all chilly it wasn't anymore. "Thanks."

"How's it going out here?" I asked, handing my dad and Henry their bottles.

My eyes went right back to Fox of their own accord. He was a great coping mechanism—somehow he had a way of pushing all of my uneasy feelings right out of my head just by looking at him. The bonus to that was it seemed like he was one of those men who'd just get better looking as we got older, like a movie star or something. Lucky was an understatement.

And the bonus on top of *that* was that he was even more beautiful on the inside than he was on the outside—with just the right amount of edge. Seemingly impossible, yes, but he proved it on the daily. I'd actually be annoyed about it if I didn't get to call him mine.

"Corn?" my father asked, snapping me out of my Fox-induced daze.

"Don't look at me," I said innocently. "I'm just the cocktail waitress."

He cracked his beer open but didn't pursue it further. "Tell your mother I need the next round of ribs."

I pried my eyes away from my husband and headed back inside, but not before I caught his raised eyebrow and tiny smile in my direction. *The answer to whatever you're asking is yes,* I tried to send him telepathically. Being married to your favorite coping mechanism came with a ton of perks.

Heather and Lucas were just walking into the kitchen when I came back inside. Lucas was loaded down with two of Heather's storage trays, while she carried a cake box.

"Hi, y'all!"

"What's all this?" my mother asked with a smile. "I thought you were just bringing pie?"

"Well, I was," Heather said, sounding slightly guilty. "But then —"

"She found a new recipe for chocolate bread pudding, so there's that, and then she also made those little tiny cheesecake things because she knows my brother likes them." Lucas gave Heather a wry look.

I could tell by the expression on her face that she wasn't having any of his sarcasm, but I held my laughter in.

"Did we forget that I *also* made pecan pie, because it's *your* favorite, an apple crumble for Mr. Kent, and my signature cherry?" Heather asked testily.

"I haven't forgotten anything," Lucas mumbled under his breath, setting the trays down where Joy indicated. "The guys out back?"

My mother nodded. "Everyone else will be here soon, and Trey and Jeremy will be back with more beer." She handed a cold bottle to Lucas and I laughed when he quickly made his escape.

"What's up with him?" I asked Heather.

"I don't know." She seemed preoccupied. "We've sort of been living together since he's been here, kind of like a trial run, and I thought it was going pretty well. But maybe he's having second thoughts?"

"Really? I doubt it. He's probably just busy with the rebuild. I know Fox has had a lot on his mind too." For a while the hits kept coming—but my J.D. plan was means to an end. I had to keep reminding myself of that.

The diner's pickup coming up the driveway signaled the return of Sloane and McDaniels, along with the arrival of the beer. Kyle, Derek, his girlfriend, and Chase pulled up at the same time, followed just behind by Tripp and his wife. Once everyone was back inside, my mom and Joy fussed around getting the food onto the table and everyone loaded up their plates.

Sloane smiled at my mother. "This looks delicious, Mrs. Kent."

"Thank you for having us," Derek added.

"Of course, boys." She looked around at everyone at the table. "You've all been so generous with your time, and we wanted to show our gratitude."

My dad nodded his agreement. "We appreciate it," he said gruffly.

Lucas cleared his throat. "Before we start on this amazing spread, I'd like to make a toast." He stood. "To Tripp, for taking on all of this—and all of us—when no one else would."

Everyone clapped, but Lucas wasn't finished.

"To the Kents—thank you for letting this guy," he gestured to Fox, "and me by default, into your family. I think I can speak for all of us when I say that we're honored to be a part of this build." Lucas raised his beer. "And to my brother, the hardest-working man I know. Not sure how you manage it all, B., but you do."

The glance that Fox and Lucas exchanged made my eyes feel suspiciously warm and scratchy. Everyone raised their glasses without a moment's hesitation, and I squeezed Fox's leg under the table. Lucas was right. None of this would've been possible without him.

CHAPTER TWELVE

FOX

"It really does look like a building," I said to Lucas at our mid-morning coffee break. "I feel good about this."

"I'm glad *you* do," Lucas said, rubbing the back of his neck. "I feel like I'm about one hundred years old. Didn't even know it was possible to be in impeccable shape at the prime of my life and also feel like my body is falling apart."

I smirked. "Maybe you need more time sweating in the great outdoors and less time hopping around in those fancy hotel gyms."

Lucas grunted over his shoulder as he headed back to his tools. "If you tell me to rub some dirt on it I'm gonna punch you."

"C'mon Luke, you haven't—" I was cut off mid-jibe by Sloane shouting.

"HENRY!"

I dropped my hammer and sprinted toward them, vaulting over the partially framed wall with Chase and McDaniels right behind me.

We skidded around the corner of the siding on the opposite

side of the build, just in time to see Henry's ladder start to list to one side. It was a tall ladder, one we used to reach the ceiling joists —and like much of our equipment, it was an older, borrowed version. Henry was halfway down, a surefire sign that when the ladder started to lean he'd already begun his descent, but it wasn't enough to maintain the center of gravity.

The ladder started to slide again, and even as I ran, I watched Sloane use all of his strength to try and keep it in place. Henry grabbed out for something to steady him, but the framing walls were short on handholds.

"Hold on!" Sloane yelled, trying to brace his feet against the sawdust-covered concrete.

We scrambled across the sawhorses and wood, every second bringing us closer to help. I could hear my heartbeat in my ears, the roar and rush of air around me as I kept my eyes locked on Henry. *Don't fall, don't fall.* I was only a breath away when the ladder gave way, slamming Henry into the rungs as it went down before crashing to the ground on top of Sloane.

I heard a grunt and a swear, and we looked around quickly for Landry, finding him a couple yards away under a bunch of burning debris. He struggled to straighten and push the tree branches up and off of him, and I heard McDaniels and Sloane yelling from above.

"Landry! Landry!"

When I reached Sloane and pulled the ladder off of him, scattering a few two-by-fours that had fallen as well, at first all I could see was Landry's face. I had to blink about seven times before I cleared the flashback from my eyes. "You good, Sloane?"

"Yeah, man." He accepted the hand I held out to pull him up. "Just knocked the wind out of me a little."

Chase and McDaniels were already pulling Henry to his feet. "I'm fine, I'm fine, get off me," the older man grumbled. "Your boy here broke my fall." He rubbed his hip. "That'll bruise, but I'm not dead yet."

The guys helped me get Henry to one of the folding chairs by the blueprint table. Paper scattered as we shoved everything aside, and Lucas grabbed a cold bottle of water from the cooler and cracked it open for Henry.

"Henry, talk to me," I said casually. I was worried, but I knew better than to show it. "Did you hit your head? Any pain?"

He smirked at me. "No head injuries, Doc. I was on my way down for the rest of those framing boards." I noticed with relief that the color was returning to his face. "Where are they?"

"What do you mean?" I looked around. "Our supply order was supposed to come this morning. Are you sure it's not here?"

"I fell off a fucking ladder, Fox, but my eyes still work. What do you think?"

I wasn't sure about his hip, but at least I knew Henry's personality was one hundred percent intact. "Okay, so where is it?" Without the lumber and other supplies, we were facing a huge setback—*another* huge setback, more accurately.

Lucas whipped out his phone. "Let me check."

"What happened?" Jim came up next to me. "I go to get food and all hell breaks loose."

"Henry's ladder fell on top of Sloane—" I looked over to where my friend was already tearing into a pulled pork sandwich and rolled my eyes. "They're okay, but we just realized our supplies aren't here."

Jim scratched his chin. "Tripp know about this?"

"I sent him a text," Lucas said. "I have the email here saying when the order was supposed to be delivered. Supplies are scarce, so they were coming from the depot in San Antonio, but the truck should've been here by now."

He scrolled through his phone until he found the number he needed. "Yes, this is Lucas Fox. We had a delivery scheduled for this morning, in Brancher?" He listened for a moment and then his eyes widened. "What? Are you serious?"

Lucas pulled the phone away from his ear, tapping the speakerphone button. "*Fuck.*"

"—he stopped for breakfast, and just after leavin' the rest stop some asshole tried to run him off the road," the man on the phone was saying. "The rig went into a ditch, and your order was crushed when the trailer flipped. We salvaged a few boards, but everything else was toast."

I couldn't believe it. My hands clenched as I tried to reconcile what I'd heard. "Is the driver okay?"

"Broke his arm, but he'll be alright." The supervisor cleared his throat. "Truck is totaled though."

Lucas swore softly. "Thanks for letting us know. Any idea when we can expect a new delivery?"

"Probably a week out, if our stock comes in on time. I'm real sorry about this, Mr. Fox."

Me too. "Not your fault."

Lucas disconnected the call and we all stood there for a moment, looking at each other. I couldn't stand the silence, the immediate dip in morale that hit our group tenfold even compared to the near-disastrous ladder incident of ten minutes ago.

"What can we work on without the delivery?" Chase asked. "There's gotta be something."

"No," I said tightly. "Not really. Everyone should just go home." Truth was, there was nothing else to do, not without our materials. I felt like pounding my fist through something, but we didn't have any drywall up yet and I wasn't dumb enough to punch a two-by-four.

"Cranky bastard," Sloane muttered around a mouthful of pork.

I spun around to face him. "You're lucky I didn't send you to the hospital. There's still time."

He stared at me. "You're kidding, right?"

"Not all. The insurance company already has eyes on us. We're should be following accident protocol to the letter. Go back to the ranch, try not to walk under any ladders on your way." It was supposed to be good-natured ribbing, but it came out wrong and I knew it.

Sloane scowled at me. "Whatever. I'm going to get another sandwich." He dropped his tool belt and headed for the street.

"Did you see Sloane's face?" McDaniels' grin was bigger than

I'd ever seen it. "He's pissed at you."

"Too bad. Better safe than sorry," I said, jogging over to where I'd dropped my phone. I hit the first button on my speed dial. "Avery? Don't freak out, okay? Everything is fine, but Henry and Sloane had a little accident and we're shutting down for the day."

"What?" Avery cried. "Oh my god. Are they okay?"

"Yeah. Both a little banged up, but nothing to be concerned about." I took a deep breath. "There are bigger problems." *Plus, Sloane's irritated with me.* I'd probably never hear the end of that.

"Anything I can do?"

"Not unless you own a lumber yard I wasn't aware of." I tried to keep the annoyance out of my voice, but I couldn't help it. This could sink us—just when we'd gotten afloat.

"I'm sorry, Fox." Her voice was full of concern. "I'm out at the ranch, my mom asked me to stay for dinner. Do you want to come out here?"

"No. I'm just going to go home." It was better for everyone if I had a little time to shake off this funk.

"I'll call Joy, tell her to expect Henry. Don't worry, okay?" Avery understood my moods, she always did.

We shut everything down fairly quickly, and within an hour my brother and I were climbing into my truck to go home. Lucas and I didn't speak much during the drive. What was there to say? We had no supplies, and that meant no work until it was resolved.

I kept thinking of Sloane scoffing at me, of Henry's face as he sat there in the chair. He wasn't an old man, but did it matter? I'd seen death come for much younger.

No one was around when I got back to the house, which was for the best. On top of the ruined materials, seeing the guys go down today fucked with me in a monumental way, and I couldn't shake it. My movements were clumsy and angry as I got out of the truck and slammed it shut, and just for good measure I slammed the front door too.

Careless. You were careless, riding the high of that family dinner. That voice in my head always came out when I felt like I wasn't doing enough, no matter how many times I convinced myself to ignore it.

I didn't blame Avery for not being here. I'd been a real dick when we'd spoken, my frustration getting the best of me. I pulled out my phone and sent her a quick text. *LOVE YOU BOTH.*

Avery's reply was immediate. *WE LOVE YOU TOO.*

I stood there in the hallway, chest heaving, my hands curled into fists. Sloane was fine, and Henry was going to be okay after a rest-up. But what about tomorrow? What if next time it was something worse? What if it was Jim? Or Lucas? No matter what I did, I couldn't save everyone. That wasn't a new concept, but it still pissed me off beyond belief.

You're having a regular day, living your life, doing your job and just being a human and BAM—ladder gives out, heart failure, big rig jackknife, cougar attack, fiery explosion, broken climbing rope, mechanical defect, busted gut, Mother Nature… the list went on and on. We were all just trying to make it home at the end of the day, and sometimes not everyone came back.

That was life, and I knew it. I accepted it. But it didn't mean I fucking liked it.

Was it easier before Avery? Before Annabelle? Was I on better terms with the idea that none of this was permanent before I had everything I'd ever wanted? When love is mostly abstract, maybe loss doesn't seem so bad.

I slammed my way into the shower to wash the day away, once again grateful that the girls weren't home. My mood was piss poor and I was testy—and even my carefully cultivated control wasn't enough to mask it. As the water pounded down on my shoulders, I rested my head against the tiled wall and considered my options.

I could let today—this week, this month, this year—throw me entirely off my game and jeopardize everything, or I could compartmentalize and move the fuck on. At the top of my list of flaws was the insane idea that I could make everything okay if I just tried hard enough. History and heartache had proven that that wasn't the case, but in this instance, I guess I was just a slow learner.

After my shower, I felt a little better, so I toweled off and threw on a pair of sweatpants, taking my laptop with me onto the couch to go over the digital versions of Tripp's blueprints. Before I could crack it open, my cell phone rang.

"Fox?"

"Hey." Just the sound of Avery's voice made me feel better. I was glad she wasn't home earlier to see me struggle, but I was missing her now.

"How are you?" she asked. "You seemed kinda out of it when we spoke earlier."

I had to remind myself that our semi-distant connection of late was still stronger than most. I knew this girl and she knew me. Whatever came, whatever was still to come, we always had that.

"I don't know," I admitted. "I can't focus."

"That's understandable. My dad filled me in on what happened," she said, her voice mostly even. I could detect a small amount of worry, which I couldn't blame her for—I didn't usually concede to anything less than solid.

"How's everything out at the ranch?" Enough with my own bullshit—this wasn't about me.

"We're good. Henry's home, and my mom brought them a casserole before we had dinner. That's partially why I'm calling—it's kind of late, and I was thinking Annabelle and I would stay the night. But if you need me to come home—"

"No, sunshine. Of course not. You should stay."

"Are you sure?"

"Absolutely."

It was nearly Annabelle's bedtime, and all I planned to do was look over some blueprints and turn in early. Avery didn't need to worry about me, plus it was a dark drive back on a pretty deserted highway.

"Okay. I'll take Annabelle to school in the morning and see you at home."

"Come by the site," I said. "I'm going to get an early start."

"Fox… why don't you take the day off tomorrow? If the

supplies aren't coming, do you really need to be there?"

"I told everyone else not to show up—sort of a mental health day."

"What about you?"

"That's the wrong kind of therapy for me," I said slowly. "I need to stay busy."

It was true. I didn't do very well with idle, whether it was mind or body. Better to keep moving, keep planning, keep doing. If I sat back and let my brain wander, it could very well head into territory I'd worked too fucking hard to get out of.

We said our goodnights and after Avery hung up I went back to my blueprints. Progress was being made, but I wanted to focus on a few areas where I felt like we weren't as organized. Everyone on the job knew a decent amount about construction, but a few people knew more than others—Tripp, Derek, and Kyle.

Derek and Kyle tended to work together, didn't they? I immediately closed out the blueprints and clicked over to my video clips. I thought I remembered seeing that—maybe if I consciously split them up, they could each anchor another guy and make two tasks go faster instead of one. I scrolled through the videos that I'd started to organize last night, keeping this idea in mind. When I found the one I wanted, I pressed play and sat back.

The scene opened just as I'd put the GoPro on my tripod, with everyone rolling in for the morning and getting their tools out. Chase and Kyle were laughing about something while Tripp talked with the espresso cart owner who'd stopped by to say hi. I remembered this day now—the football team brought us pizza and helped haul some scraps to the dumpster.

"It was Coach's idea, but this sure beats running sprint ladders," one of the kids said, and everyone laughed.

The clip continued with a visit from Heather bringing my favorite cupcakes, and it ended with the ladies from the church coming over to remind us about the pancake supper and offer their services when it came time to seed the new planter boxes we planned to put out front.

Now that I thought about it, this bevy of activity wasn't an isolated incident. A bigger city might not have cared, but every day the people of Brancher went out of their way to let us know that they were excited about what we were doing and that they were here to support it. Avery told me that from the beginning—it wasn't just a building, Kent's Kitchen was incredibly important to the town. And now I finally understood.

I'd learned this year that it took a lot to open yourself up to love, but that the alternative was fucking lonely and sad. If you went through life holding it at a distance you'd never truly experience it, and if nothing was important to you it would be impossible to see the value in caring. That part was hard, because you almost had to lose something first so you could realize how much you needed it. I'd keep holding everything close—because now I truly realized how much I had to lose.

I sent an overdue apology text to Sloane. *I'M AN ASSHOLE.*

He let me sweat a couple minutes, but when I got a reply in the form of an animated fried chicken wing, I knew all was mostly forgiven.

My phone buzzed again, and I glanced at it quickly, expecting another gif or a goodnight message from Avery.

CALL ME WHEN YOU CAN - IT'S IMPORTANT.
Heather?

CHAPTER THIRTEEN

AVERY

My sleeping habits had been less than stellar since the fire, but I was fairly sure I didn't get more than two restless hours last night. At least, that's what the circles under my eyes told me when I stared in the mirror after I got out of the shower.

"Not cute, Avery," I muttered to myself. Fox wanted to take me out tonight and I looked like a zombie.

There was no debating about why I couldn't sleep. I was lying to Fox, and I felt like an asshole about it. Period. I could keep telling myself that I was doing it for the good of my family, or because it was my score to settle, or whatever made me feel better for a tiny split second.

All of it was bullshit. I was lying to Fox about something that would make me *furious* if roles were reversed. Not only that, but my plan was unraveling. No one had heard a whisper from J.D. I'd told Fox I needed to go out of town and now I didn't have anywhere to go—was it worth it to go chasing after him at the rodeo? Everything was crashing down around me, and I didn't even care.

Let J.D. get away. Let him never do a day in jail for what he did to the Kitchen. We'd get the adoption done, so what if it took a few months longer? Let him disappear forever—maybe I'd get lucky and never have to see him again.

Just let me come clean to Fox and be done with it. I wrapped my robe around me quickly and headed out to the living room, intending to do just that.

"Give us a kiss, sunshine," Fox said as he strode out of the kitchen with Annabelle in his arms. "We're on our way to Joy's."

The small clock on the mantle chimed six, cluing me in to the fact that I'd been in the shower for twice as long as usual. We'd planned to drop off Annabelle on our way to dinner but I was definitely running late. *Oops. Blame it on the lack of sleep.*

"Oh, okay," I said, brushing my lips against Annabelle's cheek first before I set a small peck on Fox's lips. *Damn.* I hoped I wouldn't lose my nerve before he came back.

"Relax, Avery. We have plenty of time." He winked at me. "No solid agenda for date night."

"Bye, Mama!"

I stood in the doorway and waved to them as Fox got Annabelle buckled into her car seat. After the truck pulled away from the curb, I shut the door and shuffled back our bedroom to get dressed, pulling on the first decent outfit I could find. *Maybe I'd just make Fox a nice meal and then we could talk.* Joy had practically begged to have Annabelle come over, and I didn't want to waste the evening.

With that idea in mind, I headed into the kitchen and started pulling things out for a quick chicken stir-fry. Frozen veggies, onion, garlic, chicken, a little soy sauce, and rice on the side. I could handle that. The food was easy. The hard part was figuring out what to tell Fox.

Hey Fox, remember when I made you promise not to go hunting for J.D.? Well, I went behind your back and decided to contact him myself. Oh, and the detectives are helping me. Also, the grad school seminar? Yeah, that was a lie. I was going to use myself as bait at the rodeo and try to get J.D. to meet me somewhere so he could be arrested. Please pass the rice.

I cubed the chicken and put it in the pan with a little oil and garlic to cook until I was ready for the vegetables.

So, Fox, I had this idea. I thought, maybe I could find J.D. and make this all go away. Except I actually had this idea a few weeks ago, and I just went with it. We're supposed to meet up soon, if he ever calls me back. But don't worry, the detectives will be there. Must've forgotten to tell you. We're cool, right?

The front door opened just as the smoke detector went off. The piercing alarm snapped me back to reality. *Oh fuck, the chicken!* I hurriedly turned the heat off and tried to scrape the burnt pieces of meat off the bottom of the pan as Fox ran into the kitchen, fanning the air in an attempt to quiet the detector.

Shit. This wasn't going well at all.

"What happened? Is that chicken?" He peered into the pan.

"I can't do this," I said.

"It's okay," Fox laughed as he set the hot pan aside to cool. "I can take it from here. You have lots of other talents."

"What? No, I didn't mean the chicken. I mean, it's terrible, clearly. But that's not what I'm talking about." I moved to sit down at the table, and he followed, sliding into the chair next to mine. "I have to tell you something."

Fox could go still like no one else. I always recognized that as having his full attention. "Okay."

"Detective London asked me to help them bring in J.D." I said in a rush. "It was a while ago, and at first I said no, obviously, because we'd already talked about how to handle everything."

Fox's expression was painfully neutral, but I took that as a sign to just keep going. "But then I started thinking, you know, it's not fair that you always take on so much, and J.D. is in our lives because of me—I had to do something. So I told her yes."

Still no reaction from my husband.

"And we looked into it, you know, contacting him," I rushed on. "If I were J.D., where would I go? There's a rodeo in Abilene offering a big cash prize, and I thought I could start there."

"Avery, I know."

"But I really didn't think that he would—wait, what?" Fox's words finally registered. "You know? What do you know?"

"Heather told me everything." He looked me square in the eye. "Although it should've been you."

"I—" I'd gone from word vomit to speechless. "When?"

Fox lifted one shoulder in a shrug, his dimple showing just a tiny bit. "Three days ago."

Three days ago. *Three days?* He'd known for *three days* that I was planning something behind his back, and didn't say anything? I couldn't believe it. And Heather! She'd completely betrayed my trust.

"YOU LET ME SQUIRM!" I cried. "I was so stressed out about keeping this from you. Why didn't you say anything sooner?"

His eyes turned serious. "Avery, I almost had a heart attack when Heather told me. It took every single bit of willpower I had to wait and not say anything. I wouldn't have made it another day. In case you haven't noticed, I've barely let you out of my sight since you got home from the ranch. I would've lost my shit if I found out while you were in Abilene."

"It was probably another dead end anyway," I said.

Fox shook his head. "Your safety is so important to me, sunshine. Please don't do things to jeopardize yourself. Nothing is worth that."

Immediately, I felt contrite. Fox never tried to control me— he always said my independence was one of his favorite traits. But now I'd used our trust to lie to him. It was shitty, even if my intentions were pure.

"Damn it, Fox. Why do you always know what to say, good or bad?" I blinked back tears.

He grabbed my hand, bringing it to his lips. "Come here."

I slid into his lap. "I'm all conflicted now. I thought I was doing something good, but it didn't feel right. And then you knew but didn't tell me. I don't really have a leg to stand on here, I realize, but I'm not sure if I should be mad at you or not."

Fox laughed once, winding his arms around my waist. "Same."

"I wanted to help us," I said, leaning into his warmth.

"I love you for it. But we promised, together." His voice sounded extra deep with my ear pressed to his chest.

"That's why I had to tell you. I would've been so hurt, Fox, if roles were reversed. I really am sorry."

"How far did it get?" I could feel his muscles tensing slightly when he asked the question. "Did you speak with him?"

I sighed. "No. His phone number is disconnected, and the few friends I tried said they hadn't heard anything from him in months."

Fox nodded. "Lucas came up with similar results before the fire."

"Could he try again? Lucas, I mean? I know you both had ideas before—maybe it's time to implement them."

"I think you're right," Fox mused. "A group effort. We haven't exhausted all of our resources yet—I can make some calls."

"Good."

"And Avery? I'm not completely innocent in this. I've thought about going after him, many times. Lucas and I discussed it, we made more than one plan. I just didn't act on it—yet. But I was close. I'd already looped in Rambo Garrett and let Lucas do some of his spy shit." Fox's mouth quirked up on one side. "No more secrets. Full disclosure, okay?"

"Full disclosure," I agreed. "Forever." I rolled my shoulders, trying to relieve some of the residual tension. "What do you want to do now?"

He stood, taking me with him. "Now we go eat, because I'm not sure if that stir-fry is salvageable."

I tightened my grip as he carried me to the front door. "Sorry about that."

Fox grabbed my purse and his keys before he shut the door, keeping me in his arms as he walked around to the passenger side of the SUV. I loved that he could hold me like this, loved that I could be so close to him and feel his heartbeat.

"It's okay," he said softly, his face just a breath from mine. "I don't care about the food."

Slowly, ever so slowly, I slid down his body until my boots hit the driveway. "Me neither."

He opened the door, never taking his eyes from mine. "Good to know."

I nodded, backing up slightly into the open door. I put one foot on the running board, preparing to boost myself into the truck. My skirt rode up as I maneuvered into the seat, baring my legs to the upper thigh. I pretended like I didn't notice, shifting to bring the material even higher. *Did I mention that I didn't care about going out to eat?*

Fox's eyes darted down to my exposed skin, finally breaking our eye contact. He cleared his throat, and my face broke into a grin. I fastened my seatbelt quickly, smoothing my skirt down just a tiny bit. "Ready to go?"

My words snapped his gaze back to me. "Um. Yes."

I stifled a laugh as Fox ran around to the driver's side and jumped in. I caught him looking at my legs twice more as he reversed out of the driveway and turned the truck onto the street. It was subtle, the clench of his hands on the steering wheel, the way he leaned his body toward me reflexively, but I caught it.

The conversation we had in the kitchen was necessary and long overdue. Keeping secrets had muted our connection, making me feel fuzzy and uncomfortable. I was used to being my authentic self with Fox—whatever that was on any given day. Just going through the motions of marriage wasn't anything I was interested in. I wanted our ups and downs to make us stronger because we were both all in, all the time. I needed to know I could depend on Fox, and that he was *real*. He understood that and found ways to show me whenever he could.

When he reached for my hand like usual, I knew it was time to make my move. I slid our joined hands up my leg, up my raised skirt, until I could feel Fox's fingers brushing the lace of my underwear. *Was that enough of an invitation?*

He was too conscientious to actually swerve the truck, but I was rewarded with a very heavy clearing of his throat. "What do you, um—"

"Pull over."

I was nearly giddy with excitement and anticipation when Fox immediately glanced in his rearview mirror, flipping the turn signal to indicate our exit from the highway. He slid truck onto the shoulder, just around a slight bend that would protect us both from any curious passersby and also an accidental collision. *Perfect*.

"Are you okay?" I could see the fire burning low in his eyes. He was Fox, so he wanted to make sure before he acted, but he knew.

That was fine. To avoid any confusion, I'd spell it out for him. "Make-up sex, Fox. Get on board."

In a split second, the burn in his eyes sparked into full flame. I gasped with delight as he pulled me against him—hard. Every part of him was hard, actually. I wiggled even closer, loving the growl that escaped his throat. Fox was usually so in control—these little moments where he left himself go were incredibly hot.

"Let the record show, I am always on board. You name the time and the place, and I'll be there." He pressed his lips to the thin, sensitive skin under my jaw, making me shiver. "I was just *surprised*, is all."

"Surprised I'd want to make up?" I tugged on his shirt and he obliged me by slipping it off.

"Surprised because we didn't really have a fight." I watched the muscles in his chest flex as he snapped open his jeans and reached for me again, his biceps golden and tanned even in the low light.

"We could call it something else." I had my hands on him already, smoothing over his skin as I climbed onto his lap.

"Whatever you want."

I didn't even have a chance to answer before his mouth was on mine, his fingers up under my skirt. I couldn't process everything I was feeling, from the relief of being honest, to the apprehension of our outside lives, to the incredible way his body made me feel. It was too much—and still not enough. I needed everything.

"You're sure? Here?" His voice was ragged, laden with the effort of control.

"If you don't get inside me right now I might die." I clung to his shoulders, urging my hips forward. "Please."

"That's a little dramatic, but since the feeling is mutual, I'm happy to oblige."

He moved under me, into me, my body exploding into shudders as he crushed me to his chest. He pulled out slightly, lifting me to meet him, and the waves of pleasure were overwhelming. My head tipped back, my nerve endings singing as he buried his face between my breasts. His tongue, his body, the scratch of his jaw against my skin, the way his lips left fire in their wake—I couldn't process fast enough. *Could anything else be this good? Could anyone relate to how I felt right now?*

Fox caught my chin in his hand, bringing my focus back to him. "Right here, sunshine."

I looked at him, fighting to keep my eyes from glazing over in lust. Of course, *someone* could relate, the very someone whose expression mirrored my own—the person who brought these feelings to the surface for me, who touched me like I was priceless, who brought me to the brink time and time again. *My* person. Fox.

My fingers gripped him hard enough to bruise, but I knew he welcomed it. *Mark me. Let everyone know.* He was right—there was nothing else for either of us. He kissed me desperately and then I was caught up in him, only him—the rest of the world ceased to exist when he was everything.

⚬

My kitchen door slowly opened, and I saw a perfectly manicured hand pop through, holding a cupcake with a tiny white flag on the top.

"Avery?"

"Yes?" My natural reaction would've been to laugh, but I kept my response clipped, with just a hint of frost to it.

Was I honestly mad that Heather told Fox everything? Not really. If I had to admit it, I'd expected nothing less. But still, I had a right to be slightly annoyed. *Even though our "fight" had ended with the pinnacle of make-up sex—maybe I should be thanking her?*

The cupcake withdrew itself slowly, and then Heather herself appeared, looking chastised. "Can I come in?"

"Sure."

She closed the kitchen door behind her, bringing the cupcake as she came to sit across from me at the table. She placed it in front of me ceremoniously. "Here."

"What's this for?" I asked innocently.

Heather gave me a long look. "You know, I'm not going to apologize for telling Fox what you were up to. He should've known from the beginning, and it was only because you knew he'd freak that you didn't tell him in the first place." She paused. "But I am going to apologize for betraying your confidence, even if I thought it was a secret you never should've kept."

How To Disagree With Your Best Friend 101: Always have their best interests at heart and use that to defend yourself and your actions. It's a foolproof strategy, because how can you be mad at someone who loves you so much they'd be willing to piss you off to make sure you're okay?

"That is the worst apology I've ever heard," I said with a straight face. "But I'll take it, because you're right. We were both keeping things from each other—but mine was worse."

She grimaced. "Is he mad?"

"Not really," I admitted. "Hurt that I didn't tell him, concerned for my safety—but he's Fox. He understands even when I can't figure out how to explain it myself."

"It wasn't right, Avery. Y'all are supposed to be a team." Heather's voice trembled a bit as she spoke. "I could tell, when I came over the other day, that you knew it wasn't the right thing."

"I kinda wish you would've let me get there on my own—" I gave her a side-eye, "but your intentions were in the right place."

She nodded vigorously, not looking the slightest bit guilty

anymore. "So you're good? With each other, I mean?"

"Yeah."

"And no more sneaking around?"

Now that everything was on the table, the relief I felt was so immense, I wondered how I'd considered anything else. "I promise."

"And you'll come out for a girls' night tonight?"

"Trying to sneak that one in there while my guard is down?" Such a Heather move.

She grinned as she nodded. "Did it work?"

I couldn't help grinning back. "I'll be there."

~\/~

"Avery! Are you ready yet? C'mon girl, the night is young but I'm gettin' old!"

I heard the low rumble of Fox's laugh down the hall where he was supposed to be entertaining Heather as she waited for me.

"I'm coming!" I called back to her as I fastened my favorite bracelet on my wrist. "Just a minute!" I shoved my feet into my boots and ran into the living room. "Sorry, sorry."

"Now that is a cute dress, Avery Fox." Heather gave me a once-over. "Who was the girl who didn't have a thing to wear just a year ago?"

I looked down at my dark floral mini dress. "Fox picked it for me."

Just the edge of Fox's dimple showed as Heather nodded sagely at him. "Makes total sense."

"What's that supposed to mean?" I asked her, but I already knew. Clothes were so much better now that I could gauge my husband's reaction to them. Wide eyes meant one thing, narrowed meant another. Both were good.

"Bye," I said, stretching up on tiptoes to kiss Fox's cheek.

He gave my butt a little smack and my thighs tingled in anticipation. That man could speak without words. "Have fun."

"Oh, we will, Fox," Heather drawled. "A night out in Brancher is *guaranteed* to be the party of the year."

I rolled my eyes. "We're just going to Lucky's."

"Everyone's coming, Avery. Don't be a party pooper. It's girls' night!"

"Who's everyone?" I asked curiously.

"Well—you, me, Joy, your mom, Sue Ellen and her sister, those girls from your advertising class, Derek's girlfriend—I can never remember her name, a couple of your mom friends, Claire—"

"Claire is only eighteen!" I protested.

"Oh. That's right. Well, Lucky is her uncle. No one will serve her anyhow. We'll draw those big X's on her hands, just in case," Heather decided. "Let's get a move on!"

"We're going to party with my mom. Don't wait up!" I called to Fox as she pulled me toward her car.

Heather smacked my arm. "She can drink you under the table and you know it."

I glanced back at Fox, who was shaking his head with laughter as he shut the front door. "Love you!"

The porch light flicked in response.

"That man," Heather said with a sigh. "So strong and silent—his brother could learn a thing or two from him." She frowned. "Mainly like when to shut up."

"Are you guys still arguing?" I asked as I opened the car door. "I can't believe you haven't hashed this out yet. You've been saying he's acting weird, but he seems like the same old Lucas to me."

I knew I'd been pretty preoccupied with all things J.D. while Fox was at the site all day. But even with my distractions, I still noticed something was still awry in Heather-and-Lucas-land and had been for a while now.

Heather violently shoved the key into the ignition. "He'd like for you to believe that."

Her tone had me laughing, and I couldn't stop even when she speared me with a dirty look. I closed my eyes and took a deep, sobering breath. "Okay, seriously. What's up?"

"He's just being *different*," she said. "I don't know how to explain it."

"Different like how?"

I cracked the window as we cruised down the road on the way to Lucky's. The air felt clean tonight, the humidity of the past few weeks finally giving way to what I hoped would be an early fall.

"A little distant, a little preoccupied, I guess? Nothing major, but I've noticed. I feel like maybe he's keeping something from me."

"Like... someone?" I couldn't believe Lucas would do that to her, but I had to get to the root of what Heather was saying.

"No. Maybe." She pulled into a parking spot in front of Lucky's and turned to me. "I know he's juggling a lot to spend so much time out here."

I felt guilt flood through me. "We really appreciate—"

"Avery, hush up. That's not what I meant. There's nowhere else that man would be other than his brother's side, and you know it. They bicker like catty sisters, but they come through for each other every time." She picked at the beading on her top. "Something's up with Lucas, and I don't know what it is. He's been a little distant, he's spent even more time on the phone lately than usual. When I ask, he says everything is fine. And now he's been back in California for a week, and it feels weird."

There was nothing worse than relationship limbo. "Maybe you should just trust him." If it were anyone else but Lucas, I'd probably be giving different advice. But he and Fox were more alike than different, and I believed in Lucas.

"We can talk about this later. Let's get out of here and go party," Heather said, stepping out of the car. "I need a tequila. And a margarita."

"There's tequila *in* a margarita," I pointed out.

"No." She shook her head. "I need *just* tequila first, and then a margarita."

"Starting off strong." I slung an arm around her shoulders as we walked into the bar. "I like your style."

We walked into Lucky's and the hoots and catcalls coming from the back booth immediately clued me in to where the rest of our friends waited. "Avery! Heather! Get your asses over here!"

"I think they started without us," I said to Heather.

"Then we'll have to catch up."

A couple margaritas later—Lucky's poured them sour and strong, if not very good—and I desperately had to pee.

"Look who we have here," I heard a voice coming from a nearby bar stool as I made my way out of the ladies' room.

I glanced to my left and felt my buzz start to melt away. "Hi, Elise. You know, for someone who claims not to like this place, you sure seem to be here a lot."

Heather stumbled out of the restroom and nearly careened into me. "Was that door always so heavy?"

"You know my daddy gets hungry when he works late, and this is the only place still open. I heard the diner is coming along... just another thing that goes right for Avery Kent, despite everything." The sneer in Elise's voice was so evident I nearly cringed.

I wasn't sure if it was the tequila coursing through my veins or if I was just tired of her nonsense. "Chase told me you tried to keep him from coming to help Fox, tried to tell the other guys not to come either. Why, Elise? Why would you do that? This is my parents' livelihood! Whatever your problem is with me—that's fucking low of you to take it out on them, Elise."

"*I'm* low? Me? You've got to be kidding. For years all you talked about, you and my brother, was how you couldn't wait to get out of this town and get a *real* life. Like you were too good for Brancher and everyone in it."

"That's not true, Elise," I protested. "I care about Brancher and what happens in it. Just because I wanted to make something of myself—"

"There you go again! Can't build a future in a one-horse town, right? *'That Avery, she has ambition, she has drive. She wants more than what dead-end Brancher has to offer.'* If I heard that once, I heard it a thousand times. And I started to think, what was wrong with me that I didn't want that, too?"

I just stared at her. "Elise—"

"No, let me finish. I love Brancher. My family loves Brancher. Maybe Chase didn't, but we like our lives here. All I ever wanted was to be like my mama—queen of the state fair four years in a row, the best hostess in three counties, chairwoman of the children's hospital philanthropy board and about a million other charities. That's not *nothing*, Avery. It was enough for me, but you made it seem silly. And I hated you for it."

Elise's words cut me to the quick. Had I behaved that way? In the pursuit of my own dreams, had I trivialized the scope of others? Brancher was my hometown, it was a place where people lived who loved me and who I loved in return. "I—I had no idea."

She drew her mouth into a thin line. "The day I found out you'd decided to stay I was so angry. Poor Avery, couldn't go fulfill her big plans. She was stuck here with us in this backwards town that she despised. But you made it okay, didn't you? Got your degree, snagged the only new eligible bachelor who has ever moved here in like, a hundred years. I watched everything turn out for you, Avery, just the way you wanted. And I kept thinking—she's full of shit. She doesn't even like it here. She doesn't deserve all of this."

"And you did?" I asked. There was no venom in my words. I was tired of fighting with Elise. Whatever was done had already happened, and I was looking toward the future now. If I ever lived in Brancher again, it would be because I wanted it, not because I felt like I was stuck.

"More than you," she countered.

"Maybe you shouldn't be such a bitch, then." Heather surveyed Elise with her arms crossed. "You're entitled to your feelings. But as women, aren't we supposed to build each other up, not take every opportunity to tear the other down?"

"You're smart, Elise. And you're beautiful. It doesn't matter what I think about your dreams—my opinion doesn't mean shit. Whatever you want for your life, I have no doubt that you'll make it happen. I've never seen you give up on anything yet." As the words came out of my mouth I realized I truly meant them. "And I'm sorry if anything I said ever made you feel like your plans weren't as important as mine."

"You have no idea what it's been like to live in your shadow—yours and Chase's. Between the girl who beat the odds and the town hero, I didn't stand a chance." Elise paused. "And you're right. I was a bitch. I *am* a bitch," she amended. "Even my mama likes you now, and she can hold a grudge longer than anyone." She looked like she was caught between the urge to laugh and cry. "But I'm sorry about what I said to the guys—about not helping with the rebuild. What's between us should never have spilled over onto your folks."

I chose my next statement carefully. "You're right. The diner—the diner is for everyone, Elise. It means a lot to this town."

She took a deep breath. "I want to thank you for what you and Fox did for Chase. He's so much—we're very different," she said finally. "He's lucky to have friends like the two of you. Thank you for not writing him off after everything that happened."

"I care about Chase," I told her softly. "So does Fox. And we're really grateful that he came out here to help us with the diner. He didn't have to do that."

"I know!" Now Elise really looked on the verge of tears. "That's what I meant, I tried to tell him, but... he'd probably do just about anything for you still, Avery. And since he's my only brother, and you and your family matter to him—the main reason I came over here is to say I'm tired of feeling this way. It's time for me to grow up and take responsibility for my own shit. I know this has been largely one-sided, but I want a truce."

She'd done her best to stall our rebuild, and after high school had given me enough reason to hate her forever, but if there was something I'd learned through all the bullshit it was that there was always two sides to every story. That didn't mean that any of the sides were in the right, but I was done hanging onto bullshit. If I couldn't be the bigger person, I was exactly the way Elise had misconstrued me for all these years. And I had no way of knowing if she was being sincere, but what did I have to lose?

"Truce." I stuck out my hand. "Does this mean we're friends now?"

She hesitated. "How about 'not enemies'?" she suggested, placing her hand into mine.

"Deal."

"This nearly warms my heart," said Heather.

Elise shot her a dagger look.

"Whatever. I said, *nearly.*" Heather rolled her eyes. "Want to get a drink with us, Elise? We're about to order another round."

She cocked her head to one side as she considered Heather's offer. "Maybe next time." She wrinkled her nose as she glanced around at our group. "I was just leaving."

The expression on Heather's face as she watched Elise abruptly walk away made me burst into laughter.

"Did I just hallucinate?" she asked dramatically. "Because a minute ago, I thought that girl said she was trying to change."

"Baby steps, Heather. Baby steps."

CHAPTER FOURTEEN

FOX

"You got a minute, Fox?"

Jim Kent's voice surprised me, and I paused from where I was cutting and loading wood on the back of my truck. "Sure."

"Come for a drive with me." He turned and headed for his SUV parked on the street.

"Okay." My mind started spinning as I shucked my tool belt and unplugged the saw. *Where were we going?*

Chase grinned at me over a stack of drywall. "Is this gonna be like one of those survival things where he dumps you in the middle of nowhere and you have to find your way back?"

I snorted at him. "I could do that."

His grin turned wicked. "What if you were *naked*?"

"This conversation is over." I shoved a multitool into my pocket, just in case, and Chase started laughing. "Shut up. Tell Tripp we'll be back soon."

"What should I tell Avery if Jim comes back without you?" he snickered.

"I'm ignoring you," I called back to him as I loped over to the SUV.

"Won't take much of your time," Jim said as I buckled in and we headed down the road toward the highway.

"Not a problem," I told him. "Can I ask where we're going?"

"Just up the road a ways." He fiddled with the volume on the stereo, turning it down a notch. "Nice to see you and Chase gettin' on so well. There was a time I wasn't sure if that would mend."

Me either. "I understand him, I guess. What he went through— what he still probably goes through. Compassion beats out anger if you let it. I'm not always good at that, but I try."

Jim nodded slowly. "S'all you can do."

We drove in silence for a while. I had my general bearings of where we were—not too far from the ranch, but we'd come from a different direction. Lots of open land here, fields and grass, dotted with trees and miles of fence line. I looked around curiously when Jim pulled over—there was nothing here.

"Doesn't look like much, does it?"

I wasn't sure what he referred to—the road? The pasture? I was about to open my mouth and ask the obvious question when he spoke again.

"I never got y'all a proper wedding present."

Jim looked out again over the flat expanse of land. It was a nice, mild evening, with a small breeze rustling the few oak trees clustered around. The air smelled clean, as clean as air can smell with cattle close by. This was another thing I'd miss about Texas— the *space*. Nowhere else I'd been even came close.

What? "You don't have to get us anything, Mr. Kent," I said. "You've done so much for us already."

And it was true, he had. He had given me a job when I was hurt, and without that, I wouldn't have had a chance to know his daughter. That was worth more than I could ever repay. He gave me a place to live when I wasn't sure where my home was anymore. And mostly, he'd given me a purpose when I was lost. In short, he'd given me everything.

And then after Avery and I got married—between the months I was gone for my last Hotshot season to navigating the J.D. situation, Avery's father had been there for her and Annabelle at every turn. When my memory was in ruins, he'd kept the faith that I'd get my shit together. He'd given me the benefit of the doubt when I fucked up and welcomed me back with open arms when I finally pulled my head out of my ass.

No, this man didn't need to give me anything else. I would have nothing if it weren't for him.

"Well, that's too bad," Jim said dryly. "Because you're sitting on it."

I snapped back into reality at his words. "What?"

"I'm gettin' on in years, Fox. I wanted to take a chance on breeding cattle again, but the truth is that I have enough on my plate. So I sold my bull, and I bought you this place." He gestured out to the fields in front of us. "There's an old farmhouse about a half mile down—you can't see it until the road curves. Needs some work, and the barn and fences too, but I happen to know you're handy with a hammer."

"You—" I was having a hard time understanding what was happening.

"Our fences border each other on the north side. Up on a little ridge where Avery always liked to ride. She'll know the spot." He cleared his throat. "I hope you all will like it. Maybe you'll come back someday, and we'll try that cattle thing together."

I looked out over the land again. *Our* land, bought for us by my father-in-law. Land where I could farm or raise cattle, where I could have horses for Annabelle and my wife, where I could run on my own ground, maybe get a dog to go with me.

I had property already, but nothing like this. I owned two thousand square feet in Seattle, but it was a couple of stories in the air. This was real, this was dirt and trees and grass and sunshine and blue sky. This was Texas, the place where I'd met my wife, where my life started to make sense again. Avery was right about Seattle— it was where we'd reconnected. But Texas was where we had found each other in the first place.

I could imagine our life together here. He was right—we could go do whatever we needed to do and we could always come home. If Avery's hesitation over leaving was any indication, I thought she would feel the same way.

"Does Avery know?"

He looked at me. "No. I'll leave that to you to tell her. My Avery—she's always focused on the geography. It means something to her, going away. But I'm starting to think maybe coming home could mean something to her too."

"I don't know what to say, Jim. Thank you." *Thank you so much for everything.*

"It'll keep until you get back. You and Avery go and do what drives you. This land, it'll keep."

⁓⁓

I could've just let it go. Avery and I were on the same page now, everything out in the open, and no harm done. But that gene I had, that hero complex that wouldn't let it rest—well, it got the best of me. I'll admit it. And that's how I found myself out at the police station with a bone to pick regarding a certain detective's recruitment of my wife.

Sure, it wasn't the only reason I was in Midland. There were rental tools waiting for me at the home improvement store. But I could've sent Sloane and McDaniels for those. This thing, this thing with Avery and London, it was personal.

And I'm sure the look on my face spoke volumes about my displeasure when O'Connor spotted me at the station's front desk.

"Is everything okay?"

"I'm not here for you." I turned toward him slowly. "I came to ask your partner why she tried to recruit my wife into a recon mission behind my back."

His face blanched but he recovered quickly. "She's not here."

"I'll set up an appointment. You and I have nothing to say to each other." I didn't like him much either, I realized. It was unfortunate, because I actually *did* like London, in spite of everything. I just wasn't very happy with her at the moment.

O'Connor looked at me for a long moment, then gestured to back in the direction of his office. "A word alone?"

For a split second, I wondered if I needed a lawyer, but dismissed the idea quickly. He could talk, I didn't have to.

"Why?"

"Follow me please, Mr. Fox." His voice was pleasant enough, but I had a feeling I wasn't going to like what happened next. We passed by his office and boarded a nearby elevator.

And the minute the elevator doors opened and I saw the department sign, I knew I was right.

No one likes a morgue.

I mean—some people probably do, but I wasn't one of them. I glanced at O'Connor, but his face was impassive. Much more stoic than during his interrogations. As I said, no one likes a morgue.

We were quickly joined by the coroner and led to a metal gurney in the corner. I tried to focus on anything but the heavy coldness in the air, but the alternative was to think about the drawers that lined one wall of the room. *Why were we here?*

I was about to find out.

"Do you know this man?"

Sandy brown hair... solid build... road rash... tattooed forearm. I wasn't familiar with the mark or the man. So at least I could be honest when I answered.

"No."

Detective O'Connor nodded as the coroner pulled the sheet back over the body. "Thank you."

I slammed my eyes open and shut once, twice, trying to blink out images of fiery skies, of low-flying helicopters, of soot-and-tear-streaked faces pleading for help. *Don't, Fox. Don't go there. It's not the same thing, all of that happened years ago. That's your damaged brain trying to fuck with you, it's not real.*

Reality was here, in the quiet morgue with the detective and the coroner both looking to me for answers. At this point, I wasn't sure which was worse.

"Mr. Fox?"

"Sorry." I stepped away from the metal table. "Is there anything else?"

According to protocol, I shouldn't even be here. Most people didn't get asked to come to the basement and identify remains—but protocol as I knew it had flown out the window two years ago in the midst of a firestorm. Protocol meant less to me than ever before, and I was trying to be helpful. We were in the eye of a cluster-fuck, the simmering, raging calm before a disaster where the extent of the damage would encompass more than anyone could imagine.

This was typically where I thrived. But nothing about this situation was typical.

I was used to sifting through the aftermath to find what still lived. Mother Nature usually left just enough for a fresh start. Man-made ruin was different—that night was a total loss for everyone involved.

"Appreciate your time. We'll contact you with anything further."

I had to say it. "You thought this was J.D.?" We'd swept the building. I'd done it myself, against protocol, again, always. In my dreams, even. I knew he hadn't died inside the fire. And yet—I needed to be sure.

"He *is* a J.D.—John Doe, for now. He was unconscious on the side of the highway about ten miles away from Brancher." O'Connor shook his head. "Official cause of death is complications from lung damage, including untreated smoke inhalation. We're still waiting on identification."

That was why he'd wanted me here—a tie to a similar crime. It was likely they'd be waiting on that I.D. forever. Some people had a way of slipping through the cracks of life with nothing to tie them to a specific place or time. But this wasn't the man I was looking for. Or even the reason I'd come, but things always had a way of coming back around to the central problem.

"He was alone?"

His gaze was even. "Someone left him there. Bystanders at a nearby rest stop think they saw a car go by in a hurry."

Lung damage could be anything, and O'Connor knew it. Meth lab, hazmat exposure. This didn't have anything to do with J.D. It was just a shot in the dark.

My temple started to throb again and I closed my eyes, seeing the flash of fire as my brain flicked through images of that night—the real ones, not the dreams. I smelled the burn, heard Avery's sobs. The smoke reached high into the black sky, shutting out the stars until the fire became the only light. And in the periphery of my memory, something moved. Something fled. Some*one*—someone still out there.

"Sorry I couldn't be of more help." My right hand clenched into a fist, an involuntary movement that only belied a small amount of the rage that was seeping in no matter how much I tried to keep it out. I wasn't sorry at all, and the detective knew it.

"Are you sure J.D. burned down your diner, Fox?" The look on O'Connor's face implied that he clearly thought I was.

My jaw was set when I met the detective's eyes. "Are *you*?" I'd voiced my suspicions during the interview, long before Avery's involvement. They'd obviously had enough evidence if they tried to bring her into it.

His non-answer was the only one I needed.

I took one deep breath, then two. Then another, while I came to the only decision available. "I'll keep in touch."

I meant it, but only partly. I had other plans now, plans that didn't necessarily include London and O'Connor. They did, however, include my brother and some of our new friends. I thought about it all the way back to Brancher, through the busywork of the morning while I tried to shake off the cold feeling of the morgue that stayed with me even in the Texas sun.

I flexed my shoulder, stretching the tense muscle. I could never admit it to Lucas, especially after I'd given him shit the other day for that whole "impeccable shape, prime of my life" thing, but I was definitely starting to feel the effects of twelve hours a day of construction.

My coffee was already cold, but I finished it anyway. Derek and Kyle would be here soon—they usually came after lunch and we did a hard push until sunset. I didn't want to be home too late tonight, but there was plenty of work to be done. We'd finally gotten our supplies in and were back on track. *Of course, my days would be going so much better if these jerks didn't keep trying to kill themselves.*

I just needed to keep my head in the game. When Heather had told me what Avery was planning to do, I'd nearly broken the phone I held in my hand. Why she would ever feel like she needed to take that on without me... I had no idea how I would've confronted her about that. The fact that she came to me with the truth, that she trusted me with that, meant so much to the solidity of our marriage.

We were partners, and any time we didn't feel that one hundred percent, it was time to revisit and revise. Yes, the idea of Avery going to meet with J.D. on her own scared the ever-loving shit out of me—but the thought of her not feeling like she could share things with me was infinitely worse in the long run.

I'd remember that every time my hands started to clench when I thought about that asshole being around her. J.D. needed to stay the fuck away from me and mine. The only way I was interested in him being in our proximity again is if he were wearing handcuffs in a courtroom. I'd go to the ends of the earth to facilitate that if I had to. And even though I didn't like London and O'Connor very much right now, I knew I'd have backup if I needed it. We had a common goal. It was time to get organized.

"Hey Luke, you got lunch plans tomorrow?"

Lucas set his sports drink down with a thud. "Yeah B., I thought I'd go to Paris. I like their cheese." He rolled his eyes at me. "I'll be here, obviously, just like you. What's up?"

The exasperated expression on his face almost made me snicker, but I didn't want to give his dumb joke the validation.

"Wanna go for a drive with me to see your older, cooler counterpart?"

Lucas raised an eyebrow. "Rambo Garrett?"

"You have another person in mind?" I asked mildly. "Yes, Rambo Garrett. I think it's time for plan C. Or D—I'm not sure where we left it."

I had his full attention now. "You want to go after J.D.? Why now?"

"It's a long story—you and Heather should come over for dinner and we'll fill you in."

"Well, now I'm curious. Count us in—we'll bring dessert."

"Cool. Now get off your ass, we have shit to do."

⁓⁖⁓

I should've known, because it was Heather, that dessert would have a theme. We'd strategized while eating something named "Co(conut)-Conspirators Pie", which was pretty much just like coconut cream pie except it had an unexpected layer of chocolate lining the crust. I wasn't really into puns, but I was into pie, no matter what it was called.

And now Lucas and I were driving out to Rambo Garrett's with a box of donuts and muffins—those didn't have a special name as far as I knew, but then again I didn't ask.

"Do you ever wonder what Garrett's backstory is? Like, was he special ops? A SEAL?" Lucas chewed his muffin thoughtfully.

I glanced in my mirrors as I exited off the highway. "I figured you would've run a check on him already."

"I did," Lucas admitted. "But whoever does his web stuff is extremely thorough, because according to the internet he doesn't exist. That's how you know someone is really legit."

"When you can't find anything about them online?" I took a bite of my chocolate donut.

Lucas nodded. "Ultimate stealth mode."

We parked in front of Garrett's compound and got out of the

truck. The security gate buzzed us in before we even rang the bell, a true testament to Garrett's surveillance system. I couldn't see any of the cameras, but I knew they were there.

"Garrett?" Lucas called as we walked into the courtyard. "Hello?"

"In here," a gruff voice answered.

We turned right, to the big two-story garages where Garrett kept his extra equipment. I never knew what to expect when I came here, but Garrett still surprised me every time. Once he was wrapping up a jiu-jitsu session where it seemed he was the instructor. Another time he was bathing his 150-pound mastiff. And still another, he was chopping down a tree. This time he was very carefully sharpening what looked like a foot-long knife, his head bent intently over his task.

"Come on in." Another scrape of the knife.

"Um, we can come back another time, if you're busy," Lucas said quickly, and I stifled a laugh.

"No, no. I'm all done. What can I do for you boys?"

Garrett sheathed his survival knife and turned, giving us his full attention. Calling that weapon a knife was actually a little insulting —it was more than halfway to a machete.

"We need to find a man."

As it turned out, Garrett's grin was more frightening than any of his equipment. "I was hoping y'all would say that."

CHAPTER FIFTEEN

AVERY

"**J**ust the person I wanted to see," I said brightly, getting out of my car. I reached up to grab Annabelle from her car seat and set her on the sidewalk.

My father looked up from the back of the SUV where he was packing his tools away. It was the end of the construction day, and Annabelle and I had come to pick up Fox. My husband occasionally got it into his head some mornings that he'd like to jog to work, as if he didn't get enough exercise on his regular runs and, you know, making buildings with his bare hands.

We'd arrived early today, just in time to catch the rest of the crew leaving, my father included. Annabelle knew the rules of the site by now, and she waited until Fox saw her before entering the gate. He raised an eyebrow curiously at me when I didn't budge from my spot by my dad's car, and when I offered him a grin he just shook his head and plunked his hard hat down on Annabelle's head. I guess the past couple days had proven that Fox could typically tell when I was plotting something.

"Avery?" My dad's voice snapped me back to the task at hand. "What's goin' on?"

I took a deep breath. "Well, Daddy... Thanksgiving is on Thursday."

We'd all been tip-toeing around the holiday, not mentioning any plans, but I couldn't stand it anymore. It wasn't Thanksgiving without our annual Kitchen Dinner.

"I know." He didn't offer anything else, and for a moment I regretted my decision to have this conversation.

"We have to do something," I said, my voice softer now. "The Kitchen—we *always* have a Thanksgiving dinner. Some people, they count on it."

It was true, and my dad knew it. There were parts of our little town, some of the more rural parts, that were very impoverished. Without the event at the Kitchen, I knew some families would skip Thanksgiving altogether.

He looked at me and then turned to look at the half-finished shell of the building. "I don't know what we can do."

It was those words that nearly broke me. My father always knew what to do, he was the most steady, patient, solid person I knew. Fox was a very close second—but my dad won just for sheer longevity.

"I do, Daddy. Let me do it. You take care of the food, and I'll do everything else."

"I don't understand how this will work, Avery," my mom said when I told her. "I know you want to make this right, but we might have to skip this year."

"Not an option, Mom." I had faith, and after I explained my ideas, she did too. "It'll be like a cookout, the biggest one we've ever had. Tables everywhere, in the street even. Speaking of that, do you have the mayor's number? We might need a permit."

Always put your money on a determined woman, because we could mobilize an army like no one's business. I only had three days to pull together a makeshift Kitchen Thanksgiving, but I wasn't going to let a little thing like time stop me. The minute I put out the call, Brancher answered.

"Avery, we heard you're doing the Kitchen Dinner. Magnolia and I, we bought too many yams. Have someone come take them off our hands, will you?"

"I was just gonna get rid of these old coolers. You'll find a use for them, won't you?"

"Avery, I made you some table decorations. Send your young man by to collect them."

I was floored by the generosity, although I shouldn't have been surprised. Fox had gently reminded me that our town cared about the Kitchen, cared about our family. They'd donated to the Thanksgiving dinner before, but not like this.

And it didn't end there. Heather always seemed to have a pie or two up her sleeve at all times, but she produced a miracle and delivered a true Thanksgiving cornucopia of baked goods, more than anyone could eat. I recruited a bunch of the high school football players, under the supervision of Chase and the other Hotshot guys, to clean up the site and hang twinkle lights over everything that would stay still.

Annabelle's teacher got permission for us to use all of the tables and chairs from the school cafeteria, which Fox and Derek hauled over to the build site and set up family-style. My mom's friends donated extra silverware and linens, my dad went to Midland for all the food supplies, the barbecue place let us use their kitchen, and we were in business.

The weather had been a bit cold lately, but Thanksgiving day dawned warmly, and for that I was glad, considering our makeshift venue didn't have finished walls. The open space was a bonus, I decided. More room for people.

I was putting the finishing touches on the table settings when my husband came strolling up, wearing one of my favorite outfits on him—a food-stained apron and a bandanna. Not a good look for everyone, but a winner on Fox.

"Turkeys are almost done," he said, kissing my temple. He looked around at the makeshift dining room. "It looks great in here."

"I didn't do it alone," I said, adjusting a rogue fork. "Everyone helped."

"Sure." His dimple popped. "But take some of the credit, Avery. You deserve it."

"Let's just agree that we have a good team." I slipped an arm around his waist.

We watched the first few families come in, followed by some young cowboys, and after that it was a steady influx of people, coming to spend their Thanksgiving with us or just stopping by to offer a laugh, a story, or a casserole.

My dad finally had some time to catch up with his ranching friends, their wives all gathered at one of the long tables while the men smoked cigars in the street. I glanced over more than once, relishing the smile on his face. He didn't speak much, content to let the others do the talking, but that was okay. For the first time in at least a month, my father looked like himself, without a trace of his worried frown. I was incredibly glad to see it.

My mom kept busy with Joy, both of them in their complete element with people to fuss over, babies to kiss, and general gossip to enjoy. Admittedly, when I thought of the Kitchen, my father usually came to mind. But now I realized that this was my mother's social outlet, and she'd been sorely missing her time in town. Without the Kitchen, she spent most days at the ranch with only my dad to keep her company. I knew they loved each other, that their foundation was something solid to strive for, but the Kitchen filled different needs for each of them—needs that were separate but connected by the same source.

And Heather—she was baking for an army, just the way she liked it. I watched her hold court over the dessert table, accepting praise and delighting in the catty looks from girls with much lower confection skills than her own. *"Catch 'em by the stomach, keep 'em with the attitude."* I'd laughed at that saying for years, ever since the first time I'd heard it come out of her proper mouth. But with the way Lucas looked at her, I knew there was something to it. Heather had him locked down, there was no doubt about that.

Even the small rainstorm that passed through couldn't beat us. Derek and Chase jumped on a couple ladders and had tarps up within minutes, ready for anyone who wanted to take shelter. And everyone else? They danced in the rain.

Fox caught it all on his camera—another year immortalized, likely our most eventful one yet, in ways both good and bad.

"You're happy," my husband said at the end of the night. It wasn't a question.

"I am." I turned his arms, looking up into his handsome face. "Not just a good team—we're the best team."

I saw it on my parents' face the day of our barbecue at the ranch, and I saw it again today. The Kitchen meant something to everyone, but to them it was everything. We had a long-standing tradition of serving a Thanksgiving dinner, and this year despite the odds, we did it.

It wasn't perfect, but it was exactly how it was supposed to be.

⁓⁕⁓

I woke up the next morning still smiling from our successful Thanksgiving. Who needed a restaurant with actual walls? Not the Kents. We could serve two hundred people without a building, no problem. In fact, I liked the freedom of the construction site. Spilled some iced tea? No problem, throw some sawdust over it and sweep it up later. Nowhere to put the buffet? That's fine, assembly line plating works just as well.

It wasn't a permanent solution, of course, and Fox's crew was getting closer every day to finishing the build. But it made me feel good that we could be so adaptable, that we were operating at the highest possible capacity in spite of whatever was thrown at us. We'd come a long way from the hopelessness of just a couple months ago.

Fox headed out early because he couldn't sit still to save his life, even on a day most people would've stayed home. I was antsy too, and since Annabelle was home for vacation, I decided we'd get out and do a little grocery shopping. Fox had pulled every available ingredient from the ranch kitchen and our own little pantry to make the Thanksgiving dinner, and now we needed a restock.

"Annabelle! Are you ready to go?"

After I bundled her into the car, we drove toward the main streets of town while I contemplated my grocery list. I was sick of turkey—tonight I wanted brisket. But I also didn't want Fox to have to cook it seeing as he'd spent all day on the stove yesterday. And after my disastrous attempt with stir fry I was hesitant about ruining another meal, so that left takeout.

"We're making a detour, kid. I've got a taste for barbecue." I pulled into the alley parking behind Ribs, the barbecue place. There were only two spots left, and I was happy to snag one of them because street parking on this block was always scarce.

I got Annabelle out of the SUV and straightened up as another car pulled in to the other empty spot, nearly on my bumper. He was out of the car and trying to edge his way around the driver side before I'd even fixed Annabelle's headband.

Geez, this guy parked like a total jackass. I moved aside a little to let him pass, squeezing closer to the wall with Annabelle. I looked down at her and was about to open my mouth to ask if she was ready for lunch when the man turned around.

"Hello, Avery."

His voice and proximity caused me to stop short, and when I looked up, I got my first glimpse of Annabelle's father in what seemed like a lifetime.

He was the same, except he wasn't. This man was older than his years, he was thin, his hair had already greyed at the temples and started to recede, and his skin looked weathered and dull.

J.D.'s eyes widened just a fraction, then narrowed as he took two steps toward us. The walk, I should've recognized. But even that had changed—it was the now slightly stilted stride of a man who'd lately spent more time in the dirt than on the back of the bull.

It was the look in his eyes that sent a lick of dread down my spine. "J.D.?"

Five years ago, he'd been handsome, charming—if a bit rough and unpredictable. He'd been fit and wiry, his eyes sharp and his laugh quick. I used to look at him in envy of how he took everything as it came, measuring life in eight-second cycles of glory. I looked at him now and just saw broken. And desperate.

He slid closer, bringing the smell of cigarettes and, if I wasn't mistaken, whiskey with him. With his gaze trained on me, I told myself not to stare. Was Annabelle in there, somewhere? I almost never thought of J.D. when I looked at her. But face to face with him, I couldn't stop searching for signs of my daughter.

I was so intent on trying to decode his DNA that I didn't notice what he wore at his belt until he casually placed a hand on the holster.

Everything started closing in on me then. We were in an alley on the last block of town proper, the Friday after Thanksgiving when half of the population was in Midland for a football game. J.D. was here, he knew I'd be here—so that meant he'd followed me. The nearest salvation was on the other side of a solid brick building. Annabelle and I were all alone.

"What do you want?" I asked him, my eyes now trained on his right hand.

He wouldn't hurt me. He wouldn't hurt us. I took a deep breath. *He hates Fox, but—he hated Fox enough to burn down the Kitchen*, I reminded myself. *He's capable of anything.*

"You two are comin' with me."

Another step closer, and then two, and suddenly my wrist was locked into his iron grip, the grip that had won him belt buckles and kept his skull above the dirt for countless rides on the backs of wild beasts. My bones didn't stand a chance.

Every single cell in my body was on fire, a thousand internal voices screaming at me to get as far away as I possibly could, to grab Annabelle and *run run run* until the last three minutes were a distant memory.

"C'mon, Avery. Don't make a scene." J.D.'s breath was hot in my ear. "Can't have that kid start screamin'. Not unless you want somebody to get hurt."

And then I heard the unmistakable click.

CHAPTER SIXTEEN

FOX

I was well aware that my wife was a spectacular person, but even I couldn't fully grasp it sometimes. Morale was up after Thanksgiving, way up. Avery had given the town and the crew exactly what they hadn't known they needed. Everyone was hyped after the big turnout, and I wanted to keep the momentum going.

Except, I also wanted my guys to be rested and refreshed. Which was why I was the only one on site today while everyone else was at home. *Those who cannot do, teach.* That was me when it came to taking a break. But I was fine with it. Being alone in the half-finished restaurant gave me a chance to really look, to see what still needed to be done and how far we were from getting there. Or, at this point—how close.

"A real old-fashioned barn raisin'," one grizzled cowboy had said to me yesterday. "That's what this is."

I supposed in a way he was right. It was a group of people getting together to help, not for money or individual profit, but for the greater good. This was a marvel of small towns that I'd miss when we went back to Seattle. Hell, when we went just about anywhere except Brancher, Texas. I'd never been to a place like this, and I doubted I'd see another like it.

My coffee grew cold as I moved from one end of the building to the other, jotting down notes and numbers. We were so close. Visually, miles away. But in a project sense, we had a structure. It was primitive at best, but it was half the battle.

I was calculating some costs when a private call came through. "This is Fox."

"Fox, it's Garrett." Of course he had a blocked number. No surprise there. "Can you talk?"

Garrett didn't strike me as the type to call someone up just to chat, so of course I was going to listen, no matter what else I had going on. "Yeah, sure. What's up?"

"Took some work, but I have a sighting from a reliable source."

"Already?" Rambo Garrett had done in a few days what Lucas's P.I. hadn't been able to accomplish in months. I couldn't believe it. *Wait until I broke the news to Lucas.*

"Just takes knowing who to call," Garrett said easily. "You guy's still in the wind, you knew that. Been seen travelin' up through a couple counties in a late model blue sedan, busted fender. I don't bother with plates because they're always lifted. Not much to go on for now, but it's something."

"It's better than something," I told him. "Now we know he's still around, and what to look for."

"There's more. On a hunch, I got a copy of the police report from when your truck driver got in that accident. Did they ever tell you where it happened? Because it wasn't too far from here, only about eighty miles. And the driver, he didn't know much, but he did get a vehicle description."

My vision narrowed, darkened. "Let me guess—a blue car with a busted fender." *Fuck.*

J.D. wasn't a criminal mastermind, I didn't believe that for a minute. All he'd need was a CB radio, because he had enough connections to know what was happening around town. And he was typically drunk and stupid enough to try anything. History had proven that more than once.

"It's a big state, Fox, but we just started lookin'. We'll find him."

"Thanks, Garrett. You've made good progress already."

We disconnected, and I immediately dialed Lucas as I got into the truck. Avery would be home soon, and I had a lot to tell her.

"We've got a lead, Luke," I said when my brother answered the phone. "Garrett found J.D."

"You're kidding."

"Nope," I said. I wasn't sure if this was good news or not, but it was definitely a breakthrough. On one hand, J.D. was still lurking. On the other, he was close enough to catch.

Lucas swore. "I'm going to fire the P.I."

"And I'm going to leave him a one-star Yelp review," I said dryly. "Where'd you find that guy, anyway?"

Ribbing my brother about this wasn't as fun as I anticipated, probably because it was concerning something important. But I already had adrenaline coursing through my veins, making me jumpy. Combine that with the coffee, and I was wired, ready to go. If it were just me, I would've been gone on the hunt already.

But no moves would be made until I could talk to my wife. Avery knew J.D., she knew this state, and I was certain she'd be instrumental in finally locating Annabelle's biological father. After that, we'd put him behind bars and hopefully never think of him again for at least ten to twenty years.

"Fox?" My brother's voice broke through my internal monologue.

"Sorry. What's next?"

"You decide whether or not we take this information to the detectives," Lucas said thoughtfully. "Or we do it my way, stealth mode."

I considered for a moment. London and O'Connor could be helpful when it came to more eyes out there, now that we had something to go on. But with police involvement, I would be taking a chance that J.D. could spook and take off. Maybe stealth mode was the way to go.

"Let me talk to Avery first. Beers tonight at Lucky's? And maybe a little recon?"

"Two of my favorite pastimes," Lucas said.

We were close, I could feel it. I just wasn't sure yet if that was a good thing.

CHAPTER SEVENTEEN

AVERY

It was a cliche, it was a movie, it wasn't really happening. *Who actually comes back so near to the scene of the crime?* I'd seen this part before, the part where the female lead is forced into the car at gunpoint, the part where everything is out of focus and you're screaming at the TV to try and shock the poor girl out of her trance and get her to start fighting back.

But when you're in it—when the movie is real—you can't move. You know you should, but you can't. My limbs wouldn't cooperate, my mind spun uncontrollably, and I had only one coherent thought.

"Not her." It didn't even sound like my voice. I cleared my throat and tried again. "Not her. Not Annabelle."

We had a plan. *Fox and I had a plan, and this was not part of it. Did I bring this on? Was it happening because he heard I tried to contact him?* My thoughts were spinning, but I knew I had to keep Annabelle out of this. There was no other option.

He laughed. That motherfucker actually laughed. "Yeah, right."

Some of the feeling in my body was returning as I stood up a little straighter, stepping away from him as far as I could with Annabelle still tucked behind my legs. My hand and wrist ached from when he'd grabbed me. "I'll go. You know Fox will give you whatever you want in exchange. But Annabelle stays."

"No way."

"She'll only slow you down. She'll cry, she'll need to eat and go to the bathroom all the time. Plus, the cops will get involved a lot faster if there's a child involved." Every word out of my mouth was painful but true.

J.D. glanced around nervously, probably gauging the likelihood of someone coming upon us soon. We weren't exactly concealed by the side street, but the nearest salvation was around the alley to the barbecue place's door, and I didn't think I could make it there before he caught me.

The look in his eyes was calculating, clouded only by what I assumed was a decent amount of whiskey. "You wouldn't just leave her here."

Get Annabelle somewhere safe, somewhere Fox can find her. "I'll send her into Ribs for barbecue," I said, gesturing at the sign painted on the alley wall. "They know her there."

J.D cocked his head, studying me. I was surprised his focus was as sharp as it appeared, given the way he smelled. *This was a nightmare. I am going to wake up and we'll be home, safe in bed.*

"Give her your phone."

Any hope I had shattered into pieces, but I tried to pretend like I didn't understand what he was getting at. "What?"

"Give her your fuckin' phone, Avery. You think I'm stupid? That I don't know about GPS? Give the kid the phone—or should I shove you both in the trunk right now?" His voice was low and so dark.

"Annabelle." I crouched down so we were eye to eye. Could she see my fear? Could she possibly know what was happening? I didn't want her to be afraid. I couldn't shield her forever—but I could protect her from this. From him.

"It's lunchtime!" I told her brightly. "How about barbecue chicken?"

I'd already mentioned it in the car, and maybe this way she wouldn't be as confused. She nodded slowly, her eyes trained on me, and I thought I could feel my heart breaking right then.

"You walk right around the corner and through the front door, okay? Nowhere else, only there." Everyone in this town knew her. Even if she missed the door, someone would find her. *Someone would find her.*

I kept telling myself that, repeating it in my head as I gave her the rest of my instructions. "You sit down and tell Ms. Mary or Ms. Sue Ellen that Mama is coming. And that we're hungry!"

I wanted to cry as she nodded at me again, her blue eyes bright. "Can I have chocolate milk, Mama?"

"Sure, baby." I had to think of a way to warn Fox, to give him any bit of information, no matter how ambiguous. "You tell them I said it was okay to order our food. I'm going to have a salad with bleu cheese dressing. Can you remember that?" I didn't dare sneak a glance at J.D. to see if he was paying attention to my words.

"A salad with bleu cheese," Annabelle repeated obediently.

I smiled. "Good girl." My eyes roamed over her whole face, holding it in my brain, reminding myself exactly why I was doing this. For her. Always for her.

"The phone, Avery. Now."

There was no time to type a message, not with J.D. hovering over my shoulder. I hoped Fox would put something together from my restaurant order, if Annabelle remembered. He had to get it. He knew me—better than anyone.

"Take my phone, okay?" I tucked it into the side pocket of her little backpack. "You can play the birds game if you want."

Any other time Annabelle would've been thrilled to be in possession of my cell phone, but she knew something about today was different. I watched her eyes dart to J.D., and I shifted to put myself directly in front of her. The last thing I needed was for him

157

to suspect that Annabelle knew anything was wrong and decide not to let her go.

I kissed her little cheek. "It's okay, baby. Go on, I'll be right behind you."

My voice nearly broke on the words, but I willed myself not to cry. I was going to let her go. Just like that day on the Ferris wheel. I would let her go to save her. I watched her walk around the corner, and then I was jerked around to face J.D.

Acid boiled in my stomach as he smirked at me, his grip like iron on my arm. "Let's go."

I wanted to scream, but I willed my face into a neutral expression. I needed to know Annabelle was safe so I could do whatever I had to do. My entire focus shifted to survival, to self-preservation, and I was terrified—but I was also fucking *mad*.

J.D. had crossed the very last line. He had threatened the most important thing in my entire life, and there would be no more sympathy. And there would be no saving him.

CHAPTER EIGHTEEN

FOX

I'd barely hung up with Lucas and walked up the driveway when I felt the phone buzz again. My lips curved into a smile at the face and name flashing on my screen as I headed into the house. "I was just thinking about you."

"Fox?"

The woman's voice had me checking my screen again even as the back of my neck started to prickle. Who was calling me from my wife's phone? "Yes?"

"This is Sue Ellen down at Ribs—I was just, well I was just wonderin' what y'all's time frame was for Annabelle?"

Her words had me at a loss. And my gut didn't like it. "I—what?"

"Well she's no trouble, of course," Sue Ellen said hurriedly. "We love having her here, she's just as sweet as can be, sitting and coloring away. But um, it's been a little while now and I didn't know how else to contact Avery."

"Annabelle is there? Without Avery?" They were supposed to

be picking up groceries and something else—a library book? I wracked my brain trying to remember what Avery had said. Nothing out of the ordinary, just errands.

"Yes, she came in nearly an hour ago. Sat herself down at a table and placed an order, like she was all grown up. Mary couldn't keep a straight face. It was the cutest darn thing—"

"She's been there an *hour*?" I was already halfway out the door again, keys still in my hand. I jumped into the truck and the call patched through to my bluetooth immediately.

"— held up the menu like she was reading it and everything," Sue Ellen was saying. "Smart girl, that one."

Sue Ellen's kindly drawl meant well. I kept telling myself that even as I screeched around a corner. My mind raced in time with the truck's wheels. The site was only a couple blocks from Ribs, and I'd been there until just minutes ago without a clue. What was Annabelle doing alone? Where was Avery? Why did Annabelle have her phone? *Where was Avery?*

"Can you tell me exactly what happened?" I hoped my voice sounded calmer than I felt.

"Well, Annabelle came in and sat down, like I was saying," Sue Ellen continued. "Ordered a salad for her mama first thing. A salad, with bleu cheese dressing. Said Avery was coming along behind her and that she was allowed to have chocolate milk."

The houses sped by in a blur, but not faster than my thoughts. "A salad?" That detail stuck out in the whirlwind. Avery liked salads, sure, but not when barbecue was an option.

"I know! I thought that was so strange too—everyone knows that Avery always orders the—"

"Brisket sandwich with no sauce," I finished for her. She liked it with ketchup, my wife of the interesting palate. *Where the fuck was she?*

"Exactly! And don't tell nobody, but our salads aren't that great." Sue Ellen sounded guilty. I revved the truck engine harder.

"I'm almost there." A salad with bleu cheese? Avery hated bleu cheese. Annabelle must've gotten it wrong.

"I packed up Avery's salad to-go—do you think she still wants it? And Annabelle had some chicken and a corn cob but it's on the house, Fox, don't worry 'bout the bill."

"I—thanks, Sue Ellen." The bill was absolutely the least of my concerns but I knew she was just trying to help.

My tires screeched as I flipped a U-turn in the middle of the street, nearly jumping the curb in my haste to park illegally in front of Ribs. As soon as my boots hit the pavement I was half-running through the barn-style doors. I skidded to a halt in front of the table where Annabelle sat, her little chin tucked down as she concentrated on her coloring book.

"Hey, Bells," I said, forcing calmness into my voice. "Sorry I'm late."

Annabelle looked up at me and blinked. "Where's Mama?"

There were a million things I needed to do, phone calls I needed to make, action steps I needed to take, but the look on Annabelle's face stopped me cold. There was confusion and a little fear there, and it clutched at my already-roiling gut. Annabelle was here, and Avery wasn't—and it was on purpose. Annabelle was here because Avery would not allow her to be wherever she was. And that thought terrified me.

This was about J.D.—I knew it. My gut knew it. There was no other answer. Avery and I had decided to work together, to stop keeping secrets that were only designed to tear us apart. We'd promised. I couldn't believe that my wife, the person I knew her to be, would renege on that. Something was very, very wrong.

But right now I had to push all of that aside. "She sent me to get you," I said, sitting down next to Annabelle. "She went to the store." It was the only thing I could think of.

Annabelle nodded slowly. "With the man?" she asked.

All I saw was red, but I tried to blink it away. *Where the fuck was my wife?* "I think so." I already knew. But I needed her to tell me. Everything. *Anything.* "What did he look like? Do you remember?"

"He had a hat," she said softly.

"Okay," I said gently. "I like hats. Do you?"

She nodded, sliding closer to me.

I tried again. "Did they go in Mama's car? Or another car?"

Annabelle shook her head. "It was big and dirty."

"Do you remember what color?"

Annabelle screwed up her face in thought. "Blue."

Blue car. Bleu cheese. *A blue car with a busted fender. A bleu cheese salad.* This was not a coincidence. Avery didn't know anything about J.D., his whereabouts, or his car. I hadn't had a chance to warn her. *I couldn't warn her.* She was trying to tell me what happened the only way she could, and thank god I had the rest of the info to fill in the blanks. But it still wasn't enough.

I needed to call Rambo Garrett, to call Lucas, to call Jim, to tell the General and the police and everyone who could help me locate an old blue car somewhere on the highway in Texas. And I had to do it right now, before I broke this table and trashed this entire restaurant with my bare hands.

But I willed myself to smile, to gentle my voice again. My little girl would not be afraid, ever, not if I had anything to say about it. "Let's take a ride out to the ranch, Bells."

Quickly I gathered Annabelle's things and put a hundred dollar bill on the table before I swung her up in my arms. "Bye, Sue Ellen, and thank you."

Sue Ellen's smile was relieved—because she didn't know the whole story. "We'll see you soon, Annabelle. Take care now."

⸺⁂⸺

"There was nothing in the SUV." I slammed my hand down on the solid wood table top. "Parked and locked behind Ribs."

Chase drove me back to town to get it, his foot tapping agitatedly between switching gears.

"I'll call everyone I know, Fox," Chase said. "Kyle and I, we have football friends all around the county, and Derek's brother has rodeo connections—someone might know where he'd go."

I was clenching and unclenching my hands in the passenger

seat, but I nodded. "Appreciate it."

"You'll find her." Chase took his eyes off the road to look at me. "It's what you do."

What I do is protect people I love. *What I do* is take the necessary precautions, prepare in advance so things like this don't happen.

These thoughts screamed through my head until I couldn't hear anything else, not the road noise, not the low hum of the stereo. On the way back, alone in Avery's SUV, I hadn't bothered with the radio at all. My thoughts were loud enough.

"When are the detectives supposed to call back?" McDaniels asked.

"Soon." I shoved back from the table. "She's not a missing person until it's been twenty-four hours. But they know better, so they're trying to push through the paperwork to connect it to the case and get moving sooner."

"I didn't find anything on her phone, B." Lucas looked like hell. Whether it was because it was late or because he was worried about Avery, I didn't know. Because if he looked like that, I could only imagine what *I* looked like.

Somewhere out there, J.D. had my wife. I didn't know exactly where, but I knew why. I'd set this ball rolling nearly a year ago, when I'd first called him and tried to arrange Annabelle's adoption. But things had escalated to a scenario that was unrecognizable in comparison with the original.

My mind raced, every thought worse than the last. I got up to pace the same path I'd walked a thousand times already, rolling ideas through my head. *Where would he go, what would he do? Was he working with someone, or on his own?* Each variation meant something different for Avery, and the possibilities were endless. So was my rage.

The ranch had become command central in just a couple hours. Heather was cooking, I wasn't sure what, but it smelled incredible and there was a lot of it. Annabelle was upstairs, tucked under the covers in Avery's old bedroom, with Rebecca parked in the overstuffed chaise lounge next to her, ostensibly reading a book. I knew better. She was on watch. We all were.

In fact, Sloane and Chase were outside on the porch right now. And a few miles away, Kyle and Derek sat in the dark in my house. Ready. Waiting.

McDaniels, Jim, Lucas, and I gathered at the table. And strategized. And tried to hold our tempers. We'd been in close contact with Garrett, and he had scouts out already. We'd called O'Connor and London. We'd tracked and followed every possible lead—and came up with nothing. It was like Avery and J.D. had vanished without a trace.

CHAPTER NINETEEN

AVERY

"**D**on't fall asleep," J.D.'s voice was gruff and slightly more intoxicated than the last time he'd spoken. The half-full bottle of whiskey tucked between his leg and the driver's side door could attest to that.

"I'm not," I said quietly, trying to keep my tone even. "Where are we going?"

J.D. grunted. "When we get there I'll tell you."

This piece of shit car didn't have a dashboard clock, so I wasn't sure how long we'd been driving. Were we even still in Texas? I'd cycled through quite a few emotions in the past couple hours, but I kept coming back to a cross between angry and terrified. J.D. hadn't put me in the trunk like he'd threatened, but part of me wondered if this was worse. I looked down at my wrist, handcuffed to the door handle.

Definitely worse. At least if I were in the trunk, I could've jumped out at the last rest stop. I'd seen all of those viral videos of the women kicking the taillights out of cars and freeing themselves. I was prepared for that—as much as someone can prepare for this kind of shit.

I looked over to J.D., his once handsome profile shadowed in the darkness. So much had changed. A couple more breaks in his nose, more gray hair, and his skin definitely showed some hard miles. Underneath all of that, somewhere, was the boy who'd charmed me, who'd helped me forget about Chase's absence, who'd distracted me when I needed it.

But he was also the one who'd vanished without a trace one morning, and who'd been impossible to track down when I needed him. What *happened* to this man? I was trying frantically to reconcile everything I knew of him years ago with everything I'd experienced in the past months. He was quick tempered, he was selfish. But was he *evil*? It sure as fuck seemed like it.

"So, I knocked you up. "

Now he wanted to make small talk? "Almost five years ago, yes."

I didn't want to talk about Annabelle, didn't want to make this personal. She was mine to keep and protect, far away from him. I prayed to any available saint that she'd made it into the front door of Ribs. By now, Fox would know everything—and he'd be looking for me. Of that I was sure.

"And you decided to keep it?" J.D. looked dubious. *And the charm just keeps on coming.* "Why?"

It wasn't an easy choice. Nothing about those weeks were easy—I'd had a few options and each one had its pros and cons. The right answer was different for everyone.

"Because I wanted her."

J.D. snorted and took another pull from the bottle. "I'd be a shitty dad. No surprise there. Never cared for kids—didn't know I had any." He gave me an appraising look, and my heart skipped when he veered onto the road's shoulder before quickly correcting his steering. "You ask around about me before this?"

"Not really," I admitted. "I tried for a little bit in the beginning, but not for long."

"What for? You think I'd marry you or something?"

Even in my most desperate, lonely times, I'd never really believed that J.D., Annabelle, and I would ever be a family. There had been a chance it might've worked with Chase one day, but until Fox, I didn't truly know what it meant to have a partner. Anything and anyone else paled in comparison to him.

"I just thought you had a right to know, that's all. I didn't want anything from you then, just like I don't want anything from you now. We can end this now. Just pull over, and let me call Fox." I tried to keep my voice casual. I didn't want J.D. to know how scared I was, both of his driving and whatever he may have planned.

"Nah, I'm gonna let him worry a lil while longer," J.D. said with a laugh.

Such an asshole. I bristled inwardly but tried not to let his words affect my face. "Can you pull over anyway? I have to pee." I knew my attitude was walking a fine line between shaky-scared and defiant, but I couldn't help it.

He scowled. "In a minute."

Every time J.D. opened his mouth I wanted to scream at him, but I didn't have enough faith in his temper or his driving to believe he wouldn't run us right off the road if he got angry enough. *I just want to get home to Fox and Annabelle*, I thought. *Whatever I need to do, I'll do it.*

He took another pull from the bottle, and I winced as he swung the car into a wide arc at the next exit. We coasted over a gravel parking lot, heading toward the back of the well-lit gas station. Well-lit, but to my dismay, old and empty. J.D. cut the car's engine directly in front of the restroom sign.

"Whatever you're thinking, stop," J.D. growled at me, flicking open the safety strap on his holster. He came around to my side of the car. "Ain't no one here to give a shit."

I shook out my aching arms one by one as he unlocked the cuffs and gestured toward the bathroom door. My face blanched. "You're not coming in with me."

He kicked the old metal door open and surveyed the inside, his lip curling up in distaste when he flicked on the light. "No thanks.

You got three minutes."

Three minutes three minutes—was there anything I could do in three minutes? Anything I could try? I looked around. The restroom was disgusting, stuffy, reeking of old urine, with writing on the walls and a cracked mirror—and no window.

I did have to pee, badly, so I took care of that first, trying not to touch anything as I hovered above the toilet bowl. *Gross.* I was still looking around as I went to wash my hands. *This mirror... it was already broken. Maybe I could take a shard, use it if I had an opportunity.*

The thought was so ludicrous, I almost had to laugh. *He has a gun and you're going to what? Stab him at close range with a piece of broken mirror?* But it wasn't the worst plan—and it was the only one I had.

"One minute, then I'm coming in," J.D. called from outside the door.

My fingertips were raw, near bleeding from trying to claw out a piece of mirror glass. It wouldn't budge, still, and I rested my head against the cracked surface briefly. *Okay, this wasn't going to work.* I jumped back just as J.D. shoved the door open.

"You're done, let's go." He grabbed my wrist, clicking the cuff into place.

"Why are you doing this?" I cried as he locked me to the car door again. "Why did you do *any* of it? You could've killed Fox in that fire!"

"You all promised me something and didn't deliver. I want what was promised to me, and this is the way I'm gonna get it." J.D. slammed the driver's side door and turned the ignition key. The car bumped over the gravel, back to the highway. "A trade."

"If Fox finds us first, you'll lose your advantage," I told him.

"Do you have any idea how big this fuckin' state is?" J.D. took both hands off the wheel and spread them for emphasis. "Your ol' boy Fox don't know what direction we went or which road we took! He could look forever and he'll never catch me!"

I cringed as he slapped his palm back down on the steering wheel and wrenched the car sideways. A CB radio on the dashboard crackled and he smacked that too for good measure, silencing it permanently.

"Piece of shit." He took another swig from the bottle. "You got any money?"

"I have—I have like forty bucks. And my credit card," I said. *Please let him use it.*

J.D. pulled the cash from my wallet and in a blink of an eye, tossed the rest of my bag out the window. I nearly cried out as it flew, spilling over the road and into the darkness. "Credit cards would lead him right to us, but nice try. Guess it's gonna be a cheap room."

He left me in the car when we stopped at a blaring neon motel sign, both hands secured around the door handle now after he got nervous at the pit stop. I gave a few half-hearted pulls before I slouched down as far as my bound hands would let me. I couldn't reach the horn, but even if I could there was no one around to hear. *What was the point?*

Truth be told, I was beyond tired. Staying put somewhere for a few hours increased the odds of Fox catching up to us, in my opinion. Fewer miles between me and him was always a good thing. And maybe if J.D. could sleep off a little of his bender, I could try to reason with him in the morning.

When J.D. returned to the car he led me by the handcuffs to the end of the long outside hallway. He kicked open the door to reveal a dingy room with two twin beds. The carpet was orange, threadbare in places, and smelled distinctly of wet dog. *Charming.* When the door shut behind us, I started to get a little panicky. We'd been driving for hours, but now we were completely, utterly alone. My palms began to sweat, and I felt my knees wobble just a tiny bit.

"I have to go, I have to get out of here, don't touch me, don't touch me!" I pulled as hard as I could on my cuff, my voice rising with hysteria as I dug my heels into the floor.

"What the fuck is wrong with you?" J.D. hauled me over to one of the beds in spite of my protesting and clicked my cuff to the metal frame. "Stay put. No one's gonna touch anyone."

He sat down heavily on the other bed and looked at me. With

my arm attached to the headboard, I couldn't curl up into a ball the way I would've liked, but I pulled my legs up and scooted as far away from him as possible.

"I gotta cuff you, otherwise I know you'll try to split." J.D. took off his hat and rubbed his forehead. "I'm not gonna touch you," he repeated. "I'm an asshole but I ain't *that*. And even if I was, I'd never get my money from your old man that way."

I cringed but stayed silent. *Definitely* an asshole.

"Now I'm going to the shitter, and I'm takin' the phone with me," he said, unplugging it from the wall. "Don't do anything fucked up, otherwise you'll sleep in the car."

The car might be better than this. A few rogue tears found their way down my cheeks, and I sniffled quietly. I imagined Fox right now, out of his mind with worry. On the other side of the wall, I heard the shower start, and I tried to pull myself together. I couldn't give J.D. the satisfaction of seeing my misery. Finding a comfortable place to rest my on the lumpy pillow was difficult with the restriction of the handcuffs. Tonight was a lost cause, but tomorrow was another day.

I had to find a way home.

CHAPTER TWENTY

FOX

I didn't sleep at all, in fact, I didn't even try. I spent the first night in a chair in front of Annabelle's door, phone in my hand.

J.D. had let Annabelle go, and I knew it was highly unlikely he would try to come back for her. But at this point, there was no such thing as overreaction. So Sloane and McDaniels bunked on the porch, unconcerned about the elements, Chase and Lucas were on the downstairs couches, and I sat at the top of the stairs.

Waiting.

Derek and Kyle had my house covered, and Rambo Garrett and his guys were out doing whatever they did. Lucas wanted to bring in his own men too—he'd been in contact with High Road Divide, who'd generously offered all of their resources stateside, including Lucas' handpicked members of the band's security team and access to a private jet or helicopter that they'd arranged to arrive at the local airstrip.

"Let's get the helicopter in the air first thing in the morning," I'd told Lucas. "See what we can find."

I hated that my wife could be far enough away to necessitate aerial support, but at this point, nothing should've surprised me. Avery and I didn't have a normal, not that I could recall. From the moment I laid eyes on that girl, it had been no ordinary rollercoaster. I fucking loved her for everything she tried to do, for what she wanted for us, but this had gone all wrong.

I was supposed to be there. I'd *planned* to be there—and for her to be nowhere nearby. But that was wrong too, because we were stronger as a unit. And so we'd compromised.

And now—now that plan had gone all to shit, and Avery was somewhere unknown, alone, without me, at the whim of a desperate man. One who would rue the day he ever thought he could win by reckless force. I would see to that, personally.

Time crawled by with nothing, not a whisper. We'd helicoptered over what felt like the entire state, Garrett's crew had come up empty as well, and after thirty-six hours I was manic. Rebecca didn't have to convince me to let Annabelle stay—I needed to know exactly where she was while I went to look for her mother.

Lucas had already loaded a tracing app onto my phone. "Best one on the market," he said. "I made it. With my laptop, we can track him when he calls, no matter where we are."

J.D. would call, I knew that much. He was biding his time, making me crazy, making me wait. He stupidly thought that this game would give him the upper hand, but instead, all it did was make me angrier.

"I need to go. I need to find her."

Lucas read my face and nodded. "Eat something, and we'll head out." It didn't matter where—I had to move.

We ate a terse meal cooked by Heather—not even her french dip sandwiches could lighten the mood. I was just about to take my dish to the sink when my phone rang, silencing any budding conversation around the table. No one moved, no one even took a breath. Thirty-six hours I'd waited, I'd sent out scouts, I'd flown a hundred miles. And it all came down to this.

"Hello, Fox."

I was caught somewhere between relief and fury. "Where is she?"

"Can't even say hello?" J.D. didn't strike me as a polite conversationalist, but he did seem like an all-night drunk. It was barely past lunchtime and he was already half-slurring his words.

"Where is she?" I asked again, my voice a growl. I saw Lucas shake his head, warning me to be careful as he opened his laptop. I was so far past that, so far past caring what happened to this piece of shit, but I had to keep him on the phone for the trace. Regardless, I nearly spat my next words. "I will kill you if you touch her. Make no mistake about that."

"I don't want her," J.D. scoffed. "Not like that. But I had to get your attention, seeing as the fire didn't work. Got it now, didn't I? Are you paying attention *now*, Fox?"

I was going to kill him regardless. "Where is she?" I repeated.

Lucas' fingers flew across his computer keyboard, searching, searching for any trace of the phone on his scanner software. I could tell by the increasingly loud typing sounds that he wasn't having any luck.

"She's all right, don't fucking blow a gasket."

"I want to talk to her." I clenched my hands over and over, trying to relieve some of the tension I felt in my body. "Put her on the phone, now."

"Can't do that," J.D. said. "Can't have her telling you anything." There was some rustling, some background noise. "But you're on speaker. Say hi, Avery."

"I'm okay, Fox." Her voice was faint, but even. "We're—"

"That's enough." The speakerphone clicked off and it was just me and him again. "Bye for now."

"Wait." I hated this. *I fucking hated this.* "Tell me what you want, so we can get this moving."

The longer he had her, the longer she was in danger. I blamed myself for this mess and no one else. Always wanting to believe the best about people, always wanting to give second chances. No more. Not again. Not ever.

J.D. laughed, and then I could tell exactly how drunk he was. My urge to pound him directly into the ground intensified tenfold. "Money, Fox. You know that. I want your money. How much is she worth to you?"

More than you can imagine. More than your fucking alcohol-soaked pea brain could ever comprehend. Avery was okay, for now. But the sooner I got her back, the better—for everyone.

"I'm not playing this game with you, J.D. You want to end this before everyone I've put on the hunt finds you? Give me a number. Because they will find you, I promise. And it won't turn out the way you want it to."

There were a few moments of silence, and I cursed internally, wondering if I'd pissed him off enough to hang up. I was just about to ask Lucas about the connection when J.D. finally spoke.

"Two hundred fifty grand. Small bills."

Money meant nothing to me right now. "Time and place."

"Now we're talking, Fox." J.D. couldn't hide his glee. *This fucking guy.* "I'll be in touch."

And then the connection went dead.

The phone was my only lifeline to Avery, so I couldn't throw it across the room like I wanted. I had to settle for taking a few deep breaths and staring up at the ceiling while Lucas finished up his tracing codes.

I would've paid ten times that much. I would've given him every last cent I had to get Avery back. He'd get his money. And once I knew she was safe, I would take my time, hunt him down myself for daring to take what was mine.

"I got him, B." Lucas sprang out of his seat. "He turned off his geotagging but not his location services. What a dumbass."

"Where?"

Lucas sat back down, his fingers a blur as he entered the info to find what we needed. He tapped a spot on the map. "Right here."

I peered at the screen, at the tiny dot that held my entire world. It was too far, we'd never make it in time. "I'm calling the police."

"What do we do in the meantime?" Lucas asked when I got off

the phone. "Wait?"

I didn't want to, I was terrible at it. O'Connor assured me they would send a car out right away, but I paced for fifteen minutes and had my keys in my hand, ready to go, when he called back with bad news. I didn't have to look around the room to see the disappointment and fear on everyone's face—I felt the same way, plus a big side of fury.

"No one was there, Fox. Room's abandoned. Looks like they left in a hurry."

"You have to be fucking kidding me," I snarled into my phone. "I gave you their exact location."

I knew this was a mistake. I should've gotten in my truck immediately and never trusted this to anyone else. I sent a proxy to find my wife, and all they came up with was an empty hotel room.

"He's gone, Lucas. Find him." I shoved my wallet into my pocket and grabbed my keys. "*Find him.*"

My brother was back at his computer, pounding his frustration into the keyboard. "There's a chance," he muttered. "If I can just —yes! Got him!" He looked up. "Let's go."

"What do you need from us, Fox?" Chase asked. "We got you, man."

My head was spinning in circles as I tried to think. Nothing was registering aside from the immediate goal of finding my wife. I looked at my father-in-law, his face drawn and grave. "Annabelle will be safe with you."

Jim nodded, and I could see the pain and frustration in his eyes. "Count on it."

"We'll stay with Jim," Sloane said, gesturing at himself and McDaniels. "No one will even get close."

"I'll pull up maps when we're on the road, but we don't know the area. Any suggestions?" Lucas was scrolling through his phone again.

"I drive out near that highway every other week," Derek said. "Chase, get in the truck. I know a faster way to the interstate."

Kyle nodded. "And I'll go back to your house, just in case."

Lucas brushed his lips over Heather's forehead. "Stay inside, please. And try to keep Rebecca calm. I'll text with any updates."

She nodded, then crossed the room to kiss my cheek. "Go get my girl. Be careful. And don't worry about Annabelle." I gave her a grateful smile as she slipped out of the room.

"Call us when you've got something." McDaniel's eyes were narrowed into slits. "We'll be waiting."

My fingers were already punching Garrett's number into my phone as we all ran out to our trucks. I had no fucking idea what was going on, but all I knew was that I needed to be where Avery was, right away. Lucas barely got the door closed before the engine roared to life and my tires squealed as I reversed.

"I found her. Sort of. She's—" I didn't have time to explain it to Garrett. "She's okay, I think, but she's with J.D. I'm going now. Derek and Chase might know where." The phone skidded across the dashboard as I flipped a U-turn in front of the riding paddock to follow Derek's truck, but the call was already patched to the speakers. "Can you get here?"

"Already on my way," Garrett replied, and I heard the sound of a gunning engine, and if I wasn't mistaken, the high rumble of a motorcycle or two. "You need anything else?"

"Not sure." Derek was hauling ass, but I was right on his tail. "You'll be the first to know." I jabbed the button to disconnect the call.

"B., you need to get steady. C'mon man—I know you're pissed off and scared, but you gotta rein it in."

My jaw was starting to ache from clenching it so tightly. I spared Lucas a one-second glance. "Don't."

He held up his hands. "You know I'm right. "

"He *took* her, Lucas! *Fuck*!" I slammed my hands against the steering wheel. "How did he get to her? Why didn't we see him coming?"

Lucas's face was tense at my outburst. "You and I both know that roles could easily be reversed right now. We were close, B. We had everything in place. Somehow J.D. beat us to it."

He was right, of course he was fucking right, but it didn't matter at this point. A million horrible scenarios ran through my head with every mile that passed under the truck's tires. My imagination was having a damn field day with this, and there was nothing I could do to stop it—the unthinkable idea of Avery in danger was enough to send me off the deep end.

We sped down the freeway in silence, every second bringing me closer to my wife who I was never going to let go once I finally got to the fucking bottom of this situation. When my cell phone rang I hit the button on the stereo to connect it—Garrett calling for information.

"Take the next off-ramp," Lucas said quickly. He rattled off a set of coordinates for Garrett. "It's all backroads now."

I put my signal on, and Derek's lit up a second later, confirming that he'd gotten the message. We cut over two lanes and veered onto a wide, hard-packed dirt road. "What is it? Where?"

"Close. Sixty miles as the crow flies."

That explained the back road. Despite everything, I felt a small sense of relief at Lucas' words. J.D. was a mess, but Avery was a smart girl with a level head, I kept reminding myself. I knew she would lay low as long as possible and let J.D. ride his plan out until she saw an opportunity. She would keep it together, just the way she had when I'd wrecked the bike, or when she'd sent Annabelle to Sue Ellen. We had way too much to lose. Avery knew that. I hated that she'd sacrificed herself, but I knew why she did it. I knew my girl.

"Fox? You there?" The wind noise made Garrett's connection loud with static.

I wasn't, not really. I was already miles away in the middle of a fucking unexpected covert operation, next to my wife while we figured out a way to take J.D. down for good.

That's where I should've been from the beginning. Never in the vows of marriage did I agree to let Avery take a hit, especially one that was meant for me. It might've been archaic, but this was the exact opposite of everything I believed in.

"Yeah. I'm here." I thought fast. "How close are you?" I had no idea what was about to happen, but more manpower always felt like a good plan.

"Coming from the west side," Garrett said. "Ready for anything."

After seeing the contents of his garages, I didn't doubt that. "Thanks."

Garrett disconnected and I punched the accelerator of the truck, keeping my bumper just feet from Derek's.

Ready for anything.

I was too, and God help anyone who got in my way.

CHAPTER TWENTY-ONE

AVERY

"**C**'mon, wake up."

It was only sheer exhaustion that allowed me to lower my guard for any length of time when J.D. was behind the wheel. I was certain that the only thing saving us from multiple car accidents was the fact that we were driving on backroads now and not main highways. Fewer objects for him to hit was a good thing, especially because he treated the lanes more like suggestions than boundaries.

Was I numb? Not quite yet. But after almost two days with J.D., I was past panic and firmly forced into self-preservation. How was he still going? What sort of terribly fucked up cocktail ran through his veins that allowed him to run on whiskey and no sleep?

"Where are we?" I'd asked this question so many times by now, I wasn't really expecting an answer.

I jolted forward as the car hit a hard dip, bottoming out on the dirt road. There was a clank and a screech, and smoke started coming from under the hood.

"Damn it!" J.D. pulled the car to the side of the road, roughly steering into the softer dirt.

My heart pounded—what did it mean if we didn't have a working car? This felt like the middle of nowhere. I craned my neck, looking around at the open land. There was something in the distance, I could just make out what looked like a restaurant sign. We must be near a highway—but I still had no idea where.

"Is that a rest stop?"

J.D. shoved open the driver's side door. "Where'd you think we were headin'? I'm meetin' someone."

My initial excitement waned immediately. Bringing someone else into this situation could either be very good or very bad for me. And with the company J.D. tended to keep, my money was on the latter. But if we could just get to the rest stop—maybe I could get away, or get someone to help me.

After looking under the hood for a couple moments, J.D. slammed his way back into the car looking glum. "Stupid oil pan is busted." He dug in his pocket for his phone. "Where are you?" he asked after a moment. "Yeah, well, I got a problem. I'm almost a mile south. You'll see the car."

"Who was that?" I asked quietly. I didn't want to know, but I *had* to know.

J.D. ignored me, instead taking a few swigs from his ever-present bottle. I debated trying again, and then decided it was better just to keep quiet. I had no control over what was going to happen so long as I was handcuffed to the door.

I got my answer a few minutes later when an old white truck pulled up across the road and a man got out.

"Well, well, what have we got here?" He was tall and skinny, with a mean glint in his eye. I pegged him to be about my father's age, with a weather-roughened face and well-worn, faded clothes. Nothing remarkable, nothing about him memorable, but I tried to keep his face in my mind even as I looked away. "What's your name, pretty girl?"

I stayed silent, shifting my body away from the window where he stood.

"Shut up, Spurs," J.D. said. "You ain't helping." He got out of the car and popped the hood again.

Spurs? Really? I sunk down lower in my seat while they spent a few minutes looking under the hood. The feeling of dread that had washed over me when J.D. mentioned a meet-up intensified tenfold once I'd actually *met* that someone. The sooner they fixed the car and we got away from him, the better.

"You're wasting time with this ol' car," Spurs said. "Leave it, steal another one later."

J.D. dropped the hood with a crash and I jerked against the cuffs in reflex. "Fine. Let's get out of here." He came around to my side of the car and opened the door.

"You can walk. I'll just take her, for collateral." Spurs looked me up and down and I wanted to vomit.

"She ain't yours to take," J.D. snarled at him, eyes flashing. "And you'll get your money when I got it." He unlocked my handcuffs from the car door by releasing one arm. "Gonna need your truck."

"Kiss my ass."

J.D. smirked. "Make me."

This was going nowhere fast. I looked down at the marks on my free wrist. *Ugh.* Too many hours in a cuff. *Chalk that up to a sentence you never thought would apply to you, Avery.* I immediately hated Spurs, and it didn't seem like J.D. liked him much either. It was a shitty common ground, but the only one we had.

Spurs scowled at him. "What makes you think I'd give you anything?"

"You want the money?" J.D. straightened up from a crouch, hauling me with him by my still-cuffed arm. "We need your truck. It's your fault my car is wrecked anyhow, all these damn dirt roads."

"Fuck you."

J.D. ignored him, leading me over to the pickup. He opened the passenger door and tossed his backpack inside. "Get in," he said, but instead of securing me to the door, he just cuffed both hands together. "You sit in the middle. Don't try anything funny."

My mind was spinning. I knew this was a bad idea, not that anything recently had been a *good* idea, but I didn't trust Spurs. I didn't trust J.D. either, but I felt like maybe I was starting to make progress with him. He couldn't run forever. If I could just get us to that rest stop, I was nearly certain I could get J.D. to call Fox and tell him where to meet us. Then all of this could be over, and I could go home to Annabelle.

Tears threatened to spring into my eyes at the thought of my little girl. I hoped she wasn't too scared, I hoped Fox had come up with something to tell her so she didn't know anything was wrong. I was on the verge of breaking down altogether, my vision blurring, when I saw a shadow behind J.D.

A shadow holding a gun.

J.D. must've felt it too, because he turned around quickly, just as Spurs swung his gun hand into J.D.'s face with enough force that I heard the sickening sound of contact. His head snapped to the side, blood and spittle spraying. J.D. shook his head to clear it, his hands clenched as he charged toward Spurs.

This is crazy. Too many guns, too many volatile tempers. I have to get out of here. I slid forward toward the truck's open door and tried to weigh my options quickly. If they were going to fight, maybe I could run. But if they got into the truck to follow me, I was done. I checked the ignition—no keys. *Damn it.*

I winced involuntarily as Spurs hit him again, just his fist this time, and again J.D.'s head snapped back. *I have to go. We're in the middle of nowhere—who would even hear a gunshot?* I put one foot outside the door. *If I got out and started running, how much of a head start could I get? Was the rest stop too far? Was I faster than both of them?*

J.D. swung at Spurs, stumbling forward. They were both breathing hard now, their chests heaving. My foot caught on something as I tried to make another slow move—J.D.'s backpack. I glanced up in just enough time to see Spurs raise the gun again. Clumsily, I unzipped the small front pouch with my cuffed hands, nearly crying with relief when I found a pocketknife—exactly what I needed.

"Stop it, asshole!" J.D. lunged, trying to disarm the other man.

Spurs had his gun pointed directly at J.D.'s head, a cold expression on his face.

"What the *fuck*, Spurs?" J.D. spat.

My eye fell immediately to the empty holster at J.D.'s belt. *Shit.* If J.D. didn't have his gun, that meant it must be in the car. I glanced over at the stalled sedan. The five yards might as well have been five miles. Or—I felt the weight of the backpack in my hands. *Maybe not.*

"Your part in this rodeo is over," Spurs drawled at him. "But you should be used to that. Thanks for playin'."

For the second time in too few hours, I heard that terrifying click again. And then a gunshot.

I recoiled, vomit rising in my throat, afraid to look. But when no one spoke, I forced myself to bring the men back into view.

Spurs laughed. "Scared, ain't ya? I didn't have to miss." He cocked the gun again. "I won't this time."

J.D. was still standing. I watched in horror as his face paled under the sticky blood, and I knew he was afraid. Spurs was toying with him, he would kill J.D. without another thought, and they were supposed to be friends? That meant he would kill me too, as soon as I was no longer useful to him. I had no other choice.

I took a silent, shallow breath and pulled the gun from J.D.'s backpack. Moving forward, I trained my aim on Spurs, willing my hands not to shake. I was barely a half-way decent shot on my best day—and today definitely did not qualify as my best day. *Just knock him down, and then run like hell.*

J.D.'s eyes were unfocused, darting around. I wasn't sure exactly what he could make out in his angry, drunken, and now potentially concussed state, but I could see him weave and start to wobble. And when his gaze shifted to over Spurs' shoulder, I realized he could see me, too.

"The fuck you lookin' at?" Spurs twisted his body to glance backward, keeping his gun trained on J.D. His face registered the shock when he saw me aiming J.D.'s revolver right at him. "Put that down!"

I said nothing out loud, but inside I was screaming.

You have no choice.

And then we pulled our triggers at the same time.

In slow motion I watched J.D. drop backward, a bright crimson stain of blood appearing on his chest immediately. My own bullet missed Spurs' heart by a mile and instead burrowed deep into his upper thigh, causing him to drop his gun and clutch his leg, his mouth opening in shouts and curses that my frozen brain couldn't hear.

J.D.'s skull cracked onto the hard-packed dirt as he hit the ground, and my body jolted into action. I darted forward, kicking Spurs' gun into the brush on the side of the road.

"You shot me, you bitch!" Spurs lunged at me, blood spurting from his wound as he tried unsuccessfully to staunch it with his hands.

You shot him, was the only thing I could think. Spurs shot J.D., and as much as I wanted to be rid of him, it wasn't like *this*. I dodged him and stumbled backward, hitting the ground hard, my hip cracking on the dirt as I tried to scoot away with my hands still bound.

"Get away from me." I trained the gun on him again, closed my eyes, and pulled the trigger.

No choice. I had no choice.

The gun clicked, but nothing happened. One fucking bullet, that's all J.D. had? I opened my eyes again, dropping the gun. *What now?*

Spurs shook his head and grimaced, still coming closer. "Guess I got that collateral after all."

I shook my head, creeping backward now. "No." *No no no.* I couldn't let this man take me anywhere. Would a flat tire be enough? Was J.D.—he wasn't moving. I coughed, nearly gagging, bile rising in my throat.

We were out here alone, but there were people at the truck stop —I could still see it from here, less than a mile down the road. I hadn't made it this far to go down in flames. This wasn't going to be how my story ended. I pulled the pocketknife from my boot, the pocketknife I'd stolen from J.D.'s backpack, and using both cuffed hands in one swift reach, embedded it into the rear truck tire.

Spurs limped quickly toward me, his head cocked and hands out as I scrambled until I got my feet under me, sliding sideways to avoid his grasp.

My entire body hurt, but I had to try and get away. I'd hobbled him, he couldn't run. But if he found his gun, if the truck's tire wasn't flat yet—was it too much ground to cover?

"No. I'm not going anywhere with you." I edged down the road a little further in a crouch, not wanting to make any sudden moves.

"You stupid girl. Get up." Spurs limped closer. He kicked a rock at me and missed, lurching forward like something out of a nightmare with the dark stain of blood spreading down his leg. I could just barely see J.D. on the ground behind him now. The sun was on its way down, and that only added to my urgency.

I stood up shakily to my full height, my hip screaming as I prepared to run. The cuffs dug into my wrists, limiting my range of motion. Spurs went to grab at me again, and I channeled all of my adrenaline and frustration into force, jamming an elbow into his nose just like my daddy taught me—if all else fails, be your own weapon.

"I said *no!*" And then I rammed the heel of my boot into his thigh.

He howled, blood dripping from his nose. He reached down to clutch his leg again and dropped me altogether. "Bitch!"

No looking back now. I turned on my bloody heel, determined to put as much distance between myself and Spurs as possible. I could hear him behind me, yelling and swearing—but his injured stride was no match for my determination.

With every step I ran, every inch closer to the rest stop, my relief blossomed just a little bit more. I stumbled, catching myself, my hands still bound and full of dirt and gravel, tears streaming down my face. I could make out the individual cars now, the lights inside the restaurant. There were people outside, truckers filling up at the gas station. *Closer, closer. So close.* Spurs was never going to catch me. I wasn't going to allow it.

I heard the roar of engines, and across the rest stop, I saw two familiar trucks scream into the parking lot along with a couple Humvees. Two motorcycles blared past me followed by another Humvee, but my stride didn't falter. *Almost there.*

The wind whirled down the road as the friction of all of the tires churned dust into a tornado, blurring my vision and leaving my mouth and tongue gritty and coated. Fox was nearly on the ground before his tires stopped, sprinting down the road and yelling in my direction.

"*Avery!*"

I didn't even realize I'd been waiting for him until he showed up. No time to ponder how that was basically the theme of our relationship—I just kept running.

CHAPTER TWENTY-TWO

FOX

For as long as I lived, I'd never forget the sight of my wife running full out toward me, her blond hair streaming behind her, fear and determination all over her beautiful face as she closed the distance between us.

I caught her up into my arms, fighting the urge to run my hands all over her body, to check every bit of limb and skin to make sure she was whole.

My thoughts were coming too quickly and they were murderous—if I hadn't been actually driving my truck I would've jumped out the minute I saw her running toward the rest stop. *Why was she alone, and where was J.D.? What the fuck was he doing with her way out here? Were those handcuffs?*

Two of Rambo Garrett's Humvees skidded into the lot just to our left, and out of the corner my eye I saw Garrett himself and two motorcycles head in the direction Avery had come from. It made me wonder for the tenth time exactly who Rambo Garrett was. But there would be time for that later.

I pulled back to look into Avery's face, taking in her wild eyes, her pulse jackrabbiting in her neck, feeling the shuddering breaths she took as she clung to me.

"What happened? Where is he? J.D.?"

She shook her head, burying her face in the crook of my neck as she tried to catch her breath.

Christ. "Okay," I said, running a hand down her back as I held her. "It's okay."

Avery was safe, and that was all that mattered. I pulled out my multitool and jammed it into the handcuffs' lock, springing her wrists free. Her hands were full of dirt and tiny cuts, her wrists marked with angry red lines, and I felt my fury rise again.

"Another man, he—J.D.—" She squeezed her eyes shut, breath still heaving, her face paler than I'd ever seen it. "Shot in the chest, he's still there—"

I'd taken a few vows in my lifetime. One was to the girl I held in my arms, to love and protect her for the rest of my life. I would never forsake that promise—it was the most important one I'd ever made. But the other—the other was to use my skills to help people in need. And I couldn't break that vow either.

My original plan was to hold on to my wife for at least three days straight once all of this was over, but the look on her face told me that my plans would have to change. Lucas would take care of Avery while I put my medical skills to the test. Avery's panic and my own moral code said I had to try.

So then it was my turn to run. Away from my wife, away from protocol, and straight into the mess of things. That's how I'd always been, and it probably wouldn't change any time soon. Lucas had told me more than once that I couldn't save everyone, but I knew that already. And yet… here we were, all of us.

My lungs were screaming by the time I reached the scene, but then I was on my knees, blood streaking my hands as I pressed on a wound that was too easy to staunch. J.D.'s blood was everywhere, but it wasn't enough—not enough for a beating heart.

The rules of CPR were simple, though. You didn't stop, not

until the situation was out of your hands. So I kept going as the world spun on around us, as sirens filled the air, as Garrett and his boys wrenched another bloody silhouette out of a truck with a flat back tire.

The world spun on as I tried to bring him back, a man who was already gone, a man who'd nearly taken everything from me, a man I hadn't liked but wanted desperately to save. A man who had probably sealed his fate the minute he'd lit that match.

CHAPTER TWENTY-THREE

AVERY

"I need to go home to my daughter."

Detective London gave me a sympathetic look. "I understand, Avery. I think we're done here."

She was trying to be nice, but it was only the manners that had been ingrained in me for years that kept me from biting her head off. Our debriefing at the police station had taken hours. I didn't want to talk about today anymore. I didn't want to think about J.D. Every time I did, I felt a mix of anger and guilt rise up into my throat.

Why did J.D. do all of this? Why couldn't he have just cooperated with Fox from the beginning and gotten his money? Why did he think this was the answer? And why did he bring Spurs into it? He could've traded me for his debt and even more. Not that I wanted him to but he could've just—I was out of energy for speculation. There were so many different ways for this to end up, but this wasn't an outcome I'd considered. One minute he was here, and the next gone. Fox had tried his best, but a wound like that left few survivors. And...

what would I tell Annabelle someday?

Despite all that had happened, my relationship with J.D. had given me the most important thing in my life. Everything was so incredibly fucked up. I wanted J.D. to take responsibility for his mistakes, to own up to what he'd done and also to what he hadn't —I didn't want him to die. Of course I didn't.

After Detective London dismissed me, I found Lucas, Fox, Chase, and Derek in the station's waiting room. They greeted me with tired waves and we all headed out to the parking lot. Once Lucas had driven away with the other guys and Fox and I had settled into his truck, I turned to look at him. Fox's mood had shifted, settling into the quiet, pensive mode I remembered so well from when we'd first met.

"Did they ask you a lot of questions?" I rested my cheek against the seat and watched as he put the car into reverse and backed smoothly out of the lot.

He shook his head. "Just a few."

"What about Garrett and the other guys? Did they ask how everyone was involved?"

Fox looked over at me, his small smile almost sad. "Not my info to give."

I nodded. "I felt the same way."

"Are you okay?" His voice held something I couldn't define.

"Yes." This wasn't the first time he'd asked me, or even the fifth. And I knew it wouldn't be the last. Somehow, saying yes every time made me feel better. As though even if I didn't actually think I was fine, saying I was could make it so.

Fox's eyes told me he understood. "Annabelle's with your mom and dad," he said. "Do you want to spend the night at the ranch?"

"Okay." I wanted to be wherever Annabelle was. I needed to see her with my own eyes, to kiss her little face, to reassure myself that this was all over and that I'd truly kept her from harm. If she would've been with us, if Spurs... I couldn't even think about it.

My mother had tears in her eyes when we walked through the door. "Thank god you're home." She hugged me hard. "Annabelle is upstairs in your bed."

I kissed my father on the cheek. "Go on, now," he said, gesturing to me and Fox. "Get some sleep." Even his slightly gruff demeanor couldn't hide the relief in his voice. "It'll keep till morning."

Hand in hand, Fox and I walked up the wooden staircase to my old bedroom. Annabelle was inside, sleeping under the duvet I'd had since I was a little girl. I brushed her hair back from her forehead and kissed her nose. "Sleep tight, Bells."

Seeing her there, dreaming so peacefully—that was worth all of it. Every scary hour, every bruise. I would do it all over again if I had to.

Fox followed me into the spare bedroom and closed the door behind us. I felt disgusting, grimy from the long hours on the road. All I wanted was to wash this all away and climb into bed, but I didn't think there was enough soap in the world that could make me feel anything less than exhausted right now.

"I'm going to get in the shower," I told him, pointing to the tiny en suite bathroom. "Want to join me?" I smiled at him, knowing full well there was nothing sexy about my invitation. I was the definition of a train wreck.

He gave me just a hint of dimple. "I'll wash your back."

I kicked off my boots and piled my dirty clothes next to the tub.

"Avery... *damn it.*" His hand was gentle as he turned me in a circle, but the heat of his words made me cringe. "You have bruises everywhere."

I wrapped a towel around myself reflexively. "I fell a few times."

Fox stood there, his hands balled into fists. "I hate this."

"I know."

"He hurt you." His words were ice.

"I'll be fine." I didn't want to talk about this anymore. My nerves were still shaky, my emotions on edge. Fox's anger and guilt would put me over the top.

"Avery, it's killing me." He turned, slamming his fist onto the counter hard enough to break bone. "It's *killing* me."

"I get it, Fox!" I cried, the dam breaking wide open. "You're mad! And I'm not saying you don't have a right to be—I'm saying I'm fucking mad too!"

He looked taken aback for a moment at my outburst. "I know—"

"Do you? Do you really?" My shoulders heaved as I tried to catch my breath. "For almost four years I took care of me and Annabelle, did everything myself and tried to have enough left at the end of the day to show her that she could be capable, comfortable, and happy no matter what. Because that's the most important thing I can teach her, right? That she is enough? That she can be whatever she needs or wants to be?"

He nodded slowly, his eyes intently on mine. "You've set an incredible example for her, Avery."

"Thank you," I said automatically, my heartbeat responding to the sincere look on his face. "Wait, no! Stop distracting me. That's the thing, Fox. That's my entire point!"

"I'm not sure I'm following," he admitted.

"You came into our lives and I felt safe, like I could relax," I told him. "And I love you for that and about a million other things —but somewhere along the way I started to lose the part of me that knew I could do it on my own, and I *need* that part." My voice broke and I nearly choked on a sob. "I didn't know until it was almost gone, but I *need* it."

Fox's eyes flashed and his frown deepened. "Avery... after my accident, you were the one who carried us through. You're the strongest person I know."

"Am I? I let him take me, Fox. I didn't even put up a fight, because I was so terrified. I was terrified and I was angry, but I *let* him."

"No, Avery. You convinced him to let Annabelle go, you made an incredibly difficult decision." The expression on his face was one I'd never seen before, and it tore my already tender heart to shreds. "I'm so fucking proud of you for everything you did. You saved yourself. *You* did it."

"I had to." For me, for Annabelle. For Fox and the life with him that I was determined to live.

Fox's expression turned guilty again. "I wasn't there. I should've been, and I wasn't. I'm so sorry, Avery."

I must've heard him incorrectly. "Are you crazy?" I shook my head. "You can't protect me from everything, Fox. I know you want to, I know you try to. But this—this was some next level shit. Even for us."

"But—"

"No but. You came for me. You moved heaven and earth to get to me as fast as possible. I know you did." I remembered his face on the road, the way he'd looked at me when I ran to him.

"You had it handled."

"Yes." I had a flashback of myself running down the dirt road to salvation. "But you're the best backup a girl could ask for— always."

A tentative smile finally reached his eyes. "Can we agree on an 80/20 split in your favor?"

He pulled me close and I let him, because even the strongest people aren't immune to earnest compliments and dimples and those green eyes and warm skin and everything that came with it. If loving Fox made me weak—I couldn't even finish that thought because it wasn't true.

In reality, loving Fox made me stronger than ever. That's what I'd finally realized, after I stopped doubting myself. I had the two most important things in the world to fight for, and it made me a formidable enemy. I'd never forget that again.

"It's okay." Fox held me tight, cradling my body against his like he'd done on that godforsaken backroad. "It's over."

I shook my head, pulling away to look up at him. "It's not, Fox."

He said nothing because he knew I was right, but his beautiful face was gentle and kind as he looked at me. With one finger, he wiped away a teardrop as it fell to my cheek.

"J.D. is dead, and as much as I'd like to pretend it never happened, I was there. I had something to do with it, and someday I'll have to tell Annabelle." I thought I was done crying over him when he disappeared five years ago, but my tears came with renewed force. "I'll have to tell her, Fox. What will I tell her?"

"I don't know. But whatever you decide, we'll tell her together."

⁓ˈ⁄⁓

"Thank you all for being here today," I said. "We're so happy to be reopening the new and improved Kent's Kitchen exactly where it belongs, in the heart of Brancher!"

The crowd gathered outside the diner whistled and cheered. I looked around and saw everyone grinning, and it made me even more grateful that we'd been able to rebuild.

"Are you ready to do the honors, Avery?"

I smiled at Fox when he handed me the giant pair of scissors to cut the ribbon tied in front of the doors. "Three, two, one!"

The air grew still as I closed the blades over the red satin, the low roar of the crowd inexplicably silenced. I glanced around, confused. Suddenly the street was completely deserted and it was dark, a strange chill in the silent air.

What was going on?

The scissors felt different in my hand, a heavy, almost burning heat. I needed to get this over with, to open the restaurant and then maybe everyone would come back. Where had they gone, anyway?

But then I looked down and I saw the fire. It spread over my scissors to the ribbon, reaching the front doors and licking up the walls, spreading, searching, consuming.

"No!" I dropped the scissors and stepped back in horror, but it was too late. Before I could even open my mouth to scream, the diner was once again engulfed in flame. And I was all alone.

I sat straight up in bed, my heart pounding.

My mind raced as I took huge lungfuls of air, trying to quiet the beats that I was sure could be heard for miles.

It's over, I reminded myself, still trying to breathe deeply. *No fire. You're at the ranch, safe. Brand-new restaurant, almost ready.*

And J.D. is dead. The pit in my stomach was unrelenting.

"What's wrong?" Fox asked sleepily, propping himself up on an elbow. "You okay?"

"Yes," I said, my voice small. "Just a bad dream—a different one. I was hoping they'd stop, but now that…"

"You can't expect everything to just go away." Fox put his arms around me and pulled me into his chest. "Look at what's happened the past year, or even the past twenty-four hours."

I nodded into his chest. "I know."

"I've been dreaming, too," he admitted. "About the fire, mostly."

"I'm mad that he put us through this," I said. "And that he died for it. Nothing needed to happen this way."

Fox rubbed soothing circles onto my lower back with his thumb. "He made choices, Avery. Bad ones that spiraled out of control."

"I don't think there was any getting out of this for him," I said. "Everything was too far gone even by the time you first made contact. If it wasn't Spurs, it would've been something else. Someone else."

"He burned every bridge to ashes," Fox agreed. "I know you care, Avery. You wouldn't be *you* if you didn't. But it's not your fault that he finally ran out of wood."

⁓⫯⁓

"C'mon, Annabelle," I called down the hall. "Get your shoes on!"

I heard her little feet running on the hardwood floor, and then she appeared in the kitchen.

"We're going out?" she asked, her eyes wide.

Well, that settled it. Yes, it was true that I'd stuck a little closer to home the last few days, but I was entitled to be cautious. I mean, it wasn't every day that your baby daddy abducted and subsequently tried to ransom you for a quarter million dollars.

Everything that happened with J.D. had closed a long chapter for me. It was a terrible sort of closure, honestly. It also didn't help that every time I thought about my future, I couldn't see it as clearly as I used to. Things had changed, forever, irrevocably—I knew that. But I'd always had a plan. These days I wasn't sure about anything anymore.

I closed my eyes briefly, willing myself to banish any thoughts of J.D. from my head. I needed to let him, and all memories of him, rest in peace. I couldn't do anything else about the situation—but I could do that.

My smile brightened as I turned back to Annabelle. "Yes, we're going out. And you'll never guess where!"

"To the zoo?"

"Nope." I grabbed my newly replaced purse and keys, checking the time on my new watch. Lucas had put some sort of weird GPS thing in it—it looked like a regular watch to me. But if it made him and Fox feel better I was all for it, because I think they would've microchipped both me and Annabelle if they could. For my own part, I had pepper spray and I wasn't afraid to use it.

"To…" Annabelle scrunched up her nose. "To the park?"

"Even better," I told her. "Let's go."

I let her guess all the way across town. She came up with some pretty wild ideas, but I knew I had her stumped when we pulled up in front of an ordinary looking house. A woman came out to the front porch as I got Annabelle out of her car seat.

"Avery?"

"That's me!" I smiled at her. "And this is my daughter Annabelle."

"We've been waiting for you," she said as Annabelle ran up the porch stairs. "C'mon in."

"Thank you so much for letting us come over on such short notice, ma'am," I said as we walked through the house to the backyard. "She has no idea why we're here."

"I saw your daddy at the coffee cart yesterday, and when he told me y'all were looking for a puppy, I told him to have you call me straight away," she said in a stage whisper. "Three girls and four boys, first pick is yours." She opened the door to the backyard with a flourish. "Come on, puppies!"

Annabelle turned to me with huge eyes. "Puppies?"

So much had happened since that day in her classroom when she first told me she'd like a dog of her own. I'd kept it in the back of my mind, waiting for the right time. But what I'd realized is that there *was* no exact right time, not for things you wanted to do. If you waited, there was a chance you could miss out on something wonderful. You had to grab life by the proverbial balls and just go for it, because everything could change by tomorrow.

That's why today I was getting my kid a puppy. We were done waiting around and letting life happen to us. Today we were making things happen on our own terms. "That's right, baby. Pick your favorite one."

Turns out, choosing your new best friend is a daunting task, but a little over an hour later Annabelle and her new puppy were snuggling together in the backseat of the SUV as I drove the three of us to the store so we could get some puppy essentials.

He was a cute little guy, that was for sure, although I knew that being small was only temporary. As a full-grown golden retriever, he would probably top out around sixty-five pounds. And he had that wavy thick fur, just like Annabelle wanted. I couldn't wait to see the look on Fox's face. Our family of three had very quickly become a foursome, but I knew my husband—anything that put a big smile on Annabelle's face would be just fine with him.

"What's his name, Annabelle?" I glanced at the two of them in the rearview mirror.

She looked down at the puppy thoughtfully. "Elmo?"

"Um…" *Oh god, please, anything but that.* "If you want."

"No," she said. "Maybe… Max! Like the dog from the Little Mermaid!"

I was suddenly very grateful we'd watched that movie last night instead of something else. "Max sounds great."

"Max and Fox and Mama and me," I heard her whispering to the dog.

After a whirlwind in the store, where we debated for a solid five minutes on the color of Max's bed (I won, but she picked the collar —a very flattering turquoise), we were finally on our way to the Kitchen construction site to introduce Fox to our new family member.

There was no mistaking the smile on my husband's face when he saw us pull up. "You're out of the house!" he called to me as set down what I'm assuming was a nail gun. "Hi, Annabelle!"

"Why is everyone so surprised about this?" I muttered as I got her out of the car. "Like I'm a hermit or something."

But they had a point. I'd locked myself away a little bit, not just physically. It had been about a week—one of the most uneventful weeks I could remember in the past year of my life. And I was tired of that feeling, the one that kept me inside and wary. It was time to rejoin the land of the living.

Fox and Lucas shed their tool belts and were nearly at the curb when I reached back in and carefully picked up Max, cradling him to my chest as I turned around and closed the car door.

"Fox, we got a puppy! He's going to live with us and his name is Max!" Annabelle cried.

I saw my husband's eyes widen for just a split second before his face broke into my favorite grin, complete with extra-deep dimple. If I wasn't holding the puppy, I probably would've jumped on him right there. No one made me feel like Fox did, no one, not ever.

"So, we got a dog." He stroked the puppy's head as Annabelle chattered on to Lucas about our adventure picking him out.

I smiled at him, a real smile. "Yep. Hope that's okay."

"It's okay with me," he said. "What's the occasion?"

"Because… life is short," I told him.

"Yes," he agreed. "It is. And worth living to the fullest."

CHAPTER TWENTY-FOUR

FOX

"Can't believe six weeks went by so fast," I said. "I'll never be able to thank you guys enough for coming out here to help us."

"You know I hate feeling left out, Foxy." McDaniels slung his bag over his shoulder. "There's a thousand-acre rager on the Canada border calling our names."

"That, and we already bought our return tickets," Sloane added. "Otherwise I'd be tempted to stay."

"You're heading back to the Oka-Wen?" Chase's voice held a hint of something I couldn't define.

"Yeah, vacation's over," Sloane said. "Back to reality—sleeping in the dirt, chasing smoke, the usual."

"And dreaming of Mrs. Kent's breakfasts," McDaniels added. "But it's a living."

"Yeah, I remember."

Wistfulness, that's what I heard in his voice. I'd never considered that Chase would miss firefighting—he'd left the

Hotshot crew of his own accord, but now it sounded like maybe that was exactly it.

"Wanna come, Dempsey?" Sloane must've heard it too.

I watched a multitude of emotions pass over Chase's face before he responded. "Thanks, man. But I got my own thing going on now—gonna stick with that for a while."

McDaniels nodded. "Good for you, kid," he said sincerely.

We were quiet, all shuffling our feet around for a moment, caught somewhere between the past and the present with ghosts in our midst. Before this build, the last time we'd all stood together was in the forest with Landry—or without him at his funeral. My memory loss cut a swath through vital minutes of life, but in this case, maybe I was the lucky one—I still didn't remember that day.

"Y'all ready?" A girl's voice called from across the street, breaking the spell of silence.

Chase's head jerked up at the sound, and I turned curiously, wanting to confirm who I'd heard.

"Janie? Janie's taking you guys to the airport?"

Sloane rolled his eyes, but McDaniels' shit-eating grin confirmed everything I'd just guessed. He barely had time to give Chase a quick fist bump before he was heading in her direction.

"I'm sure gonna miss Texas," he called to us, walking backward across the street. "Later, Foxy!"

Sloane gave my shoulder a friendly shove as he grabbed his bags and ran after McDaniels. "Finish strong! We'll put out a couple fires and be back for the opening."

They piled into Janie's truck and she peeled off, heading toward the freeway that led to the airport. As quickly as they'd come, they were gone again. If I didn't have a refreshed supply of unwanted dirty limericks and the recorded footage to prove that they'd been here, I might not have believed they were real. But they'd be back —maybe we'd all be back someday. I was still reeling from Jim's gift and considering how to present it to Avery.

"So now what?" Chase asked me as we watched them drive away. "We're down to barely above a skeleton crew to finish this build."

"I don't know," I admitted. "We've still got a couple weeks until the reopening, and there's a lot to do."

"I'll be here," he promised me. "I know you're trying to make Henry relax some, but we'll get it done."

"'Trying' is the operative word when it comes to Henry."

Yes, it was true that after Henry's fall I'd encouraged him to take it easier, reassuring him that we'd get everything done. But he hadn't listened, and we needed him. It was as simple as that. He'd given me about three days of cooperation before he told me to get my head out of my ass and let him work. So if he was going to keep showing up, I was going to assume he was feeling fine.

"We'll get it done, Fox. Don't worry."

"Yeah."

The home stretch was in sight, but I didn't know if it was even possible to make our deadline with the newly diminished crew. The last thing I needed was a dip in morale, which was a possibility regardless with this morning's departure. On the plus side, Lucas was due back any day. McDaniels and Sloane may not have been builders—and honestly, none of us really were except Tripp, Derek, and Kyle—but they had strong backs and a good work ethic, which made them invaluable. I know Chase meant well by telling me not to worry, but that was all I'd done on this build so far—worry.

We'd be down to the last hour and the last fucking dollar, but I wasn't letting up until it was done. For now, that's how it had to be. Inspections were coming up, and then the last bit of drywall could go in, and the appliances and furniture could finally be delivered. Maybe after that I could pause to take a breath—when everything was back the way it was supposed to be.

Chase and I decided to grab coffees at the espresso cart before heading back down the block toward the restaurant. If I gave a shit about things like gray hair I'd probably notice quite a few more of them these days. Avery's little adventure—a new term, to keep me from that hand clenching thing—was likely set me up to go all silver by the time I was thirty. My wife was incredible, brave, and completely exasperating at the same time—I wouldn't have her any other way, but sometimes it played hell on my sanity.

A few errant thoughts ran through my head about where I hoped our progress would leave us at this point—but that was all I had time for until Chase stopped short and I stopped with him. *What now?*

"We expecting anyone else today?" he asked.

Sure enough, there were two unfamiliar trucks parked in the construction zone, and I mentally let out a string of curse words. If the inspectors had come early, we could kiss the reopening goodbye. Nothing was finished, and the plumbing and electrical we did have done wasn't nearly enough to for them to sign off on the job. Did I get the dates wrong? I didn't think so, but maybe something fell through the cracks. It was bound to happen eventually, no matter how meticulous Tripp and I tried to be.

I quickened my pace, hoping to get to the bottom of this before the others showed up. I'd promised Jim I could take care of the project and get the job done, and I intended to keep that promise.

"Morning, Fox, Chase." Rambo Garrett straightened up from where he'd been leaning against the construction fence and offered me his hand. Three guys I recognized as members of his task force did the same, and we exchanged greetings quickly.

"Garrett? What are you doing here?" If I was initially surprised and relieved by their arrival, it immediately turned into concern. Security teams didn't just pop by for friendly visits.

"Shit, man. We thought you guys were the inspectors coming early." The relief in Chase's voice was evident, and remotely I filed away the fact that Chase genuinely cared about getting this rebuild done.

Garrett looked amused. "That would be bad?"

"Understatement." Cautiously I took a sip from my coffee. "What's up?"

"Help and help alike, Fox. We couldn't get out into Big Bend to save those kids, and you did it without hesitation. You needed a security system and wouldn't take my discount, so we swapped for a little surveillance. Lucas helped us out with some manpower on a job last month, and we did recon with the J.D. situation. Mr. Kent gave my brother a good deal on a bull, and now you're in a jam with this rebuild. I happen to like putting things together. What do you say?"

I raised an eyebrow at him. "You sure? You know you don't owe me shit, if that's what you're thinking. In fact, it's definitely the other way around. You need me to wax some Humvees or something?"

Garrett laughed. "Think we're all set there." He jerked a thumb over his shoulder. "These are just the work trucks."

My gut had been through the wringer lately. The aftermath of Avery's vacation (forever trying out different ways to phrase it so I didn't go into a blind rage every time I thought of J.D. taking my wife against her will) was still affecting our daily lives, and probably would for a while. The arrival of the puppy had put a balm on a few wounds, but some things were still raw. Still unpredictable, still not back to normal. So when I saw the dark SUV pull up outside of the build site and the hair on the back of my neck stood up, I wasn't entirely surprised.

"Lucas!" I jogged over to where my brother was cutting baseboard. At least he was back. I'd sort of grown attached to his complaining.

"What's up? Is Heather here yet? She's supposed to be bringing us 'builder's brunch,' whatever the fuck that is. Sounds good though. She said something about a cinnamon—"

"The General is here."

"The—what? No way." Lucas dropped the wood he held. "Where?"

"Over there." I pointed to where our father was getting out the backseat of a chauffeured SUV. "I'm assuming you didn't know he was coming?"

"Fuck no, B. I would've told you." Lucas ran his hands through his hair agitatedly. "Do I look okay?"

I snorted. "You look ridiculous. It's not a blind date, it's our dad."

Lucas gave me a dirty look. "The odds of rejection are the same."

Okay, he had a point. I had no idea what the General would be doing here, other than the fact that both of his sons currently lived at least part time in Brancher. But typically, that wasn't a good enough reason for a visit. Part of me was worried, but a tiny percentage was also sort of proud to show him what we'd accomplished.

Or I would be, for about three seconds, before he would inevitably tell us how we could've improved the build or used our time more efficiently. Life with the General had few variances. I'd already come to terms with the fact that our heart-to-heart in Seattle was a one-time occurrence. Probably for the best, because it was unnerving as fuck.

"Mom didn't come?" Lucas craned his neck, trying to see around the construction.

"I don't see her." At least with Savannah around, the General's demeanor was slightly less frosty. There was truth to the idea that the right woman could make you want to be a better man. In my father's case, my mother was the love of his life, and she still only managed to bring him up to a moderately pleasant level.

"Well, let's get this over with," Lucas said gloomily. "What do you think he'll pick apart first? Our choice of materials or the design?"

"I'll take odds on the design concept. Loser buys the beer."

"Either way, we both lose," Lucas grumbled, but he kept up with me as we walked across the site to the curb where the General stood staring up at the unfinished building.

"Beckett, Lucas." The General nodded at us. No hugs here, which was to be expected, even though neither of us had seen him in a month or more.

"Hey Dad," Lucas said easily. He'd always been the talker, so I just let him. "What brings you out to Texas?"

My father focused his laser stare on Lucas. It would've been funny, the reflexive recoil I saw from my brother, if I wasn't afraid he'd look my way next. "A consulting client. Your mother asked me to coordinate it around the reopening." He turned his gaze to me. "She's down the street, distracted by the novelties of a small town."

Thank God for small favors. "Can we show you around the site?" I heard my voice making the words, but I felt out of my body. *Sure, invite him in to drain you of all self-esteem, like a judge-y vampire.* What the actual fuck. I'd been watching too much TV with Avery.

The General nodded without comment. I was supremely glad that Jim and Tripp weren't here—they'd gone to pick up our new dishes in Odessa. The last thing I needed was my father pissing Tripp off, which would be inevitable. My father might've gotten along with Rambo Garrett, however. Too bad he had other commitments today.

I was on pins and needles during the entire tour, but miraculously the General was quiet, just taking in our surroundings. I tried to see the building through his eyes, the unfinished spaces, the overall chaos that I tried to tamp down a little more every day. Was I succeeding? I thought so. Did I need to see it in his eyes to believe it was true?

"Come meet your mother for coffee," was all he said, shocking the hell out of me. "Goodbye, Lucas."

"You want to get coffee with Beckett? And not me?" Lucas's incredulous tone implied he couldn't decide if he should be happy or offended.

"You're part of this project," the General said dismissively. "We'll see you at the opening."

"Um… okay." Lucas widened his eyes at me when my father turned around. *What's going on?* he mouthed to me.

I barely had time to shrug before the General turned back to us.

"Are you coming, Beckett, or should I call your office to

schedule another time?"

He could teach a masterclass on impatient sarcasm. "Yeah, I'm coming, Gen—Dad." I glanced back to Lucas with a panicked stare, but he was too busy trying not to laugh, so I half-jogged to catch up with my father as he strolled down the street in the direction of the espresso cart.

"Bye, Dad," Lucas called after us. "Bye B., you poor jackass." The last part was mumbled around his grin, but I caught it. *Jerk.*

My mother's eyes lit up the minute she saw me. "Don't get up," I said, leaning down to kiss her cheek.

"Sit down, Beckett," she said. "I've missed you, I've been so worried. Tell me everything." I watched as she gracefully added milk to her coffee. Savannah Miller could preside over a tiny table outside a ramshackle espresso hut in West Texas just as easily as she could host her five-star dinner parties in Malibu.

I didn't know where to start. My parents had offered their support and resources when Avery was gone, and I was grateful for that. But the details… what did I want to say?

"It's great to see you," I told her honestly. "It's been too long."

"Agreed," she said. "Let's not do that again."

I nodded, feeling myself relax some. "The case is settled," I said. "Annabelle is mine, officially. I wish—" As much as I hated to admit weakness in front of the General, I had to tell my mother the truth. "I wish it wouldn't have gone down that way, but it did."

We all sat in silence for a moment—not to honor the dead, per se, but I still thought it was warranted. Life had changed that day on the road.

"And the opening—thank you for coming." I'd known Savannah would come, but my father too?

"You're on a good track with the building." If I hadn't watched his lips move, I would've sworn I was hearing things. It was faint praise, but positive just the same.

"We've had some setbacks, but pulled through." As hard as it was for him to give, it was just as hard for me to receive.

"And as far as Avery—you did everything right, Beckett. You

kept a calm, level head. In your position, I'm not sure anyone could've done the same thing," my mother said.

The General cleared his throat. "You and your brother are convinced I'm a hardass, and that's because I am. I won't apologize for it because I think it's served you well."

I wished I didn't need his approval. I wished I didn't care about it. But I was human, and I did.

My mom put her hand on my arm. "What your father is trying to say, badly," she speared him with a look, "is the best things you can teach Annabelle are love, loyalty, and tenacity. And the best way you can teach her is to show her—you're doing that, Beckett. Every day."

CHAPTER TWENTY-FIVE

AVERY

Despite all of my nightmares from the past weeks, I'd slept solidly the night before the diner's reopening. Fox had too—when he'd finally come to bed, no doubt due to a mixture of sheer exhaustion and relief. They'd rebuilt the diner to the best of the eclectic crew's capabilities, and now it was time to open the doors and welcome whatever may come our way.

"Coffee?" Fox slipped back into our bedroom, holding two cups in one hand.

I smiled. A hot man and a hot beverage. *How did I get so lucky?* "Thanks. Is Annabelle still sleeping?"

"Wrapped up like a burrito in her blankets," he confirmed. "She was out late."

I tried to keep the worry from my expression as I looked at him over the brim of my mug. "Is everything finished?"

We'd all been working to ready the diner last night, but Fox and my dad had sent everyone else home and stayed for the final preparations.

Go home, sunshine. Tomorrow will be a brighter day.

I barely stirred when he'd finally come to bed, and I knew he'd been up for hours already. I guess it was surprisingly easy to function on such little sleep when you had an endless cup of caffeine practically surgically attached to one hand. Fox always said I was his number one vice, but coffee was a close second.

"Yes." My husband's voice belied the relief I knew he felt. "All ready for the grand reopening." He pulled back the covers with his free hand and slid in next to me.

"What time are your parents coming?"

Fox groaned. "Why did you have to remind me?"

I laughed at the look on his face. "C'mon, you said you had a good talk with them the other day. And I haven't seen your mom in so long! I miss her."

I'd hit the jackpot when it came to mothers-in-law, in my opinion. I loved Fox's dad too, despite his prickly outer exterior, but my affection for Savannah was on the next level. When she looked at me I knew she really saw *me*, just the same way I felt when I'd first met Fox.

"Mom is great. The General—he has a way of making me feel about this big." Fox held his forefinger and thumb an inch apart. "Even when he's saying nice things. I feel like he's trying to trick me."

I rolled my eyes at him. "He's proud of you, Fox. I can see it."

My husband's face turned vulnerable, his eyes softening for just one moment before his mouth quirked up and his dimple popped. "He has a weird way of showing it."

"Well, *I'm* very proud of you," I said, trying to change the subject. I set my coffee on the nightstand and slid closer to Fox, taking his cup and setting it aside as well. "Did I tell you that?"

Fox's eyes were molten when he looked at me. "Maybe."

I kept my gaze locked to his as I eased myself up to straddle his lap. "If I haven't made myself very clear, allow me to try again."

"I think I need a detailed outline," Fox said, his voice low. "Then I'll give you an oral report."

"There will be a test," I promised him, my breath catching as he slid my shorts to the side. "I'm very confident you'll pass."

And he did.

⁓⎪⁓

Fox was nervous, I could tell. It wasn't a typical emotion for him, and I'd done my best to try and calm him this morning when I'd sensed how tightly he was coiled. But apparently it wasn't enough—I'd have to try harder next time.

More sex with my super-hot husband? Challenge accepted.

For my own part, I wasn't nervous at all. I thought I would be, I would've bet on it. As it turned out, the resolution of this situation was more than I could've ever hoped for, and there was no room for nerves in my happiness. The Kitchen was back. It wasn't exactly the same, and maybe some people wouldn't like that. But to me, it was even better than before.

Fox, my dad, and our friends had put their literal blood, sweat, and probably a few tears into making it what it was—a tribute to a town that didn't give up, even when things crumbled into ashes.

"Thank y'all for coming today," I said into the microphone, looking out over the crowd. My parents and Fox stood next to me, the rest of our friends and construction crew just off to the side. Somehow I'd been nominated to speak for everyone, which was fine except I didn't feel very prepared.

"We hope you love the new Kitchen just as much as you loved the old one—the recipes are the same, but the jukebox actually works and we have central air now." I smiled when a few voices whooped their approval.

I caught a glimpse of my in-laws, Savannah effortlessly chic in a flowered sundress, a neutral expression on the General's face. *Neutral was good*, I thought. *Fox wouldn't mind neutral.* Sloane and McDaniels had finally shown up this morning after a couple of flight delays, but they were here.

Was the whole county here? It was damn close. I hoped we had enough room, I hoped the mayor wouldn't be mad if we put tables in the street again, and most of all, I hoped that this would be just the very beginning of a whole new era of Kent's Kitchen.

"We really appreciate y'all standing by us while we rebuilt. So without further ado—" My dad and Fox each grabbed one of the glass doors, swinging them open. "Welcome back, Brancher!"

The rest of the day was a blur. Fox and I put on our aprons and didn't sit down or even manage more than a sip of water for five hours as we served what felt like the entire state of Texas. I'd had busy shifts at the diner before, but today was on another level.

"This is wild!" Heather called from behind the counter as I whipped by with a tray of burgers. She grabbed a couple of bottles of ketchup and some extra napkins for my table and followed after me. "I brought three times the usual Sunday order and everything is gone! Lucas went back to the house to get whatever he could find. Thank goodness I keep frozen pies in the fridge for emergencies! Think Fox has room in the oven?"

I deposited the burgers with a smile while Heather refilled iced teas. "I don't think Fox even knows his own name right now," I said, grabbing some menus and handing them to her.

"We'll make it work," she said, and then she was off across the room to seat yet another table.

"How're you doing out there, sunshine?" My husband didn't even glance at me as I stuck another ticket on the order wheel. "We still have a waiting list?"

I grinned at him, admiring the way the muscles in his forearms flexed as he flipped burgers and chicken on the grill. "Yes, and probably forever."

"Good," he said, finally looking up with my favorite Fox grin. "That's what we wanted—that's why we worked so hard."

His smile made me forget that my feet were starting to hurt. "You're right." He usually was. It would've been annoying if it was anyone else, but it was Fox and he had a way of making it seem like you'd helped him come up with the answer.

"I'd tell you to come back here and let me kiss you, but Joy has orders up so she'll be coming for them soon." Fox raised his eyebrow just enough to let me know he was seriously considering kissing me anyway.

"Later," I told him. "Much later."

I envisioned a bath in my future, full of bubbles and one of those aromatherapy bath bombs I'd gotten the other day. Maybe Fox would want to join me. We probably wouldn't both fit in the tub unless we were on top of each other. *That would be okay.*

"Avery!" Joy's voice startled me out of my daydream. "Get your food and get on out of here! We've got people waitin'!"

Fox already has his head down, focusing on his plating, but I was honed into that dimple. I could see it from a mile away. I could feel it even when it wasn't around.

It was that dimple that kept me going through another complete table rotation, and another, until the sun went down and I had a minute to breathe. It was after midnight when I finally slumped onto a barstool. Heather took Annabelle home for us after the dinner rush, but people kept coming in until we'd shut off the neon sign. I was so tired, but I was so happy too.

The construction crew and our families had stayed, and I caught more than one of them looking around the diner in awe of what we'd accomplished tonight. It was true—all of this was nothing short of a miracle. But it was so desperately needed, and with the sense of accomplishment also came a feeling of relief. The Kitchen was back in business, and life could go on.

"Best day in the history of the restaurant," my father said, looking up from the receipt he'd printed off the cash register. "By a mile."

Fox came out of the kitchen with a case of beer, and Joy fiddled with the jukebox until she found what she was looking for. The bottles were handed out, and my family—blood, legal, and extended—raised their drinks in a toast to a job well done.

CHAPTER TWENTY-SIX

FOX

"**A**nnabelle! Are you ready?" Avery called down the hall.

I was going to derail movie night. There was no other way to put it. After the incredible support we'd gotten at the Kitchen's reopening, I wanted to do something to give back to the town, to show them how much we appreciated them showing up for us in every way possible.

So for two days I'd spent every available minute with my laptop, combing through hundreds of hours of footage, and now I had something I felt accurately expressed the spirit of Brancher, and the gratitude the Kents and I felt toward them.

But how to distribute it? Some of the ranchers would've straight up laughed at me if I asked for their email address—this was not a town built on technology.

The answer came to me via a flyer at the espresso hut, and I couldn't believe I hadn't thought of it myself. Would the town be upset about a little prelude before we got to *Singin' in the Rain*? My film wasn't that long—there would be plenty of time for Gene

Kelly and Debbie Reynolds after it was done.

Even my wife didn't know what I was up to—we'd promised no more *secrets*, but this fell under the category of a surprise so I felt like I was in the clear. I was ready and waiting when the girls finally got to the door, and in less than two minutes I had all of our gear into the truck and we were on our way.

"Are you okay?" Avery didn't know about the video, but she knew me well enough to know when something was up. "I've never seen you so anxious to get to the drive-in."

I pulled the truck into the field. We weren't the very first people there, but close. "I like movies about tap dancing in inclement weather."

"Um…" She didn't look convinced. "Sure."

I set up our blankets and food quickly, laying out everything in the bed of the truck as the other townspeople arrived and cars began to fill the pasture. I knew my in-laws and our friends would be here too—the idea of showing them my film made me even more nervous.

"There's someone I have to see," I said, catching sight of the movie operator near the bales of hay they used to prop up the projector. "Be right back."

I could feel Avery just staring after me as I loped down the field. She thought I was losing it, but she'd understand soon.

"Did you get the flash drive? Is everything working?" I asked him.

"All set, Fox. We'll start in about five minutes."

I spent that time pointedly ignoring my wife while I pretended to be very interested in the projector set up. Once the final cars were parked, the operator paused the pre-movie commercials and the screen went dark.

"Here you go." He handed me the megaphone. "Imma need that back."

There were murmurs all around the field as the projector cut out. "What happened?" someone called. "Where's the movie?"

"Turn your headlights on," I said to the nearest car, then I jumped up to the top of the stack of hay bales. Avery was staring at me like I'd lost my mind, and maybe I had. But I was determined to show my thanks, and even though I loathed public speaking, I had to get this out.

"I don't want to take up a lot of your time," I said into the megaphone, shading my eyes against the light as I looked out over the parked cars. "But this is the last movie night Avery and I have before we head to Seattle."

I paused, gathering my thoughts, and a couple people whistled —one of which I was fairly sure was Joy. "I didn't know a lot about small towns before I came here. You welcomed me to Texas with open arms, and when my family fell on hard times, you all stepped up for us. And I'm so—we're so grateful. You all are brighter and better than any big city. So Brancher, this is for you."

I heard a couple more claps and whistles as I jumped off the hay bales and handed the megaphone back. "Okay, I'm ready." *Not really, but there's no going back now.*

The projector screen flickered to life again, and I almost turned around, afraid to watch. What if it wasn't enough? What if they didn't get it? Art was so subjective.

The film started with a Brancher Bulldog pep rally, exactly one year and one day earlier than the fire that destroyed the diner. The place was packed, every booth crammed full, cheerleaders filling the aisles between tables and the entire restaurant nearly bursting at the seams while everyone sang the school fight song.

From there the scenes came more quickly, a fast summary of the last year—the *before*. We cycled through the holidays, through weather and special desserts and parties and ladies lunches and everything that made the hub of Brancher what it was. Through it all was Avery and Joy, their smiles quick, their hands always full of plates and drinks, running the diner in that second nature way that only comes with years of experience.

And then—I'd debated on how I wanted to cut to the next scene, the *after*. I had footage of the burnt shell of the building, but I didn't want it here. There was no place for it, no validation given.

So I started fresh, with a few moments of still-shot of the empty foundation. A memorial to the untimely death of a beloved friend —a friend that always welcomed you in, always had what you were looking for, always wanted you to leave happier than you arrived.

Then the video I took that very first day, the morning that I'd never forget—Day One. My voice. *"So far, it's just me."*

It may have started with me, but it ended with Brancher. The next scenes were of Lucas, of Tripp and Jim, Henry and Chase, Sloane, McDaniels, Derek, and Kyle. All of us, every day, working on something new and often out of our comfort zones. The entire pasture watched as the walls went up, as men fell down, as we made mistakes, as we laughed, and as we righted a wrong.

The football team came to help, the ladies society guild, the school kids and the teachers and Gladys from the espresso cart— they were all invested in this, in the resurrection of a landmark so much bigger than it was on the map.

We had Thanksgiving under the stars, with twinkle lights and too much food, with tables in the street and dancing on the sidewalks. We watched the town show up, again and again, as though they were putting on the tool belts and raising walls to bring an American dream back to life.

The day finally came when the glass doors were ready to open, where an early morning cup of coffee with my in-laws showed a tired but deliriously happy smile from my wife, a contented look in Rebecca's eyes, and a sense of peace of Jim's face. We cut a ribbon, we brewed coffee, we revived a tradition. The camera panned over familiar faces, over friends brought back together at new tables, over food being served and life happening just as it always should.

And then an aerial shot, one of the first I'd ever done, a drone that lifted off the restaurant's roof and went higher and higher, pulling back a little at a time to show how the Kitchen fit into the very center of the town. In more ways than one.

In the background, Eli Young sang about dreaming as the drone slipped over the fields, down the highways, and to the Kents' ranch, but it didn't stop there. It kept going, around the bend and over the small crest, to a farmhouse with a puppy playing in the yard, a little girl with blond hair running after him, and a big truck parked nearby. And then the drone was climbing again, into the blue sky, higher and higher until everything disappeared.

I held my breath—the air was so still. *Don't be disappointed if they don't clap.*

But they were Brancher, so they did more than just clap. They always did more. I watched the field come to life before my eyes— headlights flashing from every corner, car horns honking in a cacophony along with whistles and what sounded like a million shouts.

My wife ran up to me, breathless, her face full of happy surprise.

"Did you like it?" I asked her.

"Fox." She gripped one of my hands with both of her own. "I loved it. Why didn't you tell me? When did you do this?"

"I've found myself with a bit of spare time in the last few days," I told her wryly.

All of my trepidation had disappeared when I'd watched the film here, surrounded by the town. It was the best thing I'd ever done—both the film and the decision to move to Texas. There was no question about any of it.

Avery grinned, but then her face turned serious. "That last scene," her eyes looked straight into my soul. "I don't understand. That was the property next to my parents' ranch."

I looked over to Jim Kent, watching us with an unreadable expression on his face. "*Our* property," I corrected her gently.

Avery followed my gaze to her father. "Ours? Really?"

"A gift. Not for now. For someday," I told her. "If we want."

"Yes." She nodded slowly, blinking back tears. "Someday."

My eyes shifted to Jim again, just catching a glimpse of his smile in the dusk as he turned to walk away.

CHAPTER TWENTY-SEVEN

AVERY

I thought my heart would burst after I watched Fox's video. His kindness, his inherent thoughtfulness always did a number on my insides. You'd think I'd be used to him by now, but I didn't think there was any way to be immune to the Fox effect. It was too strong.

There were worse things than perpetually swooning over your husband, I realized that. It was the best problem to have—I wished it was my only one. But I was facing the very real hurdle of moving my family nearly two thousand miles away, and there was a lot to do.

I packed up everything I could around the house, leaving out only necessary toys and books for Annabelle. I re-washed and re-folded perfectly clean linens, I obsessed for days about how I wanted to crate my books, and I might have cried when Heather suggested a yard sale. Allegedly.

Fox watched me fuss over the move, giving me space until he worried for my stress level and finally stepped in. "Just bring whatever you think you might want, and leave the rest here. We can always send for it."

I'd gone back and forth about renting out the little house—did it make sense, would we want to be remote landlords, who would I trust to take care of my place—and the final answer was not yet. It was another bridge to cross on another day.

"We'll need somewhere to stay when we come to visit," I had pointed out, and Fox agreed.

The farmhouse on our new land needed work, so that was out for now. And when they'd rebuilt the Kitchen, the updated plans converted the upstairs apartment into a dry storage area along with a bigger office for my dad. The end to another era—Fox's first home in Brancher was no more. I took it as a sign that he was always meant to be with us.

My parents invited us out for a farewell dinner at the ranch. "Nothin' fancy," my mother assured me. "Just a proper goodbye."

I wanted that, but at the same time, I didn't. As ready as I finally was to go to Seattle, the reality of leaving behind everything I knew was daunting. Not even Fox could alleviate my anxiety.

"You've worked so hard for this, Avery. I want you to be excited about it. If you're not, we're not doing the right thing."

I really had to think about his words. I *was* excited, but that didn't mean I couldn't be scared too. Saying goodbye to my parents made it real. It meant that the life I was always in such a hurry to start was about to go full steam ahead. And although I'd been preparing and wishing for this day for literal years, I wasn't sure I was ready.

I tried to explain it to Fox. "When I was pregnant with Annabelle, I was blissfully happy and completely terrified at the same time. I felt both of those feelings, all day every day, until she was born."

He looked at me in his Fox way. "I can understand that."

"But then after she was here, there was only happiness. That didn't mean I wasn't still scared, but I didn't have room for fear in my heart because she took up the whole thing. The happiness eclipsed everything and made the fear easier to set aside."

Fox nodded. "It's your process—feel all the feelings until you decide which one gets to win."

I laughed. "Something like that. Does it make sense? Maybe not."

He grinned at me. "I get you."

"And I'm very thankful for that." I slipped my hand into his.

"So which feeling is currently winning?"

"Right now? Full freak-out mode. But I'm optimistic about it."

So there we were, on our way out to my parents' place. All day I pretended like it wasn't happening, like this was just any other day and any other dinner. But when it finally came down to get into the SUV, I turned to Fox with tears in my eyes.

"It'll be okay, sunshine. I promise."

And because he was Fox, he was right.

My dad grilled out, we had corn and two types of salad and my mom's famous dinner rolls. My parents, not usually talkers, were uncharacteristically chatty—about everything except us leaving. But that was okay, because once again, morale was up. The success of the Kitchen was exactly what we needed to smooth this transition. Fox had known it, and now I realized it as well.

In another lifetime, without the diner fire, things would've been very different—but it was pointless to think about that, because it happened and our only option was recovery. We were leaving a wound mostly healed.

"Avery, c'mon in the kitchen and help me with these dishes," my mom said after we'd all finished. "Won't take but a minute with the two of us working."

My father nodded to Fox. "We'll go out for night check."

When the two of them headed outside to see about the horses, my mother and I cleared the table and gathered the dishes. Annabelle wandered into the kitchen behind us, Max tucked up under one arm. They plopped down onto the tile floor, where Annabelle started brushing his silky fur. The puppy rolled over onto his back in ecstasy, all four feet straight in the air.

"He's gonna be too big for you to carry around soon,

Annabelle," my mother said with a laugh. "Look at the size of those paws!"

"Thanks for dinner, Mama." I stacked the plates next to the sink. "Everything was really good."

She turned on the sink. "You're welcome. Not sure what they eat up in Seattle but I can't imagine the steak is fresh."

A little jab, but I let it slide because I knew she was emotional. "You're probably right."

I couldn't let her bait me, not now when we were so close to leaving. We didn't have time to do our usual cycle of fighting, silent treatment, and stubborn resolution.

"I don't know what the rush is, anyway. Your school doesn't start for months."

"We want to get settled, find a school for Annabelle. It's going to be a big change for her, and I want it to be fun." I tried to keep my voice upbeat. *She's upset because it's real now. Don't let her get to you.*

"You've always been ready to run, I guess. Even before her." My mother set a dish in the strainer with a little more force than necessary. "Isn't that right?"

This time I could detect the sadness in her voice, and any anger I felt drifted away. "It was never about running away. I'm looking toward my future. I hope you can understand that."

She paused for a long minute. "I can, Avery. You might think I can't, but I really can. I've thought about your future your entire life."

Her words hit home for me. Didn't I feel the same way about Annabelle? I wanted so much for her—if our visions of her future didn't line up, would I be upset? Or would I trust that she knew her own heart best?

"I love you, Mama."

Her voice was teary when she replied. "Times a million, sweetheart."

We stood there silently for a minute—a peaceful silence—drying the last of the dishes until my father came into the kitchen.

"Don't recognize that boy without coffee in his hand." My dad looked pleased with his joke. "Thought I'd make some for all of us."

He strolled over to the coffee pot, not entirely oblivious to what he'd walked into. Max took the still-swinging door as an opportunity to scamper out of the kitchen, and Annabelle got up to run after him, her giggles trailing off down the hall.

"I—" My mother's voice faltered just a little. "Bring out some cookies too. I'm going to see about Annabelle."

That was hard. It was hard, but it was good.

We both watched her go for a moment, but then my dad cleared his throat and turned back to the coffee. "You know which cookies she means?"

"I think so." I pulled a package out of the cupboard.

"Let's open that up and test 'em out."

I grinned and broke the seal, pulling two cookies from the bag. "Aren't we too old to be sneaking cookies?"

"Nonsense." My dad's gaze was steady, but his eyes looked a little wistful. "You grew up fast, chickie... you had to. And I'm real proud of the woman and the mama you are today. I know it's time for you to go now, Avery. You need to go."

"Daddy, I—"

"We're gonna be just fine." His voice teetered on the edge of gruff. "Your mother and I, we're gonna miss you and Fox and that baby girl something fierce. But we'll be fine, Avery. Don't you worry about us."

I nodded, tears welling. "We're going to miss you too."

Memories flashed through my mind, thousands of times that we'd sat in this very kitchen and I'd chattered on and on to him while he sipped his coffee. He'd been outnumbered from the beginning between me and my mom, with only Duke on his side, but he'd taken it all in stride.

And then when Annabelle was born... my life had veered off on a tangent I wasn't sure my parents would've picked for me, but my dad was the best grandfather in the entire world. Between the ponies and the tea parties, he also taught her to bait a hook, to polish tack, and to always close the gates behind her when they walked the pasture fence lines.

He'd been her first hero, her best friend, the assembler of toys and maker of forts and patient reader of endless storybooks. He'd filled the role of father figure for her until I'd met a man we all deemed worthy of the title.

He'd done for her exactly what he'd done for me, which was build me up so I could face anything. And no matter what dream I'd ever chased, even if it took me away from him—he'd believed I could do it.

"You'll come home to visit, chickie. You, Fox, and my little Annabelle... you'll always have a place here. For whatever you decide."

"I know," I said, wiping my eyes. I still couldn't believe my dad bought us that land. It showed me he'd really heard everything I'd told him about wanting more for my life. He'd taken those words and bought me the very thing I'd been missing—*options*.

He cleared his throat. "All right then. I don't know what you said to your mother, but I hope it helped. She's been in a mood since Thursday."

I managed a laugh even through my tears. "I hope so too, Daddy."

⁓

We were set to leave Brancher on a Monday, which I felt was an appropriate start to the week. One last weekend at the new and improved Kitchen, one more Sunday morning breakfast serving pancakes and eggs, one more chance to see my husband in his bandanna before he retired it for a while. Maybe for good, but maybe not.

My parents and Joy were glad for the help seeing as our replacements were still in training. It also afforded our friends a chance to come and say goodbye to us, which I didn't anticipate. But that's how it ended up, and I was glad because you don't spend the formative years of your life seeing the same people every day without needing some closure.

There was a notable absence, however. Someone very important wanted her own private farewell scene. I knew it was on purpose, just how I knew that I'd hear a knock on my kitchen door at seven o'clock Monday morning, and a pink bakery box for us to take on the road.

I was wrong, though—it was two bakery boxes.

Heather and Lucas showed up just as Fox was packing the last of our stuff into the car. My best friend's eyes were red-rimmed, and her typically perfect hair looked slightly less than smooth. I took one look at her face and immediately felt tears well in my eyes.

"Don't cry, because if you do, I'll cry too," I warned her.

Lucas shot Fox a panicked look over my head. "Help."

Heather ignored him. "This is it," she said. "We talked about it, we were ready for it. But—"

"It's always been me and you," I finished for her. "I know."

She threw her arms around me, and I let just a couple tears leak from my eyes. Heather was a constant, and I didn't know life without her. Nearly every day for the last twenty years—through boyfriends, a baby, school, love, heartbreak—we'd been together. Now we both had opportunities that would take us far from each other. It was good—but it would definitely be different.

Heather sniffled into my shoulder. "I'm not good at goodbyes. I don't know how you jet-setters do this thing all the time."

Lucas pulled Fox in for a one-armed hug. "It's never 'goodbye,' it's always 'see you later,'" he said.

"Call it whatever you want, I still don't like it," she grumbled.

I laughed, squeezing her again. "We'll see you in a couple months when you come to visit."

She nodded. "And as soon as we move into the new house in L.A., y'all have to come see it."

"Deal."

"You guys all set?" Lucas asked. He swung Annabelle into his arms. "We'll get her in the truck. C'mon, Max."

The puppy trotted closely at his heels as Lucas and Heather took Annabelle outside to where Fox's truck sat at the curb. I'd considered flying to Seattle, but in the end, we'd decided to make it into a road trip. First heading west to California, where we'd take Annabelle on a much-anticipated visit to Disneyland, and then a couple days in Malibu with my in-laws.

From there, a leisurely drive up the Pacific coast, stopping in San Francisco, Portland, and wherever else caught our eye. We'd planned for nearly three weeks on the road—a long overdue vacation for my husband.

"Well, I think that's it," Fox said, looking around our tiny living room. "Ready to go?"

"There's one last thing," I told Fox.

He looked at me curiously. "What did we forget?"

I stepped forward, wrapping my arms around him. "Remember when you sent in all of my grad school applications because I didn't have enough confidence or money to do it myself?"

"No. But yeah." He gave me one of his signature half smiles.

Fox's memory loss would always affect our lives, but it didn't scare me anymore. We'd weathered a lot worse and still come out on top. "Well, because of that, we're chasing my dreams to Seattle. And I owe it all to you." I kissed him briefly.

"You did the hard work. I just bought some stamps." His grip on me tightened.

I rolled my eyes at him. "Anyway—we've had a crazy few months, and I know it was disappointing not to get into your grad program, even if it was a long shot."

His expression changed infinitesimally, and I knew I'd hit on a bit of truth. "A little."

"I told you once that you were already a filmmaker, and I meant it. I know you feel like you still have a lot to learn." I paused, pulling a piece of paper from my pocket. "How do you feel about on-the-job training?"

He took the paper from my hand. "What are you talking about?"

"Just read it."

Fox scanned the words quickly, and when he looked up there was confusion all over his handsome face. "I don't understand."

"I sent your video of the Kitchen rebuild to a production company in Seattle—as a job application for a cinematography apprentice." I couldn't keep the grin off my face. "Congratulations. The pay is kind of shitty and the hours are long. But you're gonna make movies."

My husband was a man of few words. He always had been—maybe a little more talkative since his near-death experience, but typically the embodiment of the strong, silent type.

And right now was no exception. I watched a myriad of emotions cross his face—excitement, doubt, amusement—but most of all, love.

"You think I can do this?" he asked me finally.

"I think you can do anything."

His dimple, that dimple I loved so much, was extra deep when he smiled at me. "I think we both can, sunshine."

EPILOGUE

AVERY
THREE YEARS LATER

"**A**very, you can stop holding your breath now."

Fox's wry grin made his dimple pop.

"Beckett Fox, I am your *wife*. I will cease breathing every time we pass the piece of highway that you embedded with your DNA. That is my God given right, do not try to take it away from me." My last few words came out a little squeaky.

He turned to look in my direction. "Avery, I—"

I clutched the hand he'd rested on my thigh. "I'm fine, I promise. Can you just watch the road, please?"

Fox shook his head, laughing. "I'm well aware that we have precious cargo," he said, nodding to the backseat where Annabelle sat reading, the dog's head on her lap.

"Don't forget these!" With my knee, I nudged the box filled with copies of my debut novel. I'd all but wedged the carton into the front seat with me, insisting they could potentially be damaged in transit otherwise.

My debut novel. *My debut novel.*

My creative writing masters' thesis, edited, rewritten, and adapted into a book. I'd bled onto the pages, agonized over every word, slept scant hours over months. But it was a story I needed to tell—the best story I knew about what happens when love finds you when you least expected it. Part truth, part fiction, all mine.

And in a few months, we would have Fox's first film premiere as lead producer/cinematographer—a tiny-budgeted, beautifully shot indie about life and love and loss and so many other things that before he'd only kept in his head. I'd cried when he showed it to me, but they were good tears.

After all that, who knew? I'd stopped trying to plan out my life to the minute. The way to enjoy was to be fully present in the present.

As if he could read my thoughts, Fox grinned at me from behind his sunglasses. "Ready?"

"Yeah," I said. "Definitely."

Because I was. We were. For whatever came next. I did what I came to do, proved to myself that I could thrive and succeed. I'd had it in me all along—had I known that, deep down? Maybe—just like maybe I'd realized that the only thing ever holding me back was my own self-doubt, not a location on a map.

So now I had only one wish, for the very thing I wasn't sure I'd miss during our exciting years in the city—wide open space.

The highway curved, and Fox pointed the truck south toward Texas. Toward home.

THE HEY SUNSHINE TRILOGY

HEY SUNSHINE
NIGHT FOX
BRIGHTER DAY

PLAYLIST

"Burning House" - Cam
"End of the Road" -Boyz II Men
"Today" - Brad Paisley
"The Boys Are Back in Town" - Thin Lizzy
"Home" - One Direction
"Forever Like That" - Ben Rector
"Blood" - Dropkick Murphys
"Pushin' Time" - Miranda Lambert
"Carolina" - Harry Styles
"Landslide" - Fleetwood Mac
"Trouble" - P!nk
"Bless the Broken Road" - James Johnson
"Greatest Love Story" - LANCO
"I Don't Remember Me (Before You)" - Brothers Osborne
"High Hopes" - Panic! At The Disco
"You Are My Sunshine" - Morgane & Chris Stapleton
"Rainbow" - Kacey Musgraves
"Guiding Light" - Mumford & Sons
"Even If It Breaks Your Heart" - Eli Young Band
"Take Me Home" - The Ennis Sisters

ACKNOWLEDGMENTS

I have three years' worth of acknowledgments that should be written for this book, but I'll try to keep it short. Finishing Avery and Fox's story is one of the greatest accomplishments of my life. I hope you all realize how much I appreciate your support. Thank you is never enough, but it will have to do.

To my husband, who is the best even when he's at his worst: It's because of the way you love me that I was able to write the way that Fox loves Avery. Thank you for our life, for how hard you work to make it happen, and for every day so far and all the days in the future. Forever, done, sold.

To my daughter, who is the joy that keeps me on my toes, keeps me laughing, keeps me adaptable, and keeps my heart full: Thank you for your sweet patience, even when you didn't know how much I needed it.

To Jenny, my ride and pie (see what I did there?), my best friend for nearly all of our lives, my editor: Thank you for never giving up on me even after a thousand missed deadlines, after years of no new work, after all of my plentiful neuroses. I am nothing without my blonder half.

To my mom, who never stopped asking me about this book: Thank you for always being willing to brainstorm ideas, for encouraging me to make uncomfortable choices, and for believing in me no matter what.

To Portia, who will answer a text message even in the middle of the night: Thank you for all of your encouragement, your advice, your friendship, and your honesty and enthusiasm.

To my friends and family, who were so happy when I finally told them about this publication date: Thank you for all of your support and love, for spreading the word, and for sharing in my excitement.

ACKNOWLEDGMENTS

To my Instagram girls, who never gave up on me even after I pushed my publication date a million times: Thank you so much for caring about my books, for your beautiful pictures, and for your willingness to share my work on your lovely feeds. It truly means the world to me.

To Sarah from Okay Creations, who brought this series to life in a way I only dreamt about: These books would not be what they are without the covers. Thank you for sticking with me and creating such an incredible project.

And to my readers: thank you for waiting for me. It means more than you could ever know. This series was a labor of love that I would not have been able to finish without you. Thank you for loving Fox and Avery, for rooting for them, and for rooting for me. You are why I am here.

ABOUT THE AUTHOR

Tia is a daytime hairstylist, former English Lit major, Harry Styles aficionado, and blogger-turned-author. After four years of writing a now-retired personal site, her work has been featured on numerous forums including Open Salon and Hooray Collective. She believes in eyeliner as a defense mechanism, equal rights, and Marc Jacobs handbags as investments. Her favorite things include One Direction, story time, and the overzealous use of punctuation. When not writing and reading, she binge-watches only the best (subjective) TV shows. She lives in Southern California with her husband, daughter, tiny dog, and big dog who thinks she's a tiny dog.

Visit her website at tiawritesbooks.com.

CPSIA information can be obtained
at www.ICGtesting.com
Printed in the USA
FFHW020921100319
50912253-56337FF